To Devin

Hope you enjoy!

Josh Clark

Dakota Defined

What am I made of?

Copyright 2012, Josh Clark, All Rights Reserved

No part of this book may be reproduced, stored in a retrieval system, or transmitted by any means without the written permission of the author.

Published by White Feather Press. (www.whitefeatherpress.com)

ISBN 978-1-61808-039-4

Printed in the United States of America

Cover design created by Ron Bell of AdVision Design Group (www.advisiondesigngroup.com)

White Feather Press

Reaffirming Faith in God, Family, and Country!

Books By Josh Clark

The McGurney Chronicles Series

The Legend of Paul McGurney

Devil's Playground

Infinity

The Ends of the Earth

Ten Thousand Strong (Coming 2013)

Dakota Divided

Dakota Defined

The Streak (Coming Soon)

For my students...
Thanks for talking me
into this one!

For cheese sake!

What are you waiting for?

Turn the page and read my story!

up·swing /ˈəpˌswiNG/

NOUN: When things are flippin' terrific after a year of less-than-cheestastic happenings.

chap·ter |'CH aptər|
noun

Chubby Toddler Fingers and Prune Juice Cars

"I'm pretty sure he has your nose," Erin said as Ethan reached for another iced animal cookie. He expertly pinched the cookie between two chubby toddler fingers and wasted no time in bringing it to his mouth.

"You think so?" I said, swiping the crumbs off the table into my hand. I walked them over to the trash receptacle and brushed them into the Glad-lined bin. If my mom weren't still on her hospital rounds, she'd be beaming. I wasn't usually the clean-up-after-myself type, and for me to actually clean up after *somebody else* was one giant leap for mankind. Glancing at the clock, I saw that Karen, the woman formerly known to me as Bimbo Baggins, would be picking Ethan up within the next fifteen minutes. I'd have to get him ready to go within the next five; my father's wife was never late.

"Don't you? See the way it's all buttony? Like yours is buttony?" Erin's deep chocolate eyes smiled. My little heart couldn't help but patter faster. Minus five points for the cliché, but Erin's eyes really did take my breath away.

"Buttony, huh? Now you're inventing words? Isn't it enough that you're gonna win state with your new painting? Now you have to invent words to rub my nose in your awesomeness." I pulled out a chair and sat down. Ethan pointed and me with a soggy, half-eaten cookie.

"Here, 'kota."

"No, buddy. I think you'd better keep that one. It looks a little waterlogged."

Ethan shrugged and put the cookie to his lips. "Okay."

"I wish you wouldn't keep telling me I'm going win state," Erin said, wiping Ethan's mouth with a washcloth. "It makes me all nervous."

"Why? You won this year's district competition by a landslide. And you would've won last year's if---"

My stomach rumbled when I thought about last year's district art competition that never was. There were some memories I wish I could just stuff into a suitcase and mail to Saturn so I'd never have to relive them again.

"If there would've *been* an art competition," Erin said, shaking her head. "I still can't believe Blake and his thugs did what they did."

My ears began to ring with the awful memory. It had been a little over a year ago that pimple-encrusted con of cons, Blake Blanton, and his goon disciples had broken into Infinity High School--with me in tow—and had obliterated two hundred ninety-nine student art projects. Wielding crowbars, they had systematically decimated sketches, pottery, sculptures and paintings alike. Only one project had survived the carnage: Erin's Jamaican beach painting called *Ocho Rios*, which now hung on my bedroom wall as a bittersweet memory of that terrible night. Even though I hadn't destroyed a single exhibit, I had been as guilty as Blake and Jacob Riley and the others; I had willingly cozied up to Blake and his life of crime because I desperately yearned for acceptance and inclusion, and I had peddled my trusty Schwinn to the Infinity High School parking lot on that fateful night under my own volition. As I thought back on that terrible episode, I couldn't help but think how things would be drastically different between Erin and me if I had taken a crowbar to her painting as Blake had demanded. I had been within a few seconds of destroying not only her beautiful Jamaican beach, but also our friendship. And all because I had been a divided person, all because I had been stupid enough to think that Blake and his band of merry thugs could plug the nasty hole my father's leaving had left. I shuddered at the thought. I had been so close to throwing away everything I loved, Erin, Ethan and my father because I couldn't accept that it was my own anger that was holding me back from wholeness and not my father's faults and failures.

"You know I don't like to think back on that night," I said, closing the box of iced animal crackers, much to Ethan's dismay.

Erin smiled and my insides turned to warm butter. "I know. No need to rehash the past, right?"

"Right."

Erin stood from the table and scooped Ethan up. "We better get all your stuff around, huh?"

Ethan squealed in delight as Erin walked him into the living room to pick up his toys that lay scattered on the carpet. I followed them, marveling at how Erin seemed so natural with my half-brother.

You've got a good one, Dakota!

"Where'd you say your dad is, again? Boston?" Erin asked, holding Ethan's toy bag open as he toddled around the room picking up his toys in a painstakingly slow fashion.

"He's got a potential client in Boston, but then he's headed to Concord for some ad design conference," I said, still not quite accustomed to talking about my father without acidic bile burning the back of my throat. To say we'd come a long way in a little under a year was an understatement. Last year at this time I would've rather kissed the back end of an angry bobcat than even breathe my father's name.

It's better this way—much better this way.

"Sounds like he's doing all right," Erin answered as Ethan stuffed his sock into the open toy bag. "Hey, little man, you need those to keep your toes warm." Ethan smiled, mischief in his hazel eyes.

"He's doing a lot better since his old boss stepped down. And he comes around here a lot more, so it's a win-win."

Erin put her hands to her hips, her coffee bean eyes sparkling. "I never thought I'd hear you say that, Dakota James Lester."

I shrugged. "What can I say? We're trying to move on. You know, heal and all that sappy jazz. And quit it with the middle name. It reminds me of my kindergarten teacher."

"I'm proud of you, Dakota," Erin said, the sincerity in her voice rich as maple syrup.

If I was honest, I was proud of me, too. I had traversed a very long and very painful road to get to the place I was. I had forgiven my father for walking out on my mother and me in favor of his secretary when I was twelve. For a while, I would rather have walked barefoot over shards of broken glass or taken a paper cut to my eyeball than forgive my cheating father. But time and fellowship had sutured the wound my father's leaving had gashed, and I was loving every second of making up for the time I had lost being mad at him. And getting to know my half-brother Ethan was more than an added bonus.

"'Kota?" Ethan asked, looking up at me with his big hazel eyes.

"Yeah, bud?" I pulled up his little pants so his Pull-ups weren't showing. I had a flash thought of my own underwear ballooning out the back of my jeans after Blake Blanton had given me the nuclear meltdown of wedgies last year. That has so not been a good day.

"I go bye-bye?" Ethan pointed to the window. Karen's blue VW Beetle had just pulled into the driveway.

I scooped Ethan into my scrawny arms and planted a kiss on his chubby cheek.

"You have good ears, man! Let's go meet Mommy at the door, okay?"

Ethan squealed in affirmation as I made to leave the room with him in my arms.

"Dakota?" Erin said, coming up behind me. She put her arm around my waist and kissed me lightly on the cheek. "I really am proud of you. And I think you're pretty cute, too."

I kissed the tip of her nose as Ethan wiggled in my arms.

"Ditto."

***

"I'm not driving a Buick. They're elderly-mobiles." I scrunched my nose at the maroon 1995 Buick LeSabre and continued surveying the lot for a vehicle that was less geriatric and more from my generation. "I can practically smell prune juice and Polident seeping out the cracks in the doors."

My mother crossed her arms as the chill December breeze mussed her hair. "Funny, Dakota. But I've heard that Buicks are safe and they run forever."

"And they have trouble pooping and they play Bingo for pretzels and canned goods every Tuesday at the local Boy Scout cabin. Come on, Mom, I can't drive a Buick. It's something Bertrand would drive."

"Bertrand Warner is a nice boy," my mother answered, stooping to check out the sticker price on a 2000 Dodge Neon.

"That's my point," I answered, wishing I had worn gloves. Sal Hampton Motors' car lot was beginning to feel like the frozen tundra.

"You know I have a price range, Dakota," my mother said. "And we're walking out of it now."

I looked down the row of "priced to sell" vehicles to the very end, where gleaming Chargers beckoned me with their sexy metallic curves and seductive chrome rims. I wasn't stupid; I knew my mother couldn't afford to buy me even a used Dodge Charger. Not with her single-mom nurse's salary and my penchant to want things like food, shelter and clothing to cover my scrawny body. But I couldn't help imagining myself behind the seat of one, Erin in the passenger seat smiling at me the way that drove me wild, Tyson Francis and the other jocks of the school ogling my pimpin' ride as I coasted into the sophomore parking lot with my system up and my bass bumpin'. I sighed.

A guy can dream, can't he?

My sixteenth birthday was December eighteenth, next Wednesday, and my mother and I had struck a pretty sweet deal: she and my father would front the money for a serviceable used car if I agreed to get a part-time job to help pay for gas and insurance. Seeing as I didn't have enough money of my own in my meager savings account, I had jumped at the idea. I knew that *used* and *serviceable* would probably translate to *junky* and *cheap*, but at least I'd have a car when I turned sixteen. Not all of my classmates could say the same thing—except the ones whose rich mommies and daddies had purchased them sparkling new Mustangs and BMWs. Not that I was jealous or anything.

"What about this one, Dakota?" my mother asked, pointing to a hunter green Dodge Daytona. I circled the car to look at the sticker.

"It's a 1993—old. Front-wheel drive with only sixty-two thousand miles on it." I looked up. "How can it have so few miles? This car was born before I was."

My mother cupped her hands around her eyes so she could see inside the car. "Look, Dakota. It's an automatic with power windows."

I didn't respond. I was taking in the car, its spoiler in the back, its low-to-the-ground feel. Yeah, it was old, but my pulse began to accelerate when I found myself imagining how it would feel to drive it. I pointed to the price sticker.

"Is this in your range?"

My mother smiled. "Right where it needs to be. How's about we ask Sal if we can take it for a test drive?"

★★★

"I'll drive over next Tuesday when I'm back from Concord and we'll sign the papers," my father said from the other end of the line. I heard what sounded like an airport parking announcement in the background and knew my father was en route to New Hampshire. "I'm glad you found something you like. I can't wait to take it for a test drive."

I smiled. I was all smiles, really. I had just picked out my first car and it had passed the mom and dad test. It was going to be mine as of four o'clock next Tuesday afternoon. And I, Dakota James Lester, would have my license (assuming I passed the driver's test, of course) the day after. Life was all peaches and cream and beds full of really great-smelling roses and all that jazz.

"Awesome. I can't wait."

"Great. We'll see you soon. And thanks to you and Erin for watching Ethan, especially on a Saturday. Karen really appreciates it."

"It's no problem. The little guy's a lot of fun. When I get my license I'll be able to either meet Karen halfway or watch him at your house." Toledo was, after all, sixty miles west of Infinity.

"Karen doesn't mind, and neither do I. We want Ethan to be in good hands. What better hands than yours and Erin's, right?"

"I guess so."

"Well hey, Dakota, I gotta run or I'm going to miss my plane. Take care, congrats and I'll see you soon." He paused for a moment and then added: "I love you, Dakota."

"Love you, too, Dad," I said, not feeling an ounce of anger or embarrassment at telling my father I loved him. I was past all that, and now it just felt plain good.

Can life get any better?

chap·ter |'CH aptər|
noun

2

HODGEPODGERS

"It only has sixty-two thousand miles on it because an old couple bought it brand new and never really drove it anywhere but around town," I said, taking a bite of my pizza and gauging Timothy and Bertrand's reactions. I had been talking nonstop about my car, and since I was the oldest in the group to get my license, I held a pretty captive audience. Well, besides Bertrand. No one could ever tell where he was looking because his encyclopedia-thick glasses lenses distorted the view we had of his eyes.

"And you get your license a day before Christmas break. How cool is that?" Timothy Astor said, wiping pizza sauce from the corners of his mouth.

"I know, right? I hope the snow holds off. There's no way my mom'll let me drive for the first time by myself if there's even the slightest chance of snow." I looked up as Jeremy Stines sat down beside me. He set his tray down and flipped his disgustingly long dirty blonde hair behind his shoulder.

"What're we talking about?"

"How you need to cut that nasty hair of yours," I said, setting my rectangular slice of pizza back onto my tray. "I can't eat with you flipping it around like that. Not when you're sprinkling my pizza with dandruff and other flaky particles."

"Really, Dakota?" Jeremy said, looking at me in an obnoxiously theatric fashion. He considered himself a master thespian, and I had to admit he was pretty good. But his hair wasn't.

"You need to lay off my hair, man," Jeremy continued. "I washed it this morning. And people say it looks good."

"Your grandma has a biased opinion. Besides, you haven't cut it since last year," I said, glancing at Timothy, who was grinning. "Don't you ever hear your scalp begging for air?" I cupped my hands around my mouth and mimicked Jeremy's scalp pleading for precious oxygen.

"Hair jokes again?" Erin said as she wove her way through a clustered group of freshmen and set her tray down across from me.

"What else would it be?" Timothy asked, scooting his chair over to make room for her. "I think you need some new material, D.L."

"And I think you need to box-step your way into a blender," I shot back. Timothy was a member of the show choir, and I loved to remind him how he couldn't possibly look cool prancing around stage in a bow tie and tuxedo bottoms singing lackluster versions of show tunes and last year's top forty radio. In reality, he had a great voice and some pretty sick moves, but as the comedian of the Hodgepodge table, working the truth into my material would suck the funny from my jokes.

"That was one of your better quips," Bertrand said with a nerdy grin. He unzipped his tan fanny pack and pulled out a pencil and a small notebook. His Garfield-orange hair seemed to set the cafeteria ablaze. "I will write it down and remind you that it made me chortle this time next year."

We all looked at each other. Bertrand was a wordsmith, an etymological genius with a vocabulary larger than the rest of the table's combined. He'd lately also taken to writing things down on his little pad if he found them funny or interesting. Timothy had asked him what the pad was for, but Bertrand had only grinned and said something about "recording inspiring nuggets of comedic and/or inspirational intelligence for posterity's sake." Whatever that meant.

As I looked around the table, I couldn't help but feel we were all kindred spirits. We had labeled ourselves Hodgepodgers because we were an eclectic mix of individuals who didn't fit in anywhere else. The only thing that mattered to us was that we fit in with each other, and after first despising my seat at the Hodgepodge table, I had grown to embrace it. It had taken me a few beatings from Blake Blanton and getting arrested and put on probation, but I had had sense knocked into me, both literally and figuratively. As for my Lester the Jester persona—well—some habits died hard.

"It's a Dodge Daytona, right?" Jeremy asked me. "I think that's what you said in your text."

"Yeah, 1993. Hunter green."

"You can really soup up a Daytona," Jeremy said. "My dad's friend has a '92, red, and it flies."

"I don't want you to drive fast," Erin said, putting her warm hand over mine. "I like you in one piece."

Timothy and Jeremy rolled their eyes at the same time. If any of us could make out what Bertrand's eyes were doing behind his glasses, I'm sure we would have seen him roll his, too.

"Stop it with the sappy Hallmark junk," Jeremy said. "I'm trying to eat."

"We'll make you a deal," I said, looking from Erin to Jeremy. "You cut your wooly mammoth shag and we'll cut the sappy stuff at the table."

The Hodgepodge table erupted into laughter, and Bertrand's pencil scribbled madly onto his little pad of paper.

***

It had taken awhile for me to cozy up to the life of a Hodgepodger. Being scrawny and weak didn't exactly lend itself to being popular, and being a sarcastic—okay, I'll say it—*obnoxious* cut-up didn't help my cause, either. But what I'd learned from the whole situation with Blake Blanton was that I could accept myself for who I was and that others could, too. I learned that Addie Wilkens, Blake Blanton and I had had far more in common than I could've ever imagined; we were all personas, all fakes. Blake and Addie had both worked hard to form-fit to their bully and blonde hotty stereotypes respectively, while I had been a wandering nomad of a human being. I had been willing to conform to whatever group would accept me, when what I really wanted was to be able to accept *myself.* It hadn't been an easy lesson to learn, but I had learned how to do just that. And as the first semester of my sophomore year came to a close, I could honestly say I was in a good place.

Josh Clark

down·slide /dounˈslīdʹ/

NOUN: When things start to go wrong and
all that jazz.

chap·ter |'CHaptər|
noun

THE FALL OF DEMOCRACY

Mr. Dennis was wearing a monstrosity of a sweater: an eggplant-colored number with the picture of a deer stitched between the points where his way-too-perky nipples tented the fabric. My former freshman history teacher and student government advisor had always had a knack for wearing pukish sweaters, but this little deer number took the cake. As he passed out the agenda for the student government meeting, I seriously wondered if his mother still dressed him.

"Okay, gang," Mr. Dennis said as he plopped into his rollaway desk chair, "this meeting's an important one. So I need everyone to focus." His head turned my way, his hairy caterpillar eyebrows rising. "I mean everyone."

Okay. So I sometimes liked to monopolize Dennis's meetings with my delightfully witty and refreshingly hilarious quips and side notes. I mean, what better way to spice up a snooze-inducing meeting about canned food drives and snowball dances? My subtly-unsubtle antics during Dennis's meetings were what kept everyone from lapsing into a coma as they robotically ate their lunches and sipped from their pint-sized milk cartons and listened to gosh-awful sweater boy drone on about refilling teachers' staplers and emptying the recycling bins in the copy rooms. Throw me a bone, here! It wasn't like I was reverting back to making farting noises, or anything. Farting noises were *so* last year. Besides, the office of sophomore class president commanded at least a little dignity. And since I had run for the office unopposed and underappreciated, that dignity was Dakota James Lester's to interpret. And my interpretation of dignity was decidedly a little different from Mr. Wayne Dennis's. So sue me.

"I hear you, Mr. Dennis," I said with a salute. I leaned back in my chair and prepared to zone out. It wasn't like his saying the meeting was important actually *made* it important. When teachers said something was important, it usually meant you were going to have to regurgitate the "important" material for a test. When Mr. Dennis said something was important in a student government meeting, it just meant he was going to assign you to sell turkey-or heart-shaped cookies in the cafeteria, depending on the upcoming holiday.

"If you look at your agenda, you will see that Principal Stemwalter is going to be making a very important announcement in about ten minutes. I don't know what he wants to say, but he said it was important. Until he gets here, let's figure out who will be reading morning announcements over the P.A. for the next two weeks."

I shook my head and surveyed the room. Call me a jaded politician, but I thought I had signed up for more than selling cookies and organizing school dances when I had tossed my hat into the ring last year to become freshman class president. In reality, it seemed like we were nothing more than an assembly line, with Mr. Dennis as our supervisor; we clocked in, did what we were told to do, but left our voices at the door. To be fair, losing Addie Wilkins—whom I had had a borderline creepy crush on before being smitten by Erin's awesomeness-- to graduation had been a big blow to the student government.

Addie had run every committee, had headed up every fundraiser, had used her chameleon personality and drop-dead gorgeous looks to sway teachers and administrators to her side. Although Addie had been nothing more than a persona, she had known how to get things done as student body president. The state of our little faux democracy had been strong, and with her graduating and Sean Thompson taking over as a disinterested and ineffective president, we had regressed into nothing more than a group of students who were only in student government to bolster our college applications.

As Mr. Dennis and his Bambi sweater were wrapping up daily announcement sign-ups, Principal Stemwalter came through the door, sipping from his obligatory mug of coffee and sporting the worst comb-over in five states. A bristly smoke-gray mustache hid his upper lip, and rumor had it that he hadn't smiled once in his twenty-five plus years in public education. I always wondered if his teeth had rotted to nubs from all the coffee he consumed, as I had never seen him without a mug of joe in his right hand. He appraised the room with his hangdog eyes and took another nip from his steaming coffee mug. Mr. Dennis cleared his throat, obviously preparing to go into boss-impressing mode.

"Okay, students. As you can see, Principal Stemwalter is here to speak to us. Please give him your undivided attention." Once again Dennis-deer-dresser looked at me.

Give me a break!

Principal Stemwalter walked to the front of the room and stood beside Mr. Dennis's rollaway chair. He sniffed once and then proceeded in his lethargic drawl. I sat back and prepared to be lulled to sleep.

"What I'm about to say isn't going to be easy." Stemwalter took a sip from his steaming mug and I sat up straight. Something was up. I glanced at Mr. Dennis, saw that his bushy eyebrows were narrowed. Stemwalter continued.

"As most of you know, Infinity High School has been hit harder than some of the surrounding school districts by the current economic downslide."

Sip.

"Over the past two school years, we have had to make many difficult decisions. We've had to cut spending to the athletic programs, and we've had to temporarily scale back on some elective classes."

Sip.

"In addition, we've had to reduce staff and eliminate a few positions altogether."

Sip.

Mr. Dennis was stroking his mustache, his foot tapping anxiously as he awaited whatever hammer Stemwalter was about to let fall.

"Last night, the school board met to discuss ways in which we can be more fiscally responsible---"

To my surprise, Mr. Dennis cut Stemwalter off.

"You can't be serious, David! Please tell me the board didn't decide to cut funding to the student government!"

Principal Stemwalter sighed, the droopy bags under his eyes seeming to sigh, too.

"I'm afraid the school board has decided to dissolve the student government for the time being."

The room was silent. Pardon the overused and frequently abused cliché, but you could've heard a pin drop. Stunned expressions played on the faces of the members of the student government, and Mr. Dennis's face turned a bright red as his rage-filled blood filled the vessels and capillaries of his cheeks and forehead.

"You can't be serious! David, this organization is the lifeblood of the school! Without funding, who is going to put on the dances—put on the *prom*?! Who is going to run the canned food drives and take care of recycling? Who is going to set up tutoring opportunities for struggling students? David—*what are they thinking*?!"

Stemwalter put up his left hand as his right brought his coffee mug to his lips. I'd never seen a teacher blow a gasket in front of the principal before, let alone call Stemwalter by his first name. Even though I thought what we did in student government didn't live up to what my standards had been when I had run, I still felt cheesed off that a bunch of paunch-bellied adults could tell us what we could and couldn't do. I raised my hand, a thought popcorning into my brain. Stemwalter pointed to me, obviously not knowing my name.

"Yes. Do you have a question?"

"Can we raise our funds ourselves? If we aren't getting money from you guys, can't we raise it the old fashioned way?"

Mr. Dennis's head snapped from me to Stemwalter. The man in the eggplant deer sweater was fuming, and for good reason.

Stemwalter inhaled and exhaled slowly. "That is the second part of the board's decision. Due to bleak economic forecast, and because next school year is a levy renewal year, the board had decided that fundraising isn't an option. The board felt the community would be more willing to pass the renewal levy if they weren't constantly opening their wallets to buy candles and cookies and Christmas wreaths."

Mr. Dennis looked like he was about to burp fire. "That's insulting, David! How can they expect us to---"

"It is the board's decision, and it is my duty to uphold it, *Mr. Dennis*," Stemwalter cut him off. "I have every intention of doing my job. And I suggest you do yours."

This was a standoff between two ticked-off adults. Mr. Dennis glared at Stemwalter as Stemwalter returned the favor. After a perilous ten seconds or so, Stemwalter's face resumed its lethargic expression, and he turned to address the room of former student government members.

Dakota Defined

"I thank you for allowing me to speak to you this morning. Even though this was a difficult decision, know the school board has to do what's best for all concerned." With one final sip and a grunt in Dennis's general direction, Principal Stemwalter turned and ambled out the door.

Alas, the fall of democracy!

By second period English I had illegally texted the Hodgepodgers to let them know the student government had been terminated. I say 'illegally' because at Infinity High School it was against the sacred handbook to be caught with your cell phone indecently exposed. I had just got the newest iPhone, and I constantly found myself on the other side of the law, texting in class and snapping pictures and taking videos of teachers doing weird and/or dumb things. What can I say, I'm technology junkie. Anyway, my fellow Hodgepodgers had texted back, stunned and afraid of what this could potentially mean for their most beloved activities. Timothy had texted me that he had seen the home economics teacher crying at her desk, and that he was convinced the department was being slashed. I could only thumb back my responses and shake my head.

Mrs. Denny hadn't caught me with my cell phone out, probably because she had no idea what a cell phone was. She was older than fossil fuel and still handwrote her tests and quizzes, convinced that the "cyber net" was a passing fad akin to pet rocks and the poodle skirt. White haired and always smelling like she had bathed in purple jelly beans, Mrs. Denny was shaped like a tube of toothpaste squeezed in the middle, her sizable rump all but slapping unsuspecting students in their faces as she waddled up and down the rows of desks. Clearly it was time for this particular artifact to retire.

I sat in the back of the class and zoned out as Mrs. Denny

droned on about transcendentalism and something about a transparent eyeball. I couldn't believe the school board had decided to make all kinds of cuts. It wasn't like Infinity and the rest of Northwest Ohio were shantytowns or anything. Sure, the recession had closed the doors of some local businesses, but the really important furniture manufacturers and the major automotive plant were still doing all right. So how could the school be losing so much money? I sighed.

I don't get economics.

I just hoped and prayed the school board would be done making cuts, but something told me if they were willing to terminate the student government, they were going to keep slashing.

chap·ter | 'CH aptər |
noun

4

BOARDING UP BROADWAY

"This school sucks," Jeremy said, slamming his tray down on the tabletop. I looked up from my pudding cup and saw that his eyes were red. If I didn't know any better, I would've thought God's gift to the theater department had been crying.

"What's the matter with you? You find out your acting doesn't merit a Tony Award or something?"

"Shut up, Dakota!" Jeremy shouted, startling me. Jeremy wasn't one to get snippy. Either he was really mastering this acting thing, or something had happened to set him off. I was pretty sure it was the latter—I had seen his acting skills, after all.

Erin pulled out the chair between Jeremy and me and sat down. I could tell by the look on her face that her girl intuition immediately sensed something was wrong. She looked at me and then at the peeved Jeremy.

"What's the matter, Jeremy? Is something wrong?"

Jeremy looked up from his tray, the red rings around his eyes more pronounced. His face softened at Erin's voice.

"They cut the theater department."

I looked at Erin and shook my head in disgust. How far

was this going to go? Didn't Stemwalter and the other suited Neanderthals realize what they were doing? Didn't they realize that by slicing and dicing the budget they were slicing and dicing their students' reasons for coming to school?

Erin placed her hand atop Jeremy's. "I'm so sorry, Jeremy. I know how much the theater department means to you--"

"It's more than that," Jeremy's voice caught, and for a moment I thought he was going to burst into tears. "It's my ticket to college. My mom and dad can't afford to send me to college unless I get a theater scholarship. And now--" Jeremy threw up his hands and whipped his hair behind his shoulder. Considering the circumstances, I held my tongue in regards to his nasty girl hair. I have a conscience, after all.

"Maybe it's just temporary," I said, knowing full well that it wasn't. Jeremy had said the phrase "cut the department," and I could all but hear the death bell tolling.

Jeremy sniffled. "It's not. I saw Mr. Sanderson cleaning out his office. They want him to be a night janitor now or something. What is he gonna do? What am *I* gonna do?"

I didn't know what to say to Jeremy to make him feel better, so I didn't say anything at all. I was fuming inside, cheesed off something fierce. It's not like I had any vested interest in the theater department, but I had a friend who did. What is more, the budget-hacking axe was beginning to fall. First it was the student government and home economics electives, and now the theater department. I had a sick feeling I knew where the axe would fall next, should the school board decide to so more budget chopping.

"I wonder about the art department," Erin whispered. She looked at me, her dark eyes sad with the realization that she might just have spoken a painful truth.

"And the music department," I added, feeling my stomach fall. "Think of how that would kill Timothy—and Bertrand, too. I mean, they're both in the music wing right now practicing for district choir and band competitions."

"I can't believe our school board would do this to us," Erin said, shaking her head. She still had her hand over Jeremy's. Jeremy had his head down so we wouldn't see him cry, but I watched as his tears spattered the tabletop and made little rivulets of sorrow on the Formica.

"Believe it," Jeremy seethed, "they're all a bunch of--"

"Is this seat taken?"

I turned and saw a girl with crinkly acorn hair and matching eyes standing behind me. She had a tray of food in her left hand and a guitar case in the other, and as she looked at the constituents of the Hodgepodge table, a warm smile spread over her face. Nobody ever *wanted* to sit at the Hodgepodge table—someone coming and asking if she could sit with *us* was unprecedented. I was willing to bet the girl was here on a dare, or she was a new student. Considering I had never seen her before, I was putting my cards on the latter. Before I could offer to pull up a chair, Jeremy jumped up and pulled one beside him. His acting skills must've been on high alert at all times, because now all semblance of sadness and frustration were gone from his face and replaced with a curious look of nervous glee.

The girl put her guitar case at her feet and set her tray on the table before sitting down. Jeremy still wore a dopey expression on his face as she smiled and extended her hand to each one of us.

"I'm Hannah. Nice to meet you." She shook all our hands and then surveyed the cafeteria. "Is it always this crazy at lunch? It's like a zoo in here. Nothing compared to my old school."

"Yeah, this is what you can expect," Erin answered. "We're a bunch of ravenous dogs here in Infinity."

Jeremy laughed a little too loudly and I shot him a look. I could practically see little cartoon hearts bubbling up from his cranium.

You've got to be kidding me! From crying over the theater department cuts to puppy love at first sight!

"So, this is your first day here?" Jeremy asked, visibly fighting the urge to seem more chill than he was. It wasn't working.

Hannah brushed a strand of her hair behind her ear and nodded. "Yeah. First day here. My dad just took a job at Straub Financial Planning, and Mom is interviewing at the bank—I forget its name."

"First National," Jeremy blurted. It sounded more like a tuba blurb. "Where'd you move in from?"

"A small school in Defiance County you've probably never heard of."

I swept my hand around the cafeteria. "We may look like a sizeable herd of rabid wildebeests, but we're pretty small here, too."

Hannah laughed and I perked up. If she could laugh at my lame attempts at humor two minutes into our first meeting I had a hunch we could be friends for life.

"Put it this way," Hannah said, taking an apple from her tray, "we're so rural and small that during harvest time corn husks blow into the hallways when you open the doors."

I laughed, but Hannah's eyes widened in utter seriousness. "I'm really not joking about that."

"Oh, wow," Jeremy breathed, his chin on his hand as he leaned toward Hannah as though she were imparting the secrets of the universe. I didn't know whether to be embarrassed for the guy or to slap him on the back for finally finding something—or someone—other than theater to be obsessed with. I'd ridden the obsession train before, and it was pleasant while it lasted. Might as well let Jeremy enjoy the ride. Chugga-chugga choo-choo and all that jazz.

"Well, welcome to the bustling metropolis of Infinity," I said. "I hope you like our McDonalds and one overpriced and highly sketchy gas station, not to mention our florist who doubles as our delightful little town's mayor."

Hannah laughed. "Thanks—what did you say your name was, again?"

"Dakota Lester," I said extending my hand to her. Never mind we'd already shaken hands, it was all part of the act. "The artist formerly known as sophomore class president, if you really want to know the truth."

"Formerly? So, you lost the election?"

Erin and Jeremy looked at me and then at Hannah's black guitar case. Looked like I was going to have to break the bad news. If the theater department and student government lost their respective heads on the chopping block, the only logical progression was the art and music departments. Hannah seemed like an indie rocking freethinker, and I seriously hoped I wasn't going to destroy her hope for Infinity High School. But the truth was the truth; the writing was on the wall and the proof was in the pudding. Pardon the clichés.

"It looks like you're into music. Let me tell you about the dark underbelly of Infinity High School. And I apologize in advance; this story doesn't have a happy ending."

chap·ter | CH aptər |
noun

5

POP

"I think I'm in love," Jeremy said as he picked up his xBox controller. He brushed his cat, the aptly named Cat, off the couch and plopped onto the cushion. Cat hair and dust particles wafted into the air. I felt like I needed a gas mask. I guess that's what you get with a nasty basement couch.

"Easy there, Channing Tatum. You just met Hannah. Don't start making out a wedding registry just yet." I picked up my controller and prepared to completely own him in *Call of Duty*. Completely owning Jeremy at *Call of Duty* was kind of my thing. That and smart aleck salutes. I was a true champ at those, too.

"But didn't you see the way she looked at me? It was like she wanted me to ask her out."

I looked at him like he had seven heads. "What are you *talking* about? All I saw was you ogling her like a creeper."

Jeremy looked annoyed as he flipped through the game's intricate maps. He absently brushed his horse-tail hair behind his shoulder. "Really, D.L.? You're calling *me* a creeper? You obviously don't remember the way you followed Addie Wilkins around last year like she was a scratch and sniff sticker."

I nodded. "True, true. You've got me there. She did smell like cinnamon buns and heaven. But that was last year, and we're talking about *you*, not me."

"Hannah likes indie rock and edgy literary fiction. How cool is that?" Jeremy said, completely wrapped up in his own pathetic fantasy world.

"And you like show tunes and Dr. Seuss. What are you getting at? And pick a map, already!"

Jeremy selected a map and I prepared to massacre his face off. It wouldn't be hard; he was so deeply enamored with Hannah I could probably slather his face with peanut butter and have his cat lick it off without his noticing, let alone completely destroy him at *Call of Duty*.

"It's just—I don't know, D.L. Hannah showed up right when I needed her the most, you know? It's like we are meant to be together."

I raised my eyebrows. "Dude, you're not a serial killer or anything, right? Because you're talking like a guy who chops people up into little cube steaks and stuffs them into the deep freeze." I glanced at the deep freeze that hummed along the basement's far wall and imagined myself dismembered and scattered among hamburger patties and bags of frozen peas. Gross.

"I'm just being real with you, man," Jeremy said as my soldier blew his to smithereens. "Besides, if I was a serial killer I would have offed you a long time ago."

"Well, you might want to tone down the 'reality.' Don't you dare even think about bringing that we're-meant-to-be-together wacko talk up in front of Hannah. She'll slap a restraining order on you faster than you can say James Lipton."

We played *Call of Duty* in silence for awhile before Jeremy finally spoke again.

"I heard a rumor that the art department's getting the axe next week."

I paused the game and narrowed my eyebrows. If this was true, it meant Erin would have no real reason to go to school anymore. She was in Art II and was taking Art III as an independent study course with the hope of applying to an art school in New York. If the school board decided to yank the funding rug out from under the department, it would mean Erin would be swimming against the current when it came time to apply to colleges. Not having four years of art classes on her high school transcript would seriously maim the chances of her dream coming true, as she would be competing with students across the country whose transcripts would be littered with such classes.

It's not fair.

"Where did you hear that?"

"My dad's friends with Bill Lawrence. He's on the school board. I guess my dad was venting a little bit about the theater program being cut and Bill let it slip about the art department. Bill says his hands are tied—that there's not enough money to go around, but I think that's bull--"

"So what about Erin?" I interrupted. "And you? What about you are your theater scholarships?"

Jeremy sighed and unpaused the game. His soldier was immediately blown up by a claymore mine.

We looked at each other. Irony was a mean cuss.

"I think that just said it all," Jeremy said. "I don't feel like playing anymore."

***

I watched the snow fall outside the kitchen window as I finished the last of my Corn Pops. The white stuff had already wiped out school for the day, and as I slurped the leftover milk from my bowl I realized it might end up postponing my driver's license test, as well as any hope I had of driving my new-used car tomorrow. Of course this would happen.

Dakota Defined

I rinsed my bowl in the sink and dutifully placed it in the dishwasher so my mother wouldn't have a conniption when she got home from the hospital. Thumbing a quick and cheesy text to Erin about the weather outside being frightful, I felt a twinge of guilt for not telling her about what Jeremy had said a few nights ago about the school board's cutting of the art department. Maybe it was best for Erin to hear it from someone other than me. Or maybe I was just trying to wash my hands of being the bearer of bad news.

On the agenda for today was living up to my end of the car bargain. Mom and Dad would front the money for the car but I had to procure a job in order to make said car run. Stinkin' gas and its stinkin' price per gallon. Having the entire day to search for employment was a good thing, although I would have to traverse the town on foot. My trusty Schwinn, although reliable and steadfast as Sancho Panza, was powerless in the ice and snow. It would be my boots made for walkin.' And that's just what they'd do. Ten points for working Nancy Sinatra into an internal monologue about the perils of snow. Score.

I walked into the living room and turned the Christmas tree on. I mean, I didn't *turn the Christmas tree on*; I'm pretty sure artificial trees aren't attracted to concave-chested, peach-fuzz-lipped adolescents. What I mean is I liked the warm and gooey feelings the lighted tree gave me. Adorned with the obligatory red, green and silver bulbs and scattered with my cheesy and hastily made elementary school construction paper ornaments, the Christmas tree reminded me of the days when the Lester family was intact and thriving. It reminded me of my father stringing the lights while my mother readied the ornaments, Bing Crosby crooning "White Christmas" in the background while a light snow fell on the front lawn. It reminded me of cookies in the shapes of snowmen and stockings pasted with just the right amount of red and green frosting, of wrapped presents waiting to be placed under the tree to goad me with their mysteries until Christmas morning. It reminded me of the times I'd never get back. We all had different lives now, and different lives meant different memories. But it was still nice to look back at the old ones sometimes. It was still nice to remember where you came from.

★★★

I nearly slipped on the icy walk as I opened the door to Pop's Diner. I gracelessly recovered and thanked God I hadn't cracked my pelvis before seeking employment at Infinity, Ohio's one and only greasy spoon diner. The place had been around since 1964—a sign by the front door boasted so—and always smelled like fried bologna. I had decided to try Pop's first before inquiring at Happy Wok, where the Chinese food gave you happy indigestion. Suffice it to say, I was hoping Pop's would take me in so I didn't have to traipse all over Infinity in my snow boots.

I walked through the diner to the cut-out window in the back. Only the die-hards were here this morning, old men whose veins flowed with coffee and remember-when stories. A middle-aged waitress with way-too-blonde hair didn't even look up from her *People* magazine as I passed the waitress station. Peeking my head into the window, I saw Pop using an iron spatula to scrape the grease and grime from the large grill in the middle of the kitchen. He seemed to be the only one back there, probably sent everybody else home when he realized the snow wasn't going to be letting up anytime soon. His back was to me, and I was immediately intimidated by his enormous body and the curly black hair that carpeted his arms. I faked a cough to get his attention, and when he turned I saw the sweat and grease that plastered his black hair to his forehead. He narrowed his bushy eyebrows, and I wondered if he allowed them to grow so bushy so he'd have a spare mustache should the one that covered his upper lip decide to move to

Dakota Defined

Vegas.

"Can I help you?" His voice was gruff, like a 1960s football coach who smoked a pack and a half a day. He set the spatula on the counter and folded his massive arms across his barrel chest and looked me up and down like I was from the IRS.

I cleared my throat and tried not to let his bulk and steely stare get to me.

"I'm just wondering if—I mean, I'm looking for a job. Do you have any openings?"

Pop tilted his chin and brought a meaty hand to his mustache. "Have I seen you before?"

"I come in here sometimes with my mom--"

Pops waved me off. "Naw, naw. I've seen you somewhere else. What'd you say your name was again?"

I haven't told you my name, sir.

"Dakota Lester. I go to Infinity High School. You might know my dad, he graduated in 1984--"

Pop held up his bear paw hands. "Wait just a little minute. Dakota Lester? Now I remember who you are."

I was confused. I was about as popular as a cinder block. How could Pop have any clue who I was?

"It was you who slashed Sandy's tires last year."

What!!?? Oh, no. No, no, no, no, no. Pop can't be Nazi Neelson's—

"Sandy's my sister. You know her—works at the school. Ms. Neelson."

I wanted to burrow under the floor and die. There was no way I was getting this job, let alone walking out of Pop's Diner without a proper tongue lashing or something worse. How had I not seen the resemblance earlier? The broad shoulders? The mustache? Pop and Nazi Neelson—Sandy??!!---might as well have been the same person.

Pop continued without my having to say anything.

"After you slashed the tires of her Ford Focus last year, she was pretty devastated." He took a step toward the cut-out and I thought I'd wet myself.

"She called me over to check out the damage. Thought it was probably Blake Blanton and his gang. You know Blanton broke in here once and made off with over four hundred dollars?" It was a rhetorical question, I knew. There was no way I was about to answer Pop's question, not when I was on his turf and I could see the knife rack in behind him.

"Never could prove it was Blanton, but I knew it was him. The kid's bad news. Good thing he's finally locked up. After what he did to that art show..." He shook his head and picked up a towel and started to absently wipe down the counter. After a long moment, Pop looked up, a softness I had yet to see coming to his eyes.

"Sandy was hurt when she found out it was you who slashed her tires. She said you were a good kid, and she wondered why you'd ever do such a thing. She showed me your picture in the yearbook, and I remember thinking 'scrawny little runt like that slashed your tires?'"

I deserved that.

"When she found out Blanton was threatening you and the only reason you did it was to save yourself and your friends from a beat down, she was relieved. Sandy has nothing but good things to say about you, Dakota."

What? Nazi Neelson likes me*?*

To say that I didn't feel about four inches tall would be the understatement of the century. I felt horrible. Horrible for slashing Ms. Neelson's tires, and worse for continually calling her a Nazi. I was such a poop.

Pop put his big elbows on the counter and leaned forward so his face was nearly out the window.

"Sandy told me you wrote her the nicest apology letter after they finally caught Blanton and his thugs. That meant a lot to her."

I swallowed hard. For some irrational reason I felt hot tears pool in the corners of my eyes.

Don't cry, moron! How embarrassing!

"I know what kids call her. She does, too. All she really wants to do teach and be happy. You kids are her life." I nodded because it seemed like the appropriate thing to do. I felt like I had just been slammed in the gut by a sledgehammer.

Pop stood up and thrust his huge hand in my direction. For a moment, I thought he was going to grab me by the collar or my throat and strangle the life out of me. It took a second for me to register that he was smiling.

"If Sandy thinks you're a good kid, you're a good kid in my book. When can you start?'

I swallowed again and reached for his hand. It was rough and completely engulfed my own.

"Uh—I don't—you're offering me the job?"

"Show up the day after tomorrow at five. We'll have to do some paperwork and get you trained, but I think you'll find it's pretty laid back here. Whattya say?"

I smiled, still feeling like more than a horse's patoot.

"I'll be here at five. And tell Ms. Neelson I said thanks."

Josh Clark

Ne·an·der·thals /nē-ăn'dər-thôlˈs/

(See Infinity Local Schools school board)

chap·te**6** |'CHaptər|
noun

WHEN THE AXE FALLS

The snow might have stopped falling, and it might have been my birthday, but that didn't stop the school board from completely dismantling Infinity High School's art department. Before the first period bell had rung, Erin had surprised me with a big bag of Cool Ranch Doritos—my favorite—and an envelope containing two tickets to a February fifteenth Skillet concert in Toledo. She had planted a perfect Erin-kiss on my cheek and had told me the other ticket was for *her*, and that I would have to spring for Olive Garden before the concert. Her deep chocolate eyes had been beaming. By fourth period, her mascara was running down her cheeks in inky rivulets as she watched Miss Delphi pack up her desk and storm out of the building.

To say that the students of IHS were in shock was an understatement. Miss Delphi had made it a point to stomp through the main hallway during passing period, and from the distant eyes of athletes, musicians and academic quiz team members alike, it was easy to see that they were waiting for the school board's axe to come after them, too.

"It's so not fair!" Erin said as she sobbed into my chest.

My back was to my locker as people filed by, some visibly just going through the motions as they waited for more terrible news to come.

"Do you know what Stemwalter said to Miss Delphi?" Erin asked as her mascara smeared all over my white long-sleeved t-shirt.

"What did he say?" I stroked her back in small circles because I didn't know what else to do.

"He told her the school board was looking for a night custodian if she would be interested in applying for the job." Erin snorted. "I would've spit in his face! The jerk!"

I glanced at the clock and saw that passing period was all but over. A few more seconds and we'd be late to our fifth period classes. And my chemistry lab was two long hallways away.

Some things are more important than a stupid tardy.

"What am I going to do, Dakota? How am I ever going to get in to a school in New--" Another wave of sobs washed over her as the cruel metallic chime of the bell scolded us for still being in the hallway. I could've cared less about the bell, or about school. Why should I care about a school that didn't care about its students?

Besides, I had to make sure Erin was okay.

***

"I told him exactly what I thought," Erin said, pushing a green bean around her tray with her fork. "And do you know what he said to me—ugh, the friggin' jerk!—he said 'thank you for your concern. Now, if you'll please get back to class.' I wanted to dump his stupid mug of coffee over his ridiculous comb-over!"

"He really should consider shaving his head," Hannah supplied. Only Jeremy laughed. Jeremy *would* laugh.

Bertrand scribbled madly into his notebook as Timothy

shook his head and sighed.

"It's us next. It has to be. If these idiots can cut the art and theater departments, the music department doesn't stand a chance."

Bertrand looked up from his pad and squinted behind his thick glasses. "I believe the worst is yet to come for this establishment. I foresee more terminations, particularly in the areas of vocational agriculture and the scholastic quiz organization. Before the school board constituents are through, Infinity High School will be ushered into a period of melancholy and woe unparalleled by any in its history."

"I understood about half of what you said, but I get the gist," Jeremy said, flipping his nasty hair behind his shoulder. No bad thoughts about Jeremy's hair from me. I was too focused on comforting Erin and directing my rage toward Stemwalter and the school board henchmen.

"He's saying we're sunk," I said. I put my hand over Erin's. She smiled with her lips, but it never reached her eyes. And that broke my heart.

***

"You're going to do great," my mother said as we sat in her idling Dodge Neon outside the driver's testing building. "And just think, your father's signing the paperwork on your new car as we speak."

I glanced at the digital clock numbers on the dash. 3:56. My appointment was at four.

"No pressure," I snorted.

The wind whipped a paper flier off the building's glass doors and tossed it mercilessly with its frigid fingers. I was in no mindset to take my driver's test, as all I could think about was the school board taking a sledgehammer to Erin's dream of becoming a professional artist. I could relate to the poor buffeted paper; my emotions felt tossed about in a cruel, unrelenting wind I had no control over.

I opened the car door as the digital clock switched to 3:57. The biting air assaulted my cheeks, my nose.

"Well, here goes nothing." I heard the unmistakable click of a digital camera, and when I looked at my mother, she was in proud-mom-post-picture glee.

"Really, Mom?"

"We'll just add that to your scrapbook. Now, go break a leg."

***

Erin put on a brave face for me—bless her dear, sweet, beautiful heart—as we sat around the table and discussed what my newly-procured license would mean for my wallet, my responsibilities, my personal safety and the safety of others. I knew Erin was emotionally destroyed by the loss of the art department, but she seemed genuinely excited to have a boyfriend who could drive. Either that or she really liked my mom's cooking.

"We'll take her for a spin after we're done," my father said, folding his napkin and placing it on his lap. "It'll be good for you to practice some night driving." To his right, Karen nodded as she tried to get a fidgety Ethan to sit up straight.

Erin wasn't the only one putting on a brave face tonight. My mother was doing her best to make nice with Karen. This was only the second time they had met, the first being last year after my probation had ended and we had all met at a Toledo Red Lobster to celebrate the occasion. That meeting had been tense, to say the least, both women chillier than the Abominable Snowman's big toe. This one was going better, my mother and Karen actually sharing polite banter and crockpot recipes. Thank goodness for crockpots and their abilities to bring people together.

"You'll have to be careful, James," my mother said. "Some

of the back roads are still slippery."

"*Dakota* will have to be careful," my father clarified. "He's the one who's going to be behind the wheel."

"Remember the law, Dakota," my mother said, passing a plate of flour tortillas. She'd made tacos, my absolute favorite. "You can only drive with one non-family member until you're seventeen."

I rolled my eyes. She'd drilled Ohio's teenage driving laws into my brain the entire way home from the license bureau.

"I know, Mom."

"And nobody else drives your car," my father said, spooning ground beef onto an open tortilla. "That's not an Ohio law, that's a dad law."

"I get it, I get," I said, throwing up I-surrender hands. "I'll be responsible, I promise."

"Let's see your driver's license," Erin said. I pulled my wallet from my back pocket and proudly handed the still-glossy plastic to Erin. She studied if for a moment and then looked up at me. She nodded her approval.

"Not bad. I thought it'd be worse."

"What's that supposed to mean?"

"Come on, Dakota, it's *you* we're talking about," my mother said, sprinkling a taco with a few onions. "I half expected you to take the picture backwards."

"Funny, funny, funny," I said, playing up the moment. "But I'll have you know that the three-thousand-year-old woman who took the picture said I was a very handsome young man."

"And modest," my father said. That got a laugh from the table.

"Do you hear that?" Erin asked, cupping her ear.

"Hear what?" I asked, thinking all the neglected warnings my mother had given me about turning down my iPod's volume had come back to haunt me.

"That crying sound," Erin said, mischief in her eyes. "It's

your Schwinn mourning the end of a great friendship."
    We all laughed. It was great to see Erin smile.

chap·ter |'CH aptər|
noun

Denying Dennis

I drove to school the next day, feeling more than awesome to be coasting into the sophomore parking lot in my own ride. My Daytona didn't have a system—didn't even have a CD player—so I couldn't pull up bumpin'. I planned on putting a system in my new beast after I had worked a few months at Pop's Diner. For now, I settled for having the radio dial tuned in to a mix station out of Defiance. Somehow I didn't think it'd be cool to crank the Kenny G cassette tape I had found beneath the passenger seat. Definitely not what I was going for on my first solo sophomore parking lot experience.

When I turned into the sophomore hallway, I saw Erin waiting for me by my locker. She wore a navy hoodie over skinny jeans, her patented red Converses adding just the right amount of pizzazz to her ensemble. Her hair was up and her dark eyes sparkled, despite the circumstances surrounding the defunct art department.

"So how was your first drive to school?"

"It'd been better if I could've picked you up," I said, stuffing my books into my nuclear meltdown of a locker.

"I know, I know. But when you have a cop for a dad, you

get a little more overprotection than the average teenager."

I couldn't fault Officer Taylor. I mean, it wasn't like I'd had my license for three months or anything. It would take a little time for him to let his one and only daughter ride in a vehicle with the kid who only last year had bashed innocent people's mailboxes and had slashed Ms. Neelson's tires. I don't think I'd trust me without a trial run either.

"He'll come around," Erin said as I slammed my locker shut. "He likes you. He just likes me more."

I smiled and leaned in to peck her on the cheek. "And he should. You're precious cargo, you know."

"You're such a kiss-up. No pun intended, of course. Oh, hey. Before I forget, Mr. Dennis was looking for you a little bit ago. I'm supposed to send you to his room."

What? Why?

"Really? Did he say what he wanted?" I set my Algebra II book on the ground. Erin slid down the wall to her seat.

"No, just that he wanted to see you." She patted my textbook. "Don't worry. I'll guard this with my life."

***

Mr. Dennis's door was open, but I knocked anyway. I didn't want to walk in on anything weird. I could just see Mr. Dennis being the kind of guy who'd bring his taxidermy hobby to school. Not that I knew Dennis was a taxidermist or anything. I kind of just assumed as much after his eggplant-deer-sweater episode. Fortunately for me, Mr. Dennis was hunched over a stack of freshman history tests. Unfortunately for him, his sweater was atrocious. He looked up when he heard me knock.

"Oh, hey, Dakota. Why don't you come in and have a seat." He motioned to the desk in front of his own. "We have a few minutes before the bell rings. I just wanted to run something by you."

I dutifully made my way to the desk and slid into the seat.

It felt weird sitting in the front of an empty classroom, like something out of a dream. But I was fully clothed and headless chickens weren't running rampant through the school, so I knew it wasn't a dream. I tended to dream a little on the eccentric side.

"Thanks for coming, Dakota," Mr. Dennis began, leaning back in his rollaway chair. I had to try hard to take my eyes off his eyesore of a sweater-- lime-green number with little black squares all over it—and focus on his words. I seriously wondered if the guy *tried* to dress like walking vomit.

"As you know, the budget cuts are difficult for all of us," Dennis continued, absently tapping a blue ballpoint pen against the corner of his desk. The empty room made the tapping almost "The Raven" unbearable.

"Between you, me and my desk here, I think it sucks. I can't believe the school board is failing to see the ramifications of their actions."

And you want me here....why? Just to rant?

Mr. Dennis continued. "I just received word that the The National FFA Organization will be dissolved. Do you know what that means, Dakota?"

I didn't know if it was a rhetorical question, so I just sat there grinning like an idiot. When he answered himself, I knew I had chosen wisely. A-plus for good intuition and all that jazz.

"It means that farmers around here are going to go berserk. We live in an agriculturally-based region of the state. If Infinity High School doesn't have an ag program, there could be some serious ramifications." Mr. Dennis shook his head and sighed.

"I'm sorry for ranting, Dakota. As a teacher, I shouldn't do that. But as a taxpayer and as a father who has kids coming through the school system, I can't take it anymore. The reason I brought you here is because I need a leader to unite the student body behind the good and just cause of getting all the programs we lost back."

Dakota Defined

Hold up. Timeout. Rewind the tape. Did he say he needed a leader? And was he implying that *I* was the leader he needed? Had he *seen* where I ranked in the social pecking order? I was only one notch higher than industrial mop heads, for cheese sake! I was only in his student government because nobody else ran against me. Freshman year had been a fluke. What could Dennis be thinking?

"Uh—I don't really understand why you're asking me--" I stammered. I started to stand. Mr. Dennis and his trip-and-a-half sweater had the wrong guy. There's no way he could possibly mean I was remotely close to being a leader. I was more of a go-with-the-flow-and-make-obnoxious-yet-refreshingly-relevant-wisecracks kind of guy. I was *not* a leader.

"Just a second, Dakota," Mr. Dennis said, extending a palm. "Please, hear me out before you leave."

I sat back down and felt my heart pattering in my chest. I felt like the weight of some big responsibility was about to be passed my way, some expectation I had no hope of coming close to fulfilling was going to be extended in my direction by a teacher I respected, and I was going to have to turn him down. Because I was not worthy of the weight. Because I was useless when it came to expectations. I'd spent my life below the radar; what made Dennis think I might be able to rise about it?

"Dakota, whether you know it or not, you are a leader."

I nearly laughed in his face. I really hand to pinch it to keep it in. What was this guy on? Dennis continued. "The way you rallied people to your cause—the way you won them over when you gave your speech last year—that was when I knew you were a leader."

Mr. Dennis was referring to the speech I gave in front of the entire student body when I was running for freshman class president. I hadn't even used my notes—I'd torn them up, to be more exact. After Jacob Riley had said something terrible from the back of the auditorium, I began to freestyle. And it had worked. People said they identified with the way I had taken a stand for all the "little people" of Infinity High School. My classmates said the way I had talked about unity instead of division, respect instead of disdain, had stuck a chord with them. Last year was all fine and dandy. I had done my thing in the heat of the moment and it had worked out for me. But what Mr. Dennis was saying was ridiculous. I couldn't just pour it on when I wanted to. People had liked my speech because it made them feel good at the moment, because they knew I was on the hot seat and wanted to see how I would weather the storm. That didn't translate to being a leader. A leader could do things like that on command. And I couldn't. Hence, a leader I was not.

"Mr. Dennis, I--" I began to protest.

Mr. Dennis waved me off. He was now on his feet and coming around his desk to stand directly in front of me.

"You have grown up a lot, Dakota. Haven't you noticed how I always ask your opinion in student government meetings? Haven't you noticed how I always put you on committees with upperclassmen?"

"I don't know, I--"

"You have a gift, Dakota. You draw people to you through humor and then you make them see your side of things. I admire that in you. To tell you the truth, last year when you told me you were running for freshman class president I thought you were joking. But now—now I think you really *are* on your way to becoming a good leader."

What he was saying felt good and felt awful all at the same time. Yeah, I wanted Dennis to look at me as more than a skinny, slap-sticking nobody. But I didn't want his praise to distort reality: I was *not* a leader.

"What about Sean Thompson? He is—was—student body president, why not ask him to rally some people--"

Dennis sighed. "Because Sean's not a leader, Dakota. He's only student body president because the election process is a popularity contest." He narrowed his eyebrows. "And that stays between us, understand."

I nodded.

"I just think if you were able to rile up the student body a little bit you could make a big difference. They're a bunch of zombies right now who are allowing the school board to take away the things that make this school great. I can't do it, Dakota. I have a family to think about. I can't lose my job. But you—you could be the mouthpiece of the school. You could really define yourself as a leader. You could help give Infinity High back what is rightfully ours."

I didn't know what to say. All of this was too much, far too much for a guy like me to handle without exploding into a gagillion pieces.

"I—I can't Mr. Dennis. I don't know how to---"

"I'll point you in the right direction," Mr. Dennis interrupted. "Come, on, Dakota. Your school needs you. Think of all the good you could do."

And think about how I could royally mess things up!

I stood from the desk. I couldn't do it—didn't even want to think about it. There had to be someone else who could step in and be the hero I couldn't be. I had just learned to drive, for cheese sake! How could I be expected to start a revolution?

"I'm sorry, Mr. Dennis. You'll have to find somebody else."

I was out the door in less than two point three seconds, leaving Mr. Dennis and his pukey sweater to find someone more worthy to advance his cause.

***

"What did Mr. Dennis want?" Erin asked, standing up from the floor. She pointed to my textbooks. "Guarded 'em with my life, by the way."

I smiled weakly, my head still in the classroom with Mr. Dennis. How he could possibly have thought I would say yes to something so beyond my scope of influence was baffling.

"Nothing," I said as the bell sounded. A few late stragglers bustled to their lockers, the tips of their noses and ears red from the frigid cold.

Erin's eyebrows showed skepticism. She could read me like the scrawny book I was.

"Just some stuff about student government. Saying thanks for being part of the organization," I lied. I hated lying to Erin. It felt about as good as licking an envelope and getting a paper cut on your tongue. But if I told her the truth, she'd be all 'that sounds like a great idea—I think you'd be really good at it' and I'd be all 'Dennis is flippin' crazy for even thinking about me doing such a ridiculous thing' and she'd be all 'you really should do it' and I'd be all 'You can't make me' and she'd be all 'I thought I was dating someone with strong convictions'… You see why I couldn't tell her. She'd convince me to do it, and I'd do it and fall flat on my face like the time my Schwinn had decided to see if I'd like the taste of asphalt after my front wheel had popped off. Not going to do. Nope.

Erin shrugged. "Still too bad about the student government getting cut. It'd be nice if someone had the guts to rally the student body to take on the school board."

I rest my case.

chap·te**8**|ˈCHaptər|
noun

Soggy Hamburger Buns

"You take the bin and empty out all the napkins, straw wrappers and other soggy crap that floats on the bottom," Pop picked through the bus-boy bin and threw out a waterlogged cheeseburger and a passel of Coke-soaked fries. I felt my stomach roll over as I looked at all the liquid sloshing on the bottom of the bin. I tried not to think of how many customers' backwash I would be shoving my hand into. Pop wiped his hand on his greasy apron.

"There. Empty. You'd think people would eat all their food. They are paying for it, after all." He walked to a stainless steel double sink and took a hose from an equally stainless steel hook. I wanted to tell him that people were actually paying double for his food; monetarily and with frequent trips to the bathroom. Pop's Diner was famous for being a natural laxative.

"You spray this here in the bin like this," Pop said, demonstrating. "Then you take the bin back to the waitress station. Got it?"

I nodded and pointed to a stainless steel contraption I assumed was the automatic dishwasher. "And how does that work?"

Pop clapped me on the back hard. "Sandy said you're a smart kid. You'll figure it out." With that, he made to leave the dishwashing room. He turned around after he had crossed the threshold to the kitchen. "If you need anything, I'll be right up here. I only have two rules for my new help." He held out two sausage fingers. "One, if you can lean, you can clean. Two, don't eat anything you didn't buy. I stopped eating this stuff about ten years ago. Figured I liked life and didn't want my old ticker clogged with double cheeseburgers and waffle fries, know what I mean? You get a free meal on your break if you want one. After emptying those bins awhile, you probably won't want it. Good luck." He turned and walked back to the kitchen. As I turned back to the stack of dishes awaiting a hearty scrub-down, I heard the grill hiss as Pop slapped another quarter-pound heart attack onto its face.

Bon appetite!

***

There was something good about mindlessly handling liquid-bloated sesame seed buns and rubbery, half-eaten hamburger patties: it gave me time to think. As I tossed old food and soggy napkins into the trash receptacle and robotically ran the dishes through the stainless steel beast, I wondered how Mr. Dennis could possibly have pegged me as a leader. The thought gnawed at my brain, and I couldn't shake the feeling that maybe I should have stepped up to the plate and swung for the fences when he had told me he thought I could handle such a monumental task.

But still, it was *me* we were talking about. I could barely remember to put my dirty underwear into the clothes hamper, could hardly be relied upon to get my homework done on time and in a manner worthy of handing in. What could Dennis possibly see in me that made him ask me to start a revolution? It was ridiculous. Stupid, if I was really honest with myself.

Dakota Defined

Yet, there was that gnawing, that *yearning* to be the leader Dennis saw in me. If I could pull off unifying the student body and getting the programs back that had been ripped away from us, I would feel that high school had been worth the awkward morphing of my body and the leprous state of my social situation. If I could get the reeling student body behind me, I might just be able to pull off the ultimate Davidic upset against the Goliath school board.

But you can't, Dakota. You know it. It's a pipe dream.

As I sprayed out bins and wiped down the counters, I thought of Erin and how her dreams of being a professional artist had taken a severe hit. Yeah, I felt bad for Jeremy, too, but Erin and I were kindred spirits. I felt things for her I had never felt for anybody before. I didn't know if it was love, because I didn't know what it meant to truly love a girl. I mean, how do you *really* know if you're in love? Is it something you wake up knowing, or is it something that grows over time, like moss on a tree. I didn't know if what I felt for Erin was love, but it sure felt more than like. We weren't like other high school couples who were together because it elevated their social statuses or helped to release some of the enormous hormones that come along with being a teenager. I knew we were different from any other couple I knew because I connected with Erin on a deeply emotional level. Yeah, I was attracted to her—her dark eyes, her soft skin and lips, had the ability to make my heart nearly beat out of my chest and my hands get all kinds of clammy—but our connection ran much deeper than physical attraction. Besides, we'd set our boundaries, and we'd never come close to toeing their lines because we respected each other and the intimate emotional connection we had too much to mess around with ruining a perfectly healthy relationship. We were *us*. And it was a beautiful thing.

As I waited for the dishwashing machine to finish its cycle, I hoped Erin was strong enough to weather the current storm not having any art classes would bring. *Had* brought. The cyclone was already sweeping its way through the halls of the school, and any extracurricular or elective class that cost the school precious cents was swept up into its devastating swirl. Although Erin was putting on a brave face, I knew she would crumble soon. It was inevitable. She was still in a state of shock, but as time passed and she sat in two study halls instead of two art classes and saw her sketch pads sitting forlorn and unused in her locker, I hoped she wouldn't crumble into a million pieces. And I hoped I was strong enough to help her navigate through the shrapnel of shattered dreams.

chapter 9

Farmer Blues

The last day of school before Christmas break. As Mr. Dennis had predicted, the The National FFA Organization and all vocational agricultural classes were the next to fall. Mr. Felton, whom the students affectionately called Farmer Felton, cleaned out his desk and walked out of the school with dignity and class. And then he proceeded to do donuts in the staff parking lot, his tires screeching like a twelve-year-old girl at a Justin Bieber concert, black smoke and the smell of hot rubber somehow seeping through the school windows and reaffirming to the student body that the school board, in all their budget-slashing glory, cared nothing about the students of Infinity High School.

Erin's first period study hall, the slot in her schedule that had once contained an art class, came and went, leaving her in a foul stupor all the way through lunch. In fact, she didn't even sit at the Hodgepodge table, instead opting to work on a chemistry lab report with her iPod ear buds jammed into her ears atop the highest level of the foldout gym bleachers. I wanted more than anything to console her, but I knew she needed some space. I doubt she would have talked to me anyway.

"I got the part as an extra in the community theater's production of *A Christmas Carol*," Jeremy said, flipping his dandruff encrusted hair behind his shoulder. I wanted to take out a hedge-trimmer and alleviate his dandruff problem altogether.

"What do you mean, you got the part? Don't you just have to show up? It's not like people are beating down the door to get a part in a community theater production," I said, picking at my grilled cheese sandwich. I know it was harsh, but when Erin was in a bad mood, I was in a bad mood.

Jeremy looked at me like I was dumber than a box of macaroni.

"The fact that they even let me be a part of the show is awesome. The first show is tonight, and I've only been to two practices. I was planning on focusing on the spring musical here, but, yeah, that's not gonna happen anymore. So, I decided to see if the community theater needed some extras."

"I happen to think that's pretty cool," Hannah said, smiling. The way she looked at Jeremy made me want to throw up.

Are you kidding me? She likes him? Has she not seen his hair?

Jeremy looked like he'd just been shot by all of Cupid's arrows. "You should come out tonight. It'll be a good show."

"I just might do that," Hannah said, smiling. I wanted to puke to the second power.

The sound of thick-soled boots clunking against the cafeteria floor made me look to my right. Lumbering up to the Hodgepodge table was Craig Henderson, the poster-boy for Infinity High School's now defunct The National FFA Organization. He wore a red and blue plaid shirt tucked into a pair of Wranglers, a brass John Deere tractor belt buckle gleaming large at his waist. As he stepped beside my chair, his expensive-looking cowboy boots stopped their assault on the cafeteria floor.

"You're Dakota, right?" Craig asked, eyeing Jeremy and Hannah.

"Uh, yeah, that's me. What's up."

Craig shook his head and hooked his thumbs into his jeans pockets. "I'll tell you what's up. Our school board ain't nothing but a bunch of--"

The thud of Hannah's guitar case falling on its side muffled whatever Craig had said about our beloved school board. Even though I agreed with him, I wasn't sure what his abhorrence of the school board had to do with me.

"Uh—what it is you want, exactly?"

Craig looked like he was about to spit out of the corner of his mouth but quickly caught himself when he realized he wasn't in a pasture. "I want an FFA program my senior year, that's what. I'm vice president as a junior, and I want to be president."

Um...

"So, I'm still not following, Craig--"

"Mr. Dennis said you were the guy to talk to," Craig interrupted.

Drat that Dennis! I see what he's trying to do!

I shook my head and grabbed my tray. Even though I wasn't finished eating, it was the easiest way for me to make a quick exit from the awkwardness of the situation. I stood up.

"Craig, I don't know why Dennis would tell you something like that. I don't even know what you mean."

Okay, so I'm lying...

The fire seemed to go out of Craig's hazel eyes. All of a sudden he looked like a sad child. "Mr. Dennis said you were organizing some sort of student rally to get all our organizations and classes back."

Why? Why is Dennis doing this?

"I'm not. Mr. Dennis must've meant somebody else."

I quickly brushed past him and bolted for the trashcans. What was Dennis thinking? Did he seriously think that if Craig approached me with his sad, puppy dog eyes I'd give in? Well, newsflash, nasty-sweater-man: I wasn't doing it! I wasn't a leader!

Just leave me alone!

chap·ter |ˈCHaptər|
noun
10

Steppin' Out

Erin was despondent for the rest of the school day. My heart bled for her, but I knew school was not the time or the place to try to console her. I hoped classes letting out for Christmas break would offer Erin a much-needed reprieve from thinking about the dissolved art department and her uncertain future.

I drove home from school and checked the answering machine to see if Pop had called. He hadn't put me on an actual schedule yet, as he wanted to make sure I was willing to do the work first. He'd said he'd had too many "village idiots" quit on him after the first night of cleaning up soggy food and scraping nasty dishes. I didn't know if he was lumping me into the village idiot category or was setting me apart from the category, so I had only nodded and smiled---like a village idiot.

I wanted to do something special for Erin. She hadn't ridden with me since I had procured my license, save for the time I had taken Dad on a night drive. I hoped her police officer father would tone down the daddy-protection for one night so I could take my girlfriend on our first real date. That would be the perfect start to a Christmas break I would spend trying to keep Erin from thinking about what happened to the art department.

I texted Erin and told her I was picking her up at six and we were going somewhere special. I hoped when Officer Taylor saw I was trying to be a genteel adolescent he would allow Erin to ride with me. I was shocked out of my tube socks when a few minutes later Erin wrote back that she would see me at six.

***

I rolled up to the Taylor residence at five till six. As my Grandpa Lester (God rest his soul) used to say, if you weren't five minutes early, you were late. The inside of my Daytona smelled like Polo cologne, not an oppressive I'm-going-to-choke-and-die smell, but just enough to show that I was a sophisticated, modern man, thank you very much. I looked good, too, not to brag or anything. I was wearing crisp new jeans and a white and blue striped button down, my new Nikes a spotless white beneath the cuffs of my jeans. I'd given my dirty-blonde hair a playful mussed look, and I'd made sure the New Jersey-shaped zit on my cheek was successfully popped and dried. Mom had spotted me the necessary cash to make this date possible, seeing as I had only worked at Pop's Diner one night and had yet to procure a paycheck. I was feeling good. My wallet was full, I smelled like a million bucks and my antiperspirant deodorant was doing its job. I was ready to rock.

I zipped up my coat as I walked to Erin's front door. The air was biting, and I prayed more snow wasn't on the way. My mother freaked out every time she watched the local weathercast, convinced that any snowfall would mean my driving demise. I have to admit, I was a little uncomfortable myself with the notion of driving in ice and snow, but there was no way I was going to tell my mother that. I didn't want her snatching my keys away right after I got my license.

When I got to the door, it opened without my even knocking. At first I thought it was Erin, but when I saw the hulking figure in an Infinity Police Department uniform, I knew it was her father. And let me tell you, having a uniformed officer open the front door when you are about to take his daughter on her first driving date is enough to make a guy want to fudge his underwear.

Oh...super.

"Dakota, nice to see you," Officer Taylor said in a clipped, all-business voice. "Why don't you have a seat. Erin will be ready shortly." His big hand motioned to the couch, where Erin's insurance-selling mother sat with a warm smile on her face.

"You know girls," Mrs. Taylor said, "always running behind."

I sat down, hoping and praying the nervous gas bubble in my stomach wouldn't inadvertently squeak out as it sometimes did when I did sit-ups in gym class. When I was nervous, my body went into produce-foul-smelling-fumes mode. I didn't appreciate my stomach's mutiny.

"What year did you say your car was?" Officer Taylor asked, looking out the window. He didn't sit down, and his hulking presence only served to make me all the more nervous. Of course, this was what he was going for. Protective dad and all that terrifying jazz.

"It's a 1993."

"How many miles?" The way he asked me the questions made me feel like I had just been pulled over. I half expected him to ask to see my license and registration.

"Sixty-two thousand. It was owned by some old peop—uh—elderly people and they took real good care of it."

Officer Taylor only nodded and rubbed the black stubble on his chin. From where I was sitting, it sounded like sandpaper on rough wood.

"That's very nice, Dakota," Mrs. Taylor chipped in, her smile still warm and mom-safe.

Is this good cop/bad cop?

"You know my wife I and like you, don't you, Dakota?" Officer Taylor asked, his dark eyes boring holes into my soul.

Oh stinkerdoodles. Here it comes.

I fidgeted and felt my stomach roil. "Yeah. I mean—yes."

Officer Taylor nodded. "We trust you, Dakota. Not only to drive safely and responsibly, but to treat our daughter with respect."

Okay. Now I was uncomfortable. What was he getting at? Did he think I was going to park somewhere and put the moves on Erin? I wanted to tell him my back seat wasn't big enough for hanky-panky, but I thought bringing up hanky-panky might make him draw his gun.

"Uh—yes," I stammered.

Officer Taylor nodded again, seemingly satisfied by the way I had started to perspire. Now my deodorant was failing. Stupid antiperspirant that wasn't antiperspirant. Didn't they test their product under this kind of stressful situation?

"You're a good kid, Dakota," Officer Taylor continued. "As long as you treat Erin with the utmost dignity and respect, we won't have a problem." His hand brushed the gun in his holster as he extended it toward me.

We won't have a problem??!! What does that mean?

I shook Officer Taylor's hand, and his grip was like a vise.

Erin walked into the room and I about wept in relief.

"You ready to go?" she asked. I didn't have to think about my response. I was off the couch faster than you could say 'he's got a gun!'

Erin was wearing her hair back, her dark eyes shining the way that made me stutter. She wore a black button-up sweater over not-too-skinny jeans and her patented red Converses. She was stunning. Moving to the couch, she kissed her mother on the cheek.

"Be good. Make sure you bundle up. It's chilly."

"I will, Mom," Erin said, walking to her father. "See ya, Daddy."

"Dakota'll take good care of you," Officer Taylor said, glancing in my direction. I didn't know if it was warning or I was just paranoid enough to read it as one.

Sir, yes sir!

"Be back by eleven thirty," Officer Taylor said as I took Erin's coat off the coatrack.

"I'll have her back no later than eleven twenty-five. You know what they say: if you're not five minutes early, you're late." To my blessed surprise, Officer Taylor actually cracked a smile.

Thank you, Grandpa Lester (God rest your soul)!

★★★

"I survived the Father-Officer Inquisition, I think I'll be able to survive a Pop's Double Bacon with Cheese," I said, as Erin smiled and shook her head.

"They're your arteries. Eat at your own risk."

"I will have you note that I *didn't* order onions on the side." I arched my eyebrows in what I thought a seductive eyebrow arch might look like. In reality, it probably looked like I was grimacing from the effects of constipation.

"Easy, lover boy. I'm a good girl. Besides, you've seen my dad's gun." Erin took a sip from her water and shot me with a finger-gun.

"And I'm pretty sure he'd use it," I said, feeling the familiar nervous flutters in my stomach. "I'm not going to lie, he scared my hormones right out of me, so you won't have to worry about fending off any of my irresistible advances."

She laughed and leaned forward. We were the only ones at Pop's Diner, the only ones who considered Pop's a great place for a date. We occupied a booth in the far right of the small, grease-smelling establishment, and even though we weren't in the most romantic of settings, I wouldn't trade the moment for the world.

My cell phone buzzed an incoming text message in my pocket and I took it out to see who could possibly have the audacity to disturb me at such a time. When I thumbed up the text and saw who it was from, I rolled my eyes.

"Who is it?" Erin asked.

"Jeremy. He needs a ride home from the community theater. Sorry, actor-boy, no can do. I'm on a hot date tonight. And besides, I can't have you both in the car at the same time. The state of Ohio's rules."

Erin stirred her water with her straw and cocked her head to the side. "You know, you could always take me home first and then pick Jeremy up. What time is the show over?"

I thumbed the text back to the screen of my iPhone. "He says ten thirty, but who knows if the show will be over by then. And there's no way I'm dropping you off early. I have you until eleven twenty-five, and I intend to savor every minute."

Erin winked. She drove me wild.

"I feel bad for Jeremy, Dakota," Erin said with a sigh. "It's not like he has many friends, let alone friends who can drive. Timothy can't, and neither can Hannah."

I snorted when she said Hannah's name. "You mean his new obsession?"

"I think she likes him, too. I've been watching the way she looks at him. Besides, I have girl intuition, remember? I know these things."

"Well, good for him. But that still doesn't mean I'm picking him up from the theater. That's what he has parents for."

Erin looked at me with eyes that shamed me into relenting. "Come on, Dakota. He's your friend."

Drat your eyes that shame me into relenting.

I slapped the water-spotted Formica tabletop. "Fine. Fine. I'll pick him up. But only because you're *making* me."

Dakota Defined

"Now you see who wears the pants in this relationship," Erin said, her eyes twinkling.

"I wouldn't look good in skinny jeans, anyway. You can wear them all you want."

"We'll figure out the logistics of the passenger situation later," Erin said. "Right now I just want to enjoy the time I have with you."

I laughed and thumbed an I'll-pick-you-up text to Jeremy. "You really know how to wrap a guy around your finger, don't you?"

Erin only winked and stirred her water with her straw as I thought about all we'd been through together. Our relationship had morphed from friends-since-diapers to a deep-rooted romance seemingly overnight. Maybe it was something we had both subconsciously known all along, but as I watched Erin—my girlfriend--stir the ice cubes in her water cup, I knew there was a God and that he worked for good. Why else would he take two marred and broken individuals and bring them into a place of mutual respect and devotion?

A silence fell over the table, and I heard the grill hiss as Pop threw my red slab of heart attack onto the grill.

"You know, Dakota, we've come a long way," Erin said smiling into my eyes. "Last year at this time you were on probation. This year—well—I'm the happiest girl in Infinity."

I laughed and tried to brush her comment off. "Really? The happiest girl in Infinity? Are you forgetting that our school board is dismantling our little school by the day?"

Erin studied me for a moment, her milk chocolate eyes probing deep into mine.

"I have you, don't I? A guy who respects me for who I am? A guy who likes me despite my eccentric tastes? A guy who'll stand by me even when my dreams are crumbling?"

I swallowed a ball of emotion. It came over me so fast I didn't know what hit me. She truly was the most beautiful person I had ever met. Not just on the outside, but on the inside. In that moment, I thought I knew what it meant to love. But should I say it?

"I'll be okay with the whole art thing," Erin continued. "It'll just be harder to get to where I want to get to, is all."

"You'll get there. That I know for sure."

Erin's smile ignited my heart and set it ablaze.

"Promise me one thing, Dakota," Erin said, reaching across the table and placing her hand on mine. "Promise me you'll always be there for me, no matter what."

I swallowed another ball of emotion. Doggone balls of emotion. I looked her square in the eye, and all of my surroundings faded into oblivion. No Pop's Diner, no greasy burger smell. Nothing but Erin and the immediacy of the moment.

"I promise I'll always be there. Regardless of whether we're a couple or not, I'll always be there. You're my best friend, how could I not be there for you?"

Erin's eyes sparkled. She didn't have to say anything. Her tears said it all.

chap·ter |CH aptər|
noun
11

DATE NIGHT:

AKA BEING ACCOSTED BY MR. DENNIS WHILE EATING UNFORTUNATELY NAMED ICE CREAM TREATS

We finished eating our less-than-delectable Pop's dishes and readied to leave the greasy-spoon establishment. Pop had given me a hefty discount when the bill came, and when I had looked back toward the kitchen, he'd given me a hairy-armed thumbs up. Good. At least Pop liked me. Hopefully his liking me would generate some serious hours on the work schedule.

"That was great. Thanks a lot," Erin said as she wrapped her coat around her slender body and slid her arms home.

"The food will probably give you heartburn until you're forty," I said slapping some one dollar bills onto the table.

"I was talking about the company," she said as we walked through the empty diner to the front door. We passed the waitress station and Peg, the platinum blonde, middle-aged waitress looked up from her *Cosmo* magazine long enough to tell us to have a good night in a smoke-husky baritone that would scare young children and mid-sized dogs alike.

"It's eight o'clock," I said, thumbing my cell phone off and putting it in my pocket. "What do you say we get some ice cream?"

"And then you'll take me home so you can pick Jeremy up, right?" Erin asked as I opened the door for her. The wretchedly frigid air assaulted us immediately.

"You must really hate being with me," I said, fishing my keys out of my pocket. My Daytona was equipped with the basics and had no power locks. Until I had got my car I hadn't realized how much I had taken power locks for granted in wickedly cold weather.

"Come on, Dakota," Erin said, bouncing up and down and hugging herself as I fumbled to get the key in the key slit. "You know what I mean. It'd be your good deed of the day to pick him up and take him home."

My key blessedly found the slit and I quickly unlocked the door and climbed in. I reached over and unlocked the passenger door and Erin hurriedly plopped into her seat.

"Must have heat!"

"It's coming," I said, starting the car. "And don't you think my one good deed was taking you out when you could've been moping at home tonight?"

"Touche," Erin said as I pulled out of Pop's Diner's parking lot.

"I'll pick him up, don't worry your pretty little head," I said as we pulled onto Main Street. "Now for the important ice cream decision: are we settling for McDonalds, or are we driving to Swirly Cream in Clearton?"

The heat in my little engine that could finally kicked on, and for a moment we let ourselves bask in its dusty-smelling warmth.

"No brainer," Erin said, finally. "Swirly Cream it is."

"Come madam, your chariot awaits," I said, turning onto West Elm Street.

"I don't think it has the same effect since I'm already sitting in your car," Erin said, leaning over the center console and resting her head on my shoulder. "But how can I argue time and place when you are being such a gentleman?"

This is perfect. Please, God, let me remember this night always.

★★★

Clearton was a fifteen minute drive due west of Infinity. The Clearton Cavaliers were bitter rivals with the Infinity Hornets, besting us in almost every sport under the sun over the course of the last two or three years. Suffice it to say, Infinity High School students crashing Clearton's only year-round ice cream and burger joint hangout was generally frowned upon. Many a legendary fight had taken place in the Seventies-era eatery, and I was hoping I wouldn't have to throw down with an angry Clearton Cavalier for infringing upon his turf. The likelihood of that actually happening was slim to none, as I was about as popular as dental floss and bombastic athletic personalities were generally the ones who found themselves in the rivalry scuffles. But I was going to be on my guard, nevertheless. A guy never knew when he'd have to fend off the enemy or protect the integrity of his girlfriend. According to Hollywood and the liberal media, stuff like that happens more than you think.

When Erin and I arrived at Swirly Cream, the only patrons of the soft-serve establishment were an older couple licking matching vanilla-chocolate swirl cones in the far corner and a mom with her two preschool-aged children occupying a booth in the center of the shop. The preschoolers, a runny-nosed boy and a heavily-banged and scruffily-dressed girl, had ice cream smeared around their lips and noses and a mother who looked ninety-four kinds of frazzled. Erin and I approached the counter and proceeded to recite our order to the blonde high schooler behind the counter, who turned out to be as soft in the senses as the ice cream she served. After messing our orders up twice, she finally gave us our Reese's Swirlies, (awful name, I know), and we took a booth as far away from the preschoolers and their hangdog mother as possible.

"She reminded me of Addie Wilkins," Erin said, referring to the girl who had taken our order.

I laughed and grabbed some napkins for us out of the pawed-up stainless steel napkin dispenser. When I did, I saw a distorted reflection staring back at me, and when I turned I saw Mr. Dennis and his wife standing beside our booth.

Crud buckets.

"Fancy meeting you here," Mr. Dennis said, patting my shoulder. He was wearing a black wool coat, but I guessed there was a monstrosity of a sweater hidden beneath. Mr. Dennis without a hideous sweater was like a sumo wrestler without stretch marks. You couldn't have one without the other and all that jazz.

"This is my wife, Anita," Mr. Dennis said, touching the small of his wife's back. She had brown hair teetering on the precipice of a steely takeover and puffy cheeks that made her look like she was pouching corn and/or assorted nuts to munch on while she gleefully ran on her hamster wheel. Erin and I shook her hand, and I wondered if Anita Dennis was responsible for Mr. Wayne Dennis's horrific wardrobe.

"So, Dakota," Mr. Dennis said in a way teachers do when they know they have the upper hand. I knew what he was going to say before it came out of his former-student-government-advising mouth.

Not here. Please.

But my internal pleas did nothing to stifle what Dennis was spewing into the atmosphere. He continued with a smirk and a "gotcha" glint in his eye.

"Have you given any more thought to what we discussed?"

My heart accelerated. I hadn't told Erin the truth about my

meeting with Sweater Boy, and if she found out I had lied to her, things were going to get ugly.

"Um, no," I said, my voice sounding like I was pinching off a squeaker fart.

"What's he talking about?" Erin asked, looking from me to Dennis. I either wanted to pop a floor tile and tunnel my way to Malaysia or bury my head in the vanilla soft serve mix. Anything would be better than this awkward moment of awkward awkwardness.

Dennis looked like he was Benedict Arnold revealing pertinent Revolutionary War military strategies. "Oh, he didn't tell you?" He raised his caterpillar eyebrows and absently fingered his bellybutton through his coat.

Leave. Go away. Buy a normal sweater.

"I asked him if he would be willing to unite the student body for a good cause," Dennis continued. I felt his eyes boring holes through me as I pretended to find my napkin interesting enough to warrant more than a fifteen second stare.

"Really," Erin said, a hint of an edge coming to her voice. Now I could feel her eyes lasering into my skull. How much more vulnerability could a scrawny post-pubescent teenager take?

"I thought Dakota would be the perfect leader to unify a disgruntled student body against the school board and all their community minions."

"Honey…" I looked up and saw Anita Dennis touch her husband's arm, her indication that he might be saying too much.

Mr. Dennis shook his head. "I need to let my students know where I stand, Anita. This school board is acting like a death squad, and it is flat-out wrong."

"Tell me about it," Erin said, shaking her head. I knew Dennis had accomplished what he set out to. When Dennis and his hamster-wife left our table, Erin would be all up in my business about being a leader and all that jazz, and I would have to deal with her pokes and prods to "do the right thing." Why couldn't Dennis just find somebody else, already?

I sighed, trying to cover my exasperation. "Look, Mr. Dennis. I'm sure you can find somebody else. There's plenty of kids in school who are leaders--"

"But there's only one you," Erin interrupted. I looked at her like I was about to puke. She might as well have said something like 'be the change' or 'it only takes a spark to start a fire.' How after-school-specialish.

I looked at Mr. Dennis. He had a cheese-eating smirk on his face that I wanted to karate chop off.

"She's right, Dakota. You're a leader. You just don't know it yet."

"And Caesar makes salad," I mumbled.

"Excuse me?" Mr. Dennis leaned forward.

"Nothing. Just let me think about it, okay?"

Mr. Dennis looked at Erin and communicated to her via his eyeballs. When I looked at her, she winked. *Actually winked!!* This was a flippin' conspiracy the size of Vermont!

"We'll let you two get back to your date," Mr. Dennis said, putting his hand back on the small of his wife's back. "Let's move on, Anita. These kids need to enjoy their ice cream."

As Mr. Dennis and his domesticated rodent wife walked away, I felt Erin's eyes all up and over me. I turned and looked at her, spooning my melted Swirly.

"What?"

"You know what," she said, not amused at my feigned ignorance. "You lied to me. That's not cool, Dakota."

I took a deep breath. "I'm sorry. It's just—I didn't want you--"

"Agreeing with Dennis? *Completely* agreeing that you are capable of doing something great for your school? Is that what you mean?"

I shook my head. "Erin, please stop. I'm not a hero. I barely shave twice a month. Can we just drop it? I'm sorry I lied to you, really I am."

Erin studied me for a moment before smiling.

"I think you'll come around. If not—I'll make you."

Oh, brother!

***

As I started my car, Erin checked her cell phone for the time.

"Nine forty-five. We'll get to the community theater building with time to spare."

I looked over at her like she had ten heads. "What do you mean *we?*"

I pulled out of Swirly Cream's parking lot and turned the heater on.

"I meant *we*," Erin said like I was the stupidest kid in five counties.

I laughed. "No, no, no, no, no. Not a chance. You know I can only drive with one non-family member until I turn seventeen. The state of Ohio's rules, not mine. I'm not the saltiest fry in the Happy Meal when it comes to numbers, but you and Jeremy make *two* non-family members. And that's a no-no."

Erin reached over the center console and hooked her left arm around my right. "Come on, Dakota. It's what—eight blocks to Jeremy's house from the community theater building? Who's going to know?"

I stopped at a red light and looked over at Erin, whose face glowed red from the stoplight.

"Did you fall and hit your head? Your dad's a *cop*, Erin. He practically read me my Miranda rights when I picked you up tonight."

"He's not on duty tonight."

The light turned green and I shook my head. "That's not the

point and you know it. All it would take is one of your dad's officer buddies to pull me over and I'm toast. I mean, it's not like they don't know who I am. I *did* get arrested last year and all."

Erin sighed and leaned over the console to rest her head on my shoulder. "If I promise not to badger you about what Dennis said, will you lighten up about it? We can tell Jeremy to duck down in the back if you're so worried. Besides, if you drop me off before you pick him up, you lose almost a whole hour with me." She kissed my cheek, her warm, supple lips sending a warm wave through my cold cheek.

I took a right at the sign advertising Infinity Automotive and groaned. "You're not making this any easier, you know that, right?"

"That's the point," Erin said, rubbing her nose on my cheek.

"It's dumb that I'm even picking Jeremy up in the first place. It's only eight blocks. The master thespian can walk home."

"In this cold? Have a heart, Dakota."

I laughed. "You're unrelenting."

"I try."

I took a deep breath and unknowingly sealed my fate. "Fine. I'll pick Jeremy up. But if your dad finds out and tasers me, I'm gonna be more than ticked. Jeremy has to duck down, and you can't say a word to anyone. If my mom or dad finds out, I'll get my car taken away or worse."

Erin kissed my cheek again and squeezed my arm.

"You're the best."

"Don't forget it."

"I won't. Besides, what's the worst that can happen?"

dis·as·ter /dĭ-zăs'tər/

NOUN: When everything falls apart.

chap·ter |ˈCH aptər|
noun

12

JOY RIDE

We arrived back in Infinity at three after ten o'clock. True to her word, Erin had not said an additional word about Mr. Dennis and the Dakota Revolution. Instead she spent the fifteen minute jaunt back to town snuggled against my right arm, occasionally kissing my cheek while she talked about art schools in New York and Bertrand Warner's new obsession with chronicling entire conversations into his trusty notebook like some nerdy scribe. All the while I drove on and added my two cents when the conversation warranted it. In reality, I was just savoring the moment, satisfied beyond measure to hear Erin's voice as she cuddled close. But when we pulled beside the curb in front of the old brick community theater building, all the good feelings vanished and were replaced with a sudden foreboding.

"I don't think I should do this," I said, looking up at the hulking brick structure and feeling its two century history loom over me. The building was legendary for its stories of Civil War era ghosts who supposedly haunted the creaky catwalks and prop rooms; and as the street lights cast weird shadows on the brick face, I couldn't help but feel an obligatory cliché chill

Dakota Defined

tickle my spine.

Erin playfully socked my shoulder. "Don't be a wuss. Everything's going to be fine. Trust me."

"Trust you? You mean like when we were five and you told me your mother used gum to make her hair shiny and it would make mine shiny, too?"

In the splash of yellow streetlight I saw Erin scrunch her nose.

"Um, yeah, sorry about that one. Although you did look pretty cute with a buzz cut."

I let out a nervous chuckle and fished my iPhone out of my pocket. Unlocking the screen, I saw the digital clock numbers read ten after ten.

"Where is he?"

"Patience, Dakota James, patience," Erin said, patting my shoulder. "There's no need to get all grumpy."

I put my phone back into my pocket and snorted. "He's on our time."

"Be nice," Erin said as the theater's door opened and Jeremy walked out. "See, there he is."

Jeremy saw my car and headed straight for it. As he crossed into the swathe of street light, I saw his lips were redder than usual. When he opened the door, I let him hear about it.

"I knew you were a secret cross-dresser," I said, as Erin got out of the car and put the seat back so Jeremy could get in the back.

"What?" Jeremy asked, situating himself behind Erin. He flipped his nasty hair behind his shoulder and rubbed his hands together in the universal 'I'm-cold-turn-the-heat-on' gesture.

"Your makeup. You're wearing makeup."

Jeremy rubbed at his lips and cheeks. "All actors do."

"Yeah, but you're not a real actor," I said, taking my frustration over having to drive him home out on him.

"Dakota, be nice," Erin said, getting back in the car and

turning the heat up.

"Whatever," I grumbled, putting the car into drive. I looked into the rearview mirror and seethed as Jeremy flipped his stupid hair behind his shoulder again. "And you need to duck down, Tiny Tim. It's against the law for you and Erin to be in my car at the same time."

Jeremy obliged without any rebuttal. For a second I felt bad for taking my frustration out on him. That is until he starting talking again.

"So, how was the big date tonight?" He socked me on the shoulder and I wanted to sock him in the mouth.

"Great until I had to pick up this really awful cross-dressing actor from a haunted community theater and he sat in the back seat of my car and got his nasty hair particles all over the interior."

"Shut it, dude. I wash my hair twice a day."

"Come on, Dakota," Erin said, "let's just drive Jeremy home in peace."

"You're taking me straight home without letting me see how this handles higher speeds?" Jeremy asked, patting the car door.

"I'm taking you straight home because you're ruining my life right now," I shot back.

"Come on, man. I've never ridden with you before, let alone in your new ride. You're telling me you aren't a little bit curious about how fast this baby goes?"

I wanted to shove a sock into his mouth. Why couldn't he just can it until I got to his house? Wasn't enough that I was taking him home when he could just as easily walk his theater-loving patoot the eight blocks home?

"It might be fun, Dakota," Erin chimed in, hooking her arm around mine. I thought my ears must've been clogged with some pretty thick wax. She couldn't have said what I thought she just said.

"Have you completely lost your marbles?" I asked. When Jeremy laughed from the backseat I secretly wished his hair would get caught in windmill.

"What can it hurt?" Erin continued. "We're already in the car. And my dad says the IPD officers go out to the country roads when there's a call."

"And?" I asked, incredulous.

"And she's saying we're teenagers who live in a small town with nothing better to do for fun," Jeremy said as I turned onto his block. "Come on, man, just this once."

"One time won't hurt anything," Erin said.

"When did you become a delinquent?" I asked, stunned at what I was hearing. Was this the part where the police officer's daughter segued into a life of rebellion? I sure as Sugar Ray Leonard hoped not. I didn't want to be on the boyfriend-end of a t'ed off daddy-cop whose daughter went off the deep end with the aid of her skinny crush. Count me out.

"I just feel like living a little bit," Erin answered, "what's the harm in that?"

"Yeah, what's the harm in that?" Jeremy chimed in.

I took a deep breath as we coasted to a stop in front of Jeremy's house. The lights were on inside, and I could just imagine Mark and Debbie Stines sitting in the living room sipping green tea and watching *Dancing With the Stars*. And there was an overwhelming part of me that knew Jeremy should climb out of the back seat, wave goodbye to me and Erin, stomp up the stairs and take his theater makeup off and join his parents in the living as they huddled around the boob tube as a family. I could feel the rightness of it. For some unexplainable reason I knew—just *knew*—that my decision on the matter would change the course of my life.

"Please?" Erin tried one last time. I didn't know what she was trying to pull, but it made me uncomfortable. The last time I was pressured into doing something illegal I ended up in the King County Jail. And that had been about as much fun as sticking a fork into a light socket. But really, what could it hurt? If Erin was saying it was going to be okay, if would be okay. I trusted her judgment. She'd chosen me to be her boyfriend, after all. She knew what she was doing.

I took a deep breath and looked at the house and then at my girlfriend, whose face was blanketed by yellow street light.

What can it hurt? Live a little, you pansy.

"Okay. But we're going *way* into the country."

"That's what I like to hear, my man," Jeremy said. He flipped his stupid hair behind his shoulder and whooped like a way-too-theatric cowboy. "Let's make this baby go vroom."

I put my foot on the accelerator and felt my stomach churn. As I turned onto Burke Street, I wondered why I felt like I was making the biggest mistake of my life.

***

Jeremy yakked all the way to County Road R about *The Christmas Carol* and how he had all but stolen the show as an extra. Instead of contradicting his every sentence with a pertinent 'yeah, right' or 'like heck', I let him talk. Better to let him enjoy his community theater experience, because goodness knew he wouldn't be gracing Infinity High School's stage any time soon.

For the most part, I was nervous as all get out. Not only was the frigid winter night black as death in the deep northwest Ohio countryside, but also I feared black ice to be slicking the road every hundred yards or so. Snow blanketed the wide-open spaces of rural Infinity, and even though the slippery stuff had melted on the roads, that didn't mean I felt any better about driving on County Road R in the dead of winter in the dead of night. It wasn't like I was the most experienced driver in the world, either.

Just stop spooking yourself. You're fine. Nobody's gonna

to know about this.

"Dude, we're out in *Deliverance* territory," Jeremy said, leaning between the seats. "Is this even part of Infinity School District?"

"I don't know if they even having runnin' water out in these here parts," Erin said, really lathering on the southern-fried hillbilly inflection.

"This is a perfect stretch of road to see what this little Daytona's made of," Jeremy said, sitting back and clicking on his seatbelt. "Open her up, dude."

I sighed and looked out my window and then Erin's. I half expected her dad to pop out of the darkness and arrest me on the spot. That is after he tasered me within an inch of my life, of course. I felt Erin's hand on mine.

"It'll be fun, Dakota. Besides, no one even knows we're here. The nearest farmhouses are back from the road at least a third of a mile. Even if Farmer Joe Bob or Hillbilly Ralph sees your lights, they're not going to do anything. Kids come out here all the time to do what we're about to do."

I had a flashback of Blake Blanton grinning devilishly from the driver's seat of his dilapidated car as I got ready to bash mailboxes on County Road F. He owned me last year because I had willingly handed him my soul on a silver platter. Why did this situation feel so much like bashing mailboxes with Blake?

I shoved the horrid image out of my mind and revved my little four cylinder engine.

Blake's locked up. Forget about him. This'll be fun. Besides, I've been wanting to see how fast this thing can go.

"Gentlemen, start your engines!" Jeremy said from the backseat. Without thinking anymore about the consequences, I slammed the accelerator to the floor. My tires responded with a banshee screech that sent stones and loose asphalt spraying the undercarriage of my car. We took off like a dart.

"Yeah! Faster!" Jeremy yelled as my Daytona's little engine

responded to my foot's pedal-to-floor stimulus. The speedometer inched toward sixty as we blew through the first stop sign at the intersection of County Road R and County Road 17.

"See! I told you this'd be fun!" Erin shouted over the growl of the engine. The speedometer blew past eighty and the small car began to rattle.

"Faster!" Jeremy whooped.

I felt my palms go moist with clammy sweat. I didn't like the vibrations that shook the steering wheel in my hands. As the speedometer hit ninety and we blew through another stop sign, I made a deal with myself that this would be a one-time experience. When we hit one hundred miles an hour, I could take it no more. I slowly applied pressure to the brake pedal and we slowed to a comfortable forty-five miles per hour.

"Dude! You could've hit one-twenty!" Jeremy said, disappointment thick in his voice.

I wiped my palms one at a time on my jeans and shook my head. "I'll let you kill yourself in your own car once you get your license. My cap is one hundred."

My heart pounded, but I was surprised to find that it wasn't out of fear, but exhilaration.

Okay, so that was a little more fun than I thought it'd be.

"Your car rattles after eighty," Erin said.

"If this car's a rockin', don't come a knockin'," Jeremy quipped.

"What if I knock you out?" I said, feeling good. Erin had been right; this was what I needed. A little fun never hurt anybody.

"I'll sue," Jeremy responded, but I really hadn't heard him. An idea had just popped into my mind. I turned on the dome light and looked at Erin and said the two words that would give me sleepless nights for months to come.

"Wanna drive?"

She narrowed her eyebrows. "Wait—what? This coming

from the kid who ten minutes ago was lecturing us on the State of Ohio's driving laws?"

"I wanna drive, I wanna drive, I wanna drive," Jeremy sang from the backseat.

I turned around. "No thespians allowed behind the wheel of my car." I turned back to Erin. "So? How's 'bout it?"

"You do realize I only have my permit, right?"

I raised my eyebrows. "So *now* we're concerned with the laws, eh?"

Erin playfully stuck out her tongue and unbuckled her seatbelt. "You think I'm chicken? You can even get in the back."

"Sweet action! I'll take front," Jeremy said as Erin opened the car door. The icy air immediately assaulted my cheeks and nose. My heart pounded with excitement.

"You game?" Erin asked, grabbing the door handle. I laughed.

"I'm game. I'll sit right behind you and tell you what you're doing wrong." I opened my door, stepped out onto the road, pushed the seat forward and buckled myself into the seat directly behind the one I had vacated. Erin circled the car and hopped into the driver's seat while Jeremy cozied himself into the passenger seat.

"Do your worst, Erona," he said, happily. "I can't wait until I get my license. Dakota, you're a lucky man, you know? New car, a chick to ride with you. It's all good for you."

"And you're barely a man with all that makeup," I shot back, feeling the adrenaline course through my veins. "Let's see what you're made of, Erin." I squeezed her shoulder as she shifted my Daytona from park to drive.

"I'm not doing the whole pedal to the metal thing," Erin said as the car picked up speed. "I'm going to hover around fifty-five. And watch who you're calling chick, actor boy."

"Wuss," Jeremy coughed.

"Yeah, come on, grandma, you've got more in you than

fifty-five," I said, feeling light as air in the backseat. Now that I had come back to earth from planet Paranoia, I felt game for anything. If Jeremy had suggested we run around the northwest Ohio countryside stripped to the waist and yelling 'The redcoats are coming!' I would have done it.

"Whatever," Erin said as she punched the accelerator. My little car growled in response as the four cylinders worked their little hearts out to pick up speed. "You ladies think you can handle eighty?"

"Please," I said cockily, "I did *one hundred,* remember?"

"Buckle yourself in, you dolt," Erin said, taking one hand off the wheel to slap Jeremy on the shoulder.

"Why? Are you planning on smashing us into a tree?" Jeremy retorted. I couldn't see him, but I knew he had just winked. Theatrical winking was kind of Jeremy's thing. "I trust you, baby."

"Watch who you're calling 'baby,' Matthew Broderick," I said, glancing over Erin's shoulder. The speedometer inched toward eighty as we blew through a stop sign.

"Still, I think you need to buckle yourself in--" Erin started, her hand raised to slap Jeremy again.

I can't explain what happened next, because I don't fully remember the car hitting the patch of black ice just after the intersection of R and 12. I don't remember the windows shattering as my Daytona pounded into the ditch, don't remember my little car crumpling like a smashed soda can as it ricocheted off the ditch's embankment and continued to roll—four and a half rotations—into Farmer Pete Bronson's snow-lathered, corpse-cold field. I don't remember my face smashing into the driver's seat headrest, don't remember my nose exploding like a Fourth of July firework. All I remember is Erin's blood-curdling scream—the scream that would haunt my dreams and claw its talons into my brain whenever I had the audacity to think the worst of that night was over.

Dakota Defined

The nightmare had just begun.

chap·ter
noun
13

MOMENTS

There are moments in life when time stands still, when your surroundings blur into oblivion and all you can feel is your heartbeat's pulsing strobe behind your eyes and the tingles of the same beat in your fingertips. There are moments when the soundtrack of your existence consists only of foreboding thunderclaps and the cruelty of shrill, wailing wind. There are moments when the taste of iron-thick blood is the only thing that confirms you are still living, when the searing burn of ten thousand migraines casts psychedelic strobes over your vision. There are times when your brain goes into shutdown mode and your perceptions of the world about seem grotesque and distorted, when a connection is lost somewhere between your optical nerves and rational thought. There are moments when seconds stretch to eternities, when each individual tick of the clock brands forever-images onto your already numbing brain. These are the moments when you know your life will never be the same; that you have a crossed a threshold into a new a new room of reality and you can never exit the way you came. These are the moments when all you thought you knew about life and its certainties shatters into a billion jagged pieces, and you know that nothing is ever certain but that all those pieces will never fit together in the same way again.

As the biting wind of the northwest Ohio night slapped me awake and the haze of my brain lifted enough for me to realize that the thick, warm substance coating my hands was my own blood, I understood I had crossed a threshold. When I realized that my head rested against the roof of what had been my Dodge Daytona and that I was actually upside down in the overturned vehicle, I knew I would never be the same again.

But that was me and my realization. My foggy brain struggled to make another connection, one I sensed was vital but couldn't place. The overwhelming urge to sleep took over my thoughts and my eyelids felt bogged down by weights.

Yes, sleep was what I needed. Sleep—maybe eternal sleep—to rectify the images of wrongness around me. I would give in. I would allow sleep to wash over me.

Maybe I'd wake to something better.

chap·ter | CH aptər |
noun

14

MATTERS OF LIFE AND DEATH

I awoke from a deep sleep cold and experiencing vertigo. My face pounded, my nose feeling like it was being knifed over and over again. An excruciating burn seared through my skull, and before I could realize where I was, I vomited until my stomach had given up its foul contents.

What? Where am I?

And then my ruptured thoughts slammed into place. I saw how I was suspended from the roof—no, the *seat*—of my crumpled Dodge Daytona. I felt the biting wind of the cruel December night wrap its fingers around my neck, felt the sting in my index finger as a shard of broken glass sliced my skin as I gingerly reached for where the back window had once been. It came back so fast, so horrifically fast.

Erin!!

She had been driving, I remembered that much. But why? Why had I let her behind the wheel of my car? And why did it matter now? I had to find her—had to get to her so I could wrap her in my arms and tell her this was all a nightmare. That everything was going to go back to the way it was before this happened. That we could fix this.

Oh, please, God—let this all be a nightmare!

I fumbled in the darkness for my seatbelt latch. I didn't know how long I had been under, but it had felt like three eternities. I knew time was of the essence, that I had to get to Erin as quickly as possible. But I couldn't find my stupid seatbelt latch!

"Erin?" I said, my voice sounding alien in the crumpled wreckage of my car. I waited a moment for her to respond. Nothing.

"Erin!" I said louder. I hurriedly tried to find the seatbelt latch as panic started to settle in the pit of my stomach. "Erin! Answer me!" Still nothing.

Please, God! Please!

My thumb finally found the button to extract me from my backseat prison. I fell with a painful thump onto the roof of my car. I realized my hand landed in my own vomit and that little jagged bits of glass had lodged themselves into the heels of my palms, but I didn't care. All I could think about was getting to Erin. She wasn't in the driver's seat, that much I knew. Even in the viciously black night I could tell the seat was empty, and that could only mean one of two things: either she had been thrown from the vehicle or she had crawled out and was trying to find help.

The car was crumpled so badly I couldn't crawl out the hatchback. I had to squeeze my way over the center console and into the passenger seat, where the shattered passenger window provided just enough room for me to wiggle out of the car, but not without first slicing my stomach on shards of broken glass. It was when I had successfully crawled out of the wreckage that I realized I had forgotten something, or rather some*one*.

Jeremy! He was in the passenger seat!

My mind swirled with all kinds of horrific thoughts and images. Both Erin and Jeremy weren't in the vehicle. They both wouldn't have gone to seek help, not with me still in the crumpled car. That could only mean one or both of them was seriously hurt.

Oh, God—no!

I crumpled over and retched into the snow. My stomach had emptied itself while I had still be strapped into the vehicle, so all I was really doing was dry-heaving and gagging on my own bile.

This can't be happening! This can't be real!

I slowly raised myself to my feet, more than surprised to find that none of my bones seemed to be broken, save for whatever damage had been done to my face I tried not to think about cannon blasts of pain that rocked my skull and my nose. It felt worse than anything Blake Blanton had ever done to me, but I had to work through it. There were more important things than my suffering. I had to find Erin and Jeremy fast.

My shoes crunched snow as I stepped back from the car and tried to get my bearings. The remoteness of the locale made the night one of the blackest I had ever been out in, and when I looked for the road, I couldn't find it.

We must've rolled three or four times!

"Erin! Where are you?" I yelled, feeling my heartbeat thunder in my devastated face. Nothing.

I need light! All I need is a little light!

I jammed my hand into my left pocket and produced my iPhone. I nearly wept when it came to life in my hand, the picture of Erin and me at the homecoming dance I had set as my wallpaper slicing an eerie blue glow into the blackness.

"Erin! Jeremy! If you can hear me, say something!" I continued on through the snow, not sure whether I was moving closer to finding Erin and Jeremy or moving farther away. All I knew was that I had to keep moving. My brain and adrenaline wouldn't allow me to stand stagnant. I prayed I was moving in the right direction.

"Erin! Jeremy!" I yelled at the top of my lungs. My voice echoed through the darkness, bouncing back to me and making me feel all the more alone. I sucked in a sob.

I have to call 911! I have to get help!

And then I heard a faint whimpering coming from my right. "Erin?"

The whimpering continued, barely perceptible over the whistling, icy wind. I started to my right, my phone out in front of me.

Come on! Where are you, Erin?

"Erin? If that's you, say something!" The whimpering grew louder, and I figured I was closing in. As I followed the sound, a wave of panic washed over me when I realized what scene I could be about to see.

Please, God! Please!

A sob lodged itself in my throat, and I swallowed it before it had a chance to burst into the atmosphere. I realized my hands were shaking, the blue glow of my phone jumping every which-way over the snow.

"Erin? Say something!"

A loud whimper immediately to my right chilled me to the core. When I swung my phone around, I saw an image that will forever be branded onto my memory.

"Erin?"

She was lying on the snow in the fetal position, blood streaming from a wound on her forehead, mixing into the snow and creating a crimson slush wherever she moved. Her head was in her bleeding hands, her dark eyes wild and wide as they peeked above her fingertips. I ran to her.

"Erin! Are you okay?" I reached for shoulder and she flinched at my touch. She was delirious, shock starting to work its way throughout her trembling body.

"Are you hurt badly? Please, tell me what I can do--"

She didn't respond, only continued to shake.

"Hold on—let me call 911, okay. Then we need to find Jeremy." I dialed the nine and Erin let out a bloodcurdling scream.

"What?! What is it?! Are you okay?"

Erin shook violently as she raised her bloody arm and pointed behind me. With everything in her, she let out an animalistic scream. "I killed him! I killed him!"

I felt my stomach lurch as I slowly swung the blue glow of my phone around.

"I killed him! I killed him!" Erin screamed over and over.

The blue light of my phone captured an oval-shaped splotch of dark blood, a few spatterings and---

"Ohhh…" I heard myself moan. My stomach lurched again, and I doubled over and dry-heaved.

Oh, dear God, no!

I had found Jeremy.

chapter |ˈCHaptər|
noun

15

NUMB

Erin was screaming, I was heaving and Jeremy was lying dead atop the snow. As I wiped the corners of my mouth with my coat sleeve and felt my skull all but explode from the booming pain, I knew I had to get an ambulance to County Road R immediately. I took one more look at Jeremy's mangled body and then made my way to where Erin was shaking violently in the snow. Her legs were curled up to her chest and her eyes were frenzied and wild.

"I'm calling nine-one-one and then I'm calling your dad, okay?" When Erin didn't respond, a wave of panic swept over me. She was in shock, or close to it, and if I didn't get her help fast, I might lose her as I had lost Jeremy.

Please, God! Please let her be okay!

***

It took the paramedics seventeen minutes to arrive. Each minute felt like a millennium as I watched the digital numbers on my phone tick away precious minutes that Erin didn't have to waste. I only left Erin's side once, and that was to go back to where Jeremy lay in a bloody heap upon the unforgiving ground. I didn't have to be an emergency worker to know he was gone. The way his body was contorted into an unnatural shape, the way his neck laid at an odd angle in a pool of dark blood, told me all I needed to know. Jeremy was dead. I didn't check for a pulse—I didn't have to. I just hoped the paramedics would hurry up and get here so he didn't have to lie in the snow very long. He deserved better than that; he had been one of my best friends.

As I walked back to Erin, I was shocked at the numbness that had overtaken my emotions. Jeremy was lying dead no more than four feet to my right, and I felt nothing. I wanted to cry, I wanted to bawl my eyes out and curse and *feel* the pain of his death—to feel *something*. But for some reason I couldn't muster anything close to the emotions I was supposed to be feeling. I couldn't even feel the pain in my face anymore. As I knelt down beside Erin and hugged her close until the paramedics came, a nagging thought lodged itself in the folds of my brain.

This is all my fault.

chap·ter |ˈCHaptər|
noun

16

WHEN EVERYTHING FALLS APART

To this day, I don't remember calling Erin's father. After I had looked on Jeremy's lifeless body the second time, the numbness had taken over every aspect of my being, and I became a zombie in all my thoughts and actions. What I do remember is that Officer Taylor and Erin's mother arrived before the paramedics. Officer Taylor ran to Erin and held her tight as Erin's mother wrapped Erin in a blanket and then gave one to me. I pulled the blanket around my shoulders even though I no longer felt the cold or the pain in my face. It was as if my synaptic gaps and nerve endings had gone into hibernation mode and all that was left of me was a husk of a human who happened to look like Dakota.

"What happened, Dakota?" Erin's father asked me, still clutching his daughter. He held his police Maglite at angle that illuminated his face, and through the beam of its powerful light I saw his eyes were wet and red-rimmed.

"We—I--" But I couldn't tell him. Not because I didn't want to, but because I physically couldn't get the words out. There was a blockage in my brain, a clog that prevented words from reaching my tongue. Instead, I just pointed and said:

"Jeremy."

Officer Taylor darted his flashlight in the direction I was pointing. He sucked in a quick breath. "Dear God."

As Officer Taylor rushed over to where Jeremy's broken body lay, the paramedics arrived on the scene, lights flashing and sirens blaring. They were into the field in a matter of seconds, two EMTs tending to Erin as her mother cried and promised everything would be okay. I stood in a daze watching the scene, and it was only after Mrs. Taylor pointed at me that one of the paramedics starting working on me.

"He's got a broken nose," I heard him say, "and he's exhibiting the initial signs of shock." The paramedic seemed to be talking from the other end of a tunnel. I could feel the pressure of his touch, but nothing more.

"You're Dakota, right?" The EMT asked. When I didn't answer, he snapped his fingers in front of my eyes. "We need you to stay with us, buddy." He pulled out a penlight and checked my eyes. "You're concussed. Stay with us, Dakota."

All of a sudden I heard Officer Taylor shout to my right. At first I thought I must've heard him incorrectly. He couldn't possibly have said—

"Jeremy has a pulse! Quick, over here! Let's go, let's go, let's go! He's got a pulse!"

***

I remembered what it felt like when I had gotten drunk with Blake Blanton and his band of goon disciples my freshman year. It had been my first—and I vowed—last time experimenting with alcohol and semi-cons. Thinking back on that night was like seeing only puzzle pieces of a larger image and gaps in time lost in universal forever, never to be recovered. I could only remember bits and pieces of the night, snapshots instead of a running film strip. It turns out a nasty concussion feels a lot like being drunk, because the rest of what happened in the field seems like a bunch of photo stills. One minute Officer Taylor was yelling that Jeremy had a pulse, and the next I was in the back of an ambulance headed for King County Health Center. All I wanted to do was sleep, but the EMT attending me wouldn't let that happen. He kept snapping his fingers and asking me stupid questions about what my favorite subject in school was and where I wanted to go to college after I graduated. I tried to ask about Erin and Jeremy, but somehow the words kept getting scrambled in my brain before I could form them into coherent sentences. I do remember him saying something about Erin joining me at KCHC, but he seemed to be avoiding any talk of Jeremy. Even in the haze of my badly bruised brain I feared the worst. Sure, Officer Taylor had discovered Jeremy to have a pulse, but I had seen his body. I had seen what the accident had done to him, how it had crinkled and crunched him like an aluminum can. How, even if he miraculously survived the ordeal, he would never be the same. But there were times to hope and times to face reality. Even though I wanted to cling to the myth that was Jeremy's potential survival, I just *knew* otherwise. In the pit of my stomach, in the back of my foggy mind, in my heart that was presently numb to emotion, I knew Jeremy was dead.

And I knew it was my fault.

chap·ter |CH aptər|
noun 17

SURREAL

When we arrived at King County Health Center, I was subjected to a battery of tests. I knew I had suffered a concussion—the EMT who checked me out in the field had said as much—but I had no idea my nose had been shattered and my right orbital bone with it. My mother and father had arrived sometime after me—or maybe they had beaten the ambulance to the hospital—like I said, I'm fuzzy about the details. All I really remember is that as they wheeled my gurney into the emergency room, my mother was crying and my father had his arm around her shoulder.

The first thing they did was hook me up to an i.v. and cover me with blankets to stave off the continuing effects of shock. That was also when the pain came back. My face exploded in the most agonizing torrents of pain I had ever experienced, and when I doctor came in to examine the extent of the injuries to my face, he concluded that I would have to go under the knife to repair my fractured orbital bone, as there were multiple shards and pieces out of place and he feared a puncture to my eyeball or worse. Fortunately I was too out of it to contemplate the "or worse" part. He also said I had suffered your "run of the mill" concussion—his words, not mine—and that he wasn't concerned about not regaining full recovery of my brain function. He said I would probably have difficulty remembering what had transpired on County Road R, and that he would monitor me closely for the next several days to make sure I was truly in the clear. What he was most concerned about was my decimated face, and I was wheeled to surgery without ever knowing what had become of Erin or Jeremy.

★★★

After a two-hour surgery, I was wheeled into a recovery room where my parents were allowed to come back and sit with me. I was groggy as all get out, and a huge bandage and gauze covered my right cheek and eye. As I slowly came out of the anesthetic haze, I was finally able to form rational thoughts and sentences. When I felt I could, I asked if I could sit up. A nurse showed my mother how to adjust the bed so I was comfortable and then left us alone so we could have the privacy to talk about the horrible night.

"How's Erin?" It was the first thing out of my mouth. I had to hear Erin was okay before I asked about Jeremy. At least her being okay would make the inevitably terrible news about Jeremy easier, or so I hoped. The pit in my stomach, the one that knew the truth about his condition, thought otherwise.

"Erin will make a full recovery," my mother said, stroking my hand. My hands and forearms were bandaged, too, probably from scratches and cuts I hadn't remembered receiving when I had crawled out of the vehicle.

"She was in shock when they brought her in," my father said, clearing his throat. "Her blood pressure was through the roof and her vitals were all out of whack. It's a good thing you called nine-one-one when you did, Dakota."

"She has a concussion, too, and had to get stiches just below her hairline," my mother said. "It's a miracle she's alive. It's a miracle you're *both* alive." She began to cry and lifted my hand to her lips. I wished the bandages could be stripped away so I could feel the warmth of my mother's lips. Sometimes a boy just needed his mother. "It's a miracle, Dakota. You're a miracle."

I hated to see my mother cry for me, and ordinarily her tears would have choked me up, too. But something she said had sent my mind to spin cycle.

God—no!

"Mom, you said we're *both* miracles—me and Erin," I swallowed a lump of dread.

Please, God! Please let Jeremy be a miracle, too!

"What about Jeremy?" I finally asked. When the words came out of my mouth it was like my whole body deflated and the only way I could be made whole again was with good news concerning one of my best friends. But when thick silence filled the room like summer air before rain, I knew it wasn't good.

My mother looked at my father. His eyes went to the floor and his jaw muscles worked twice before he sighed.

"Dakota, Jeremy—he's—it doesn't look good."

I found my breath. Maybe—just maybe he would be okay after all. "But he's alive? He's still alive?"

My father took another deep breath and let it out slowly. "For now."

I didn't understand. What did that mean? *For now!?* For now was what people said when change was imminent, when the here and now would soon change to there and then. My brain cursed the phrase, because I knew what kind of life-crushing weight those two words held.

"The paramedics said he wasn't wearing his seatbelt," my mother said, sniffling. She took her time fishing a wadded tissue out of her purse and blowing her nose, obviously not wanting to tell the truth of Jeremy's condition as I wanted to hear it.

She continued with quick exhale of breath. "He was thrown

Dakota Defined

from the car, Dakota. His spinal cord was severed and—and he had multiple skull fractures--"

I was incredulous. The past tense verbs made me want to throw something. "Why are you saying *had?* You just told me he's alive, so why are you talking like he's not?" I felt my heart thumping madly in my chest cavity, felt the thundering pain in my face and skull return in an instant.

This can't be happening! This can't be real!

My mother looked at my father again. He swallowed and looked me straight in the eyes, his own hazel ones glazed with tears. I had only seen him cry once, and that had been last year as I sat inside a jail cell and finally forgiven him and myself for our past mistakes. Now he shook his head and reached for my hand, gripping it as I gripped his back.

"They don't expect him to live through the night."

That was when I felt my whole world collapse upon me.

***

I cried for what seemed like hours. I wailed and snotted all over, my head throbbing and my heart slowing dying. How could this be? Could Jeremy really be headed for the valley of death? Wasn't I just ribbing him about his freakishly long and abnormally nasty hair? Hadn't I just told him he was bordering on creepy obsession concerning Hannah? Didn't I just make fun of his theater exploits and stage makeup? Now it all seemed so trivial, so out of place and dumb after the accident. And it was all my fault. The fact Jeremy was in a Toledo hospital battling for his life while his parents cried and his church sent out prayer chain messages. It was my fault that he would never star in a Broadway production, his dream for as long as I had known him. It was my fault that he would never again flip his hair behind his shoulder, never kiss Hannah, never live past fifteen and three quarters years of age.

I cried until I was out of tears. My parents sat patiently,

allowing me to empty my emotional tank without asking any questions or interjecting half-baked condolences. They knew the seriousness of the situation just as much as I did. And it was beyond dire.

Dear God, if You're listening—please let Jeremy live!

chapter 18
noun

The Angel of Death

That night I dreamed of Jeremy.

In my dream, Jeremy was about to go onstage for an Infinity High School production of *Oklahoma!* He was playing the part of Curly and he was decked out in cowboy getup, chaps and all. For some reason I was standing with him in the wings as he waited for the orchestra to cue the opening strains of "Oh, What a Beautiful Morning." The opening scene was set, the stage lights were on bright, and I felt in my chest a sense of urgency I couldn't define, though I desperately wanted to—*needed* to. It was as though I had some imperative piece of information to tell Jeremy, and like in other dreams where you know you have to run fast but feel like your legs are weighted with concrete, I couldn't make my mouth move fast enough. Instead I was a silent observer to the scene, although my insides were about to explode with the *something* that just wouldn't come out.

Jeremy was looking across the stage to where Hannah waited for her cue to move into the prop ranch house. Her hair was up and her eyes were shining as she held a white wicker basket full of fake eggs. Jeremy waved and Hannah waved back, blowing him a kiss for good luck. Jeremy turned to me, his blue eyes sparkling even in the dim backstage lighting. He threw a hitchhiker's thumb over his shoulder and smiled.

"You see her over there, Dakota?"

I looked at Hannah as she smoothed out her gingham dress. I wanted desperately to say something—*anything*—but I couldn't. It was like I had four layers of duct tape over my mouth and I sensed that time was running short. And it wasn't just that Jeremy was going to go on stage, it was something darker, more sinister.

Jeremy continued, oblivious to my plight.

"Someday I'm going to marry that girl. We'll move to New York City and I'll audition for Broadway shows and she'll dabble in the music scene." He laughed as the orchestra struck their first notes. Across the stage, Hannah moved behind the prop ranch house and took a deep breath. Time was running out. I *had* to tell Jeremy something—whatever that *something* was. I only knew is that it was imperative that I say it, and if I didn't, I knew beyond a shadow of a doubt I'd never get another chance.

"We'll be broke as all get-out, but we'll be happy." He lightly punched my chest. "She even thinks my hair's sexy, how's about that, D.L.?"

The orchestra was working up to the flute twills that constituted Jeremy's cue. He looked me square in the eye and smiled even bigger, if that was possible. In his smile was a bright future; a house, a few kids, some grandbabies down the road. In his smile I saw what might be, what *would* be. I also sensed that if I didn't say my piece, none of it would come to fruition. It was vital I speak to him. It was a matter of life and death.

"And you'll be the best man at my wedding D.L. How's about that? You'll have to stand up and give a speech at the reception. Not that that'll be difficult for you, D.L. You don't shut up the way it is. Maybe I'll let Bertrand be the ring-bearer. You think he can handle that?"

Dakota Defined

The flutes were twilling, and Jeremy adjusted his cowboy hat and patted me on the back.

"You'll be my best man because you've never let me down, D.L. You always have my back." With that, he gave me another pat on the back and winked.

"Wish me luck."

He walked onto the stage, his thumbs hooked into his belt like a true cowboy, his long hair sleek and shiny as it spilled out the back of his cowboy hat. My stomach dropped, my insides turned to liquid. I knew now what I had been wanting to tell him. It came to me in an instant, but it was too late.

Don't get into the car. Walk home, Jeremy. Whatever you do, don't get into the car.

I was left in the wings feeling like the angel of death.

I had let him down.

Josh Clark

guilt /gilt/

NOUN: What you feel after you've made the biggest mistake of your life

chapter 19
noun

WAITING GAME

Jeremy lived through the night.

Mrs. Stines called my mother at six-thirty in the morning to tell her to keep praying—that Jeremy was fighting, but his condition wasn't improving. The Stineses were surrounded by members of their church and family who had rushed to Toledo to be with them, My mother said Timothy and Bertrand had slept in the waiting room, and Hannah had brought her guitar and finger-picked old hymns and songs of hope for those who needed comfort. More than anything, I wanted to be with Jeremy's family and our Hodgepoder friends. It was my fault we were all part of this horrific nightmare. The least I could do was be there among the broken, because I was one of them. Although my body was at the King County Health Center, my heart was bleeding with those whose hearts bled at St. Vincent's Hospital in Toledo.

I had barely slept at all. I was an emotional wreck, my nerves feeling like they were sizzling on one of Pop's grills at the diner. The pain in my face and head was kept at bay by sweet, blessed medication, but I would have welcomed the thunderclaps of agony if I could trade my emotional pain for them. Every time I thought of Erin and Jeremy—especially

Dakota Defined

Jeremy, since I knew Erin was going to be okay—my stomach knotted into a noose. He was fighting, but how long and how hard could he fight? I had seen his mangled body, had seen the way his blood—so, much blood!—had been spilled upon the snow. How could anyone fight through that? How could anyone live through such trauma?

It was nine o'clock when I heard a knock at my door. I hadn't said much to my parents. They were giving me time to sort out my frayed emotions, and for that I was grateful. Conversation for the sake of conversation was not something I needed or wanted at the moment. There would be a time to talk later, after we saw how this macabre carousel came to a stop. They had yet to hammer me with questions like 'what were you thinking?' and 'how could you?' but I knew those were coming. They had to ask them. I couldn't imagine the torture that must be going on in their minds. They didn't have answers to all their burning questions, and I was the emotional equivalent of a paperweight.

My door opened and Karen walked into the room with Ethan on her hip. I felt my spirits lift ever so slightly. Ethan had a Get Well Soon balloon floating above him, the ribbon wrapped around his little index finger. Just seeing him had a calming effect, and he was the perfect distraction to temporarily alleviate my mind's horrendous churning.

"'Kota ouchy?" Ethan asked, pointing to the bandages on my face.

"Yeah, buddy, Dakota has an ouchy. But I'll be okay."

"Okay?" Ethan asked, reaching for me. Karen smiled politely and kept him back from the bed. How I loved that little boy! How I wished he'd stay young forever so he didn't grow up and make the same mistakes his half-brother did!

"Yeah, I'll be okay soon. And then I can play with you again."

"Okay," Ethan replied.

"Why don't you give Dakota the balloon," Karen said, unwrapping the ribbon from his finger. Ethan complied with a delighted squeal as another knocked sounded at my door. When I saw who it was, I felt tears well in my eyes.

"Is it a good time?" Erin asked.

"Come on in, dear," my mother said, making room for her to walk to my bed.

A purple bruise spread the length of Erin's forehead and a thick bandage just below her hairline covered her stiches. She may have been wounded, but she was beautiful as ever to me.

Erin wasted no time coming into the room, making a beeline for my bed. Tears were already streaming down her cheeks when she stooped down to hug me. Her embrace was more than I could bear, so necessary and perfect I couldn't hold back my own tears. We clutched each other and sobbed for what seemed like an eternity, neither of us saying anything, as no words were needed for our kindred spirits to understand each other's pain. After a seemingly long while, Erin pulled back

"We should leave these two alone for a little bit," I heard my mother say. She sniffled back her own tears as everyone filed out, leaving Erin and me alone.

"I thought I was going to lose you," Erin said, swallowing. "I'm sorry for leaving you in the car—I was in shock—I didn't know what I was doing."

I shook my head, my tears still flowing. "It's okay. I'm just glad nothing happened to you. I don't know what I'd do if—if—you know, you weren't okay."

"But Jeremy's not," Erin said, a sob catching in her throat. "He's—he might die!"

This is my fault! It's all my fault!

I couldn't respond to that. Erin was right; Jeremy's death was a possibility, there was no getting around that. It was the elephant in the room, the weight that pressed down on us to the point of suffocation. I stroked her hand and let her cry.

Dakota Defined

"How's your face?" She asked as her sobbing subsided. "Did your surgery go okay?"

I shrugged, trying to be upbeat. "As good as it could, I guess. My orbital bone was shattered and my nose was just as messed up. They put all the puzzle pieces back together. I'll be okay."

I pointed to the bandage over her stitches. "How's about you? Does that hurt?"

"It's going to scar. But it's nothing compared to what's going on with Jeremy." Her eyes filmed over with tears. "And it's all my fault."

What?! It's my fault!

"Don't you say that," I said, grasping both her shoulders. "It's *not* your fault. I'm the one who had the license, and I'm the one who pressured you into driving. It's my fault—the whole mess—it's on me."

"But I could've said no! I'm not a mindless robot; I know the difference between right and wrong! And I'm the one who put us into the field! It was me! And Jeremy's going to die and *it's all my fault!*"

She broke into sobs again and all I could do was hold her and assure her that it wasn't her fault. It was most certainly mine, and even though I knew it was mine, I did my best to make it seem like we couldn't play the blame game.

"We're not going to do this, Erin. We can't do this to ourselves. We have to be strong for Jeremy and his parents."

Erin reached for a tissue from the box that sat on the nightstand. "Have you even thought about how much trouble we're going to be in? My dad hasn't said anything yet, but I know he's thinking it. You're going to lose your license, Dakota. And if Jeremy dies--"

I shook my head and swallowed a lump of fear. "I'm not going to think about it. Our punishments are secondary to Jeremy's recovery."

"I heard my mom and dad talking this morning. They thought I was asleep, but I heard everything they said," Erin said softly.

My heartbeat accelerated. "What were they talking about?"

Erin took a deep breath and looked out the window. "My dad said he's seen things like this before. He said it'd be a miracle if Jeremy makes it through the week, that he's surprised Jeremy was even alive this morning."

I nodded and cleared my throat. "Is that it?"

Erin shook her head. "I heard them say Jeremy suffered multiple head and facial fractures. The doctors had to cut open his skull to fix a clot that had formed on his brain."

That jolted me. My parents hadn't said anything about Jeremy's having brain surgery.

"They said even if he recovers from the head injuries, he'll never walk again," Erin continued. She looked from the window, her tear-puddled brown eyes meeting mine. "Maybe it's better for him to—to die."

My heart thundered in my chest. The room seemed to get smaller, the walls closing in on us and choking the air out of the space. I couldn't think of anything to say. After hearing what Erin's parents had said, I couldn't even muster enough hope to fake a positive response. Instead, I heard myself sigh and say:

"Maybe. Maybe that would be better."

Erin and I both looked out the window. We didn't have to say anything. We both knew we were living in our darkest hours.

***

I was released from the hospital later that night. The doctor wrote enough prescriptions to medicate a small island nation and sent me on my way. My parents wanted to take me home so I could rest and recover in my own bed, but I adamantly told them there was no way I was going home; I was going to

Toledo to see Jeremy. Erin had been discharged a few hours before me, but had waited at my bedside until I got the all-clear. I'd have to return to the doctor's office in five days so he could check on my face, but, other than that, I was a free man.

Or so I thought.

It was after my mother had signed all my discharge papers that Officer Taylor and Erin's mother walked into my hospital room and closed the door. Karen stepped out of the room, Ethan wiggling his protests at her hip, and my mother and father stayed seated. I knew what was coming, knew my parents and the Taylors had planned this necessary conversation. They had allowed Erin and me to vent our emotions and lean on each other for a while, but reality needed to be faced: we were in trouble.

My father cleared his throat and took a deep breath. "You guys probably know what's up."

Erin slipped her hand around the bedrail and closed it around mine. Solidarity in a moment of tension.

"We have a pretty good guess," I said, my voice sounding pinched and constrained. I cleared my own throat and looked at Erin and then Officer Taylor. A wave of heat came to my face as the shame of seeing him in this awful situation swept over me. I had let him down; I had promised to protect his daughter and I had failed in the worst of ways. I had no doubt he would put an end to Erin's and my's relationship. After two consecutive years that saw me have run-ins with the law, why wouldn't he?

"We don't have to tell you how serious this all is," Erin's mother said, reaching for a tissue. Her eyes were red-rimmed, and seeing that she had been in tears only added to my feelings of shame.

"What you both did was reckless, irresponsible and stupid," Erin's mother continued. She looked at me, her dark eyes narrowing. "Dakota, you never should have been driving with

Erin and Jeremy in the car. You know it's against the law, yet you did it anyway. And then you decided to let Erin *drive?* We expected more from you, Dakota."

My father picked up where Mrs. Taylor had let off. "When we bought you your car, it was because we thought you were responsible enough to handle it. You've proved to us otherwise."

The sting of my father's comment sent a rippling burn throughout my body. Although I hated to hear it, and although the frankness of the comment tore me in half, it was the truth. I had let my parents down in the worst way. I had taken their trust and smeared their noses in it. I had nothing to say in response; instead, I hung my head.

"And you, Erin," I heard Erin's mother say, "I can't fathom how you could've been so—so—*stupid!* You don't have your license, Infinity had just been doused by snow and you *still* decided to get behind the wheel of Dakota's car?"

Erin swallowed and choked back her tears. I stole a glance at Officer Taylor, who stood like a stone in the corner of the room, big arms crossed over his barrel chest. He was quiet—too quiet. I knew he was going to have the last word, and I knew what he was going to say was going to be more than painful.

I put my hands up and allowed my own tears to spill down my cheeks. "Look, we're sorry. We were both stupid and beyond irresponsible. We know we're in trouble, but can't we just go to Toledo to be with Jeremy and his family?"

Officer Taylor stepped forward and sighed. "You know you're in trouble?"

My mouth went Sahara Desert dry. "Uh— I we know we're going to be punished--"

Officer Taylor silenced me with a wave of his big hand.

"Punishment from your parents will be the least of your concern, son."

My heart pounded. I felt my hands turn clammy with sweat.

"This is your second run-in with the law in two years, Dakota. And this particular offense is a lot more serious than last year's. If I had to guess, you'll be back on probation, your license will be taken from you until you turn eighteen and if Jeremy dies you could be charged with vehicular manslaughter."

All my air left me. I felt like I had just been hit in the gut by a wrecking ball. Vehicular manslaughter? I knew I was going to be in trouble, but didn't vehicular manslaughter mean jail time?

Officer Taylor looked at his daughter, who was now sobbing uncontrollably in my arms.

"I'm afraid you're looking at the same charges, Erin. There are some things I can't save you from."

"But he's going to be okay!" I shouted, my tears distorting Officer Taylor's figure into a hulking demon. "Jeremy's going to pull through!"

Officer Taylor didn't answer for a moment. With a sigh he said, "I pray so, son. For his sake and for your sake, I pray so."

chap·ter |ˈCHaptər|
noun

20

BLOOD FOR BLOOD, FLESH FOR FLESH

The drive to St. Vincent's hospital in Toledo was a silent one. I sat alone in the passenger seat of my father's Impala, my mother in the seat behind mine, and tried to process all of what Officer Taylor had just told Erin and me. How was it possible that we had been innocent teenagers enjoying ice cream treats at one moment, and a twosome with the potential to be convicted of vehicular manslaughter less than an hour later? My mind couldn't wrap around how life can change in a moment, how a trapdoor can open when you least expect it and you can fall hard and fast with nothing to break your fall but rock bottom.

Erin and her parents were going to meet us at St. V's, Officer Taylor opting to drive his daughter to the hospital himself rather than allow any more chance of disaster. At least that was how I took it. There was no way Officer Taylor was going to trust me again, and why should he? I was a magnet to poor choices, the poster boy for duh. I had successfully messed up big time to the third power two years in a row now. *I* didn't even trust me anymore.

Why? Why did all this have to happen? Why can't I reverse time and make it all disappear?

Dakota Defined

***

I was nowhere near prepared for the hell I walked into at Toledo St. Vincent's Hospital's third floor waiting room. The nauseating sterile smells of the white floor tiles and the wafting scents of fresh linen and antibacterial hand sanitizer were already mixing with my medication and making my head spin. But when I walked into the waiting room and saw it was filled with my fellow Hodgepodgers and Jeremy's relatives, I wanted to vomit. As I walked through the double doors, my parents trailing behind me, every head turned my way, and I felt every eye sweep over my revoltingly purple and hideously bandaged face. I saw their gazes travel down my unmangled and undamaged bone structure, sweep across the skin that kept my blood inside my body. As I fought back the bile creeping into the back of my throat, I sensed the room's judgment. I was standing upright and Jeremy was broken. I was breathing on my own and Jeremy was being raped by a ventilator, his oxygen given to him by a machine that had no doubt stood silent sentinel to countless deaths and horrific agony on the parts of the living. As I looked around the room and every eye met my own, I wanted more than anything to sacrifice myself to the mob of molesting eyes in order that their suffering might be somewhat appeased through my death. Blood for blood. Flesh for flesh. Life for life.

This is terrible. I caused all this—all of it is my fault.

We had arrived at the hospital before the Taylors, and I wanted more than anything to have Erin by my side. I didn't know if it was because I was selfish and I wanted someone to share the blame with me, or because I longed for her presence as a stabilizing force. I was too janked up to know for sure; my emotions were on a sick collision course and I had no idea how to flip the switch back to normalcy. All I know was I felt as naked as Adam in the Garden of Eden after he had eaten of the fruit. I will never forget the shame for as long as I live.

"Hey, D.L."

I felt a hand on my shoulder, and when I turned to the right I saw Timothy standing beside me. Before I knew what I was doing, I gripped him in a huge bear hug, fighting back the tears that threatened to topple from my eyes.

"It's okay, D.L. It's not your fault," Timothy whispered as he clutched me back. "It just happened. You aren't to blame."

There are moments in life where certain people say the right thing in the moment you need it the most. Timothy Astor did just that. As he hugged me tight, a profound intimacy we had never before experienced as friends, he whispered the words I needed the most as though he had heard them directly from God Himself.

"How are you doing?" Timothy asked as we parted. He patted my shoulder as Bertrand and Hannah joined us.

"I'm doing about as well as I can be. The medication is keeping the pain away, but that's not really my greatest concern right now, you know?"

Timothy nodded as Bertrand produced his notebook from his pocket. My parents left my side and mingled with some of Jeremy's extended family.

"It's like he's just gonna walk out and say 'what's up,'" Hannah said, holding her Martin guitar by its neck. "I can hear his voice every time I close my eyes." Her acorn eyes filmed with tears and she cleared her throat and looked away.

"How is Erin handling the immense pain inflicted upon her face?" Bertrand asked, squinting behind his thick-lensed glasses, his pencil poised over the paper as though he were a reporter covering a juicy story. I didn't know what the pad was for, but it was starting to annoy me, given the circumstances.

"Erin should be here in a second. She's holding up."

"People have been in and out all day," Timothy said, running his hand through his dark hair. "You just missed Mr.

Dennis and his wife. Heck, Nazi Neelson brought some flowers this morning."

"Her name's Sandy," I said.

"What?"

"Nazi Neelson's name is Sandy."

Timothy looked at me funny for a moment and then shrugged. "Whatever you say, D.L. It was a nice arrangement, though. I'm not a flower guy or anything, but it was pretty cool."

In any other circumstance I would have made some sort of joke about Timothy being a show choir flower boy, but I couldn't do it here. Not in this goshawful, downer of a waiting room.

"Look, there is Erin," Bertrand said with a geeky point. "The laceration above her forehead is heavily bandaged and looks like it is excruciatingly painful."

I turned around as Erin walked through the waiting room doors, her parents trailing behind her. Hannah immediately ran to her, propping her guitar against the wall and wrapping her arms around Erin. Erin burst into tears, and Hannah's back rose and fell as she sobbed with my emotionally broken girlfriend. I felt Timothy's hand on my shoulder as I watched the two girls cry.

"Let's sit down, D.L. You need to get off your feet."

Timothy led me to a chair on the far wall, one that looked out over the entire waiting room. As Bertrand sat down to my left, Timothy to my right, I took my first real look at those manning—and womanning—the seats. The first thing I realized is that I had been wrong: everybody wasn't looking at me; and those who were didn't look with hate, but with curious pity, as though they each wanted to say something to me but didn't know how. It still didn't feel good to be *that guy,* but at least I was seeing through the lens of reality and not through the distorted periscope of my emotions.

Erin pulled a chair from a line of empties and moved it across from me. Hannah sat down on the tile floor, her guitar on her lap, her fingers working the strings of her guitar to produce some nameless tune.

"I feel like I need to say something," Erin said, crossing her arms. She sniffled and quickly swiped away a tear.

"You don't have to apologize," Timothy said, gently. "We all know you and Dakota never meant for this to happen."

Erin shook her head. "But it *did* happen, Timothy. The fact that Jeremy's not sitting here with us is proof enough."

"He's not getting any worse," Timothy reasoned. "The doctor said the first twenty-four hours are crucial when it comes to injuries like Jeremy's."

"But he's not getting any *better*," Erin answered, another tear spilling down her cheek. "No offense, but it's easy for you to say it's not our fault when it's not *your* fault."

Hannah stopped picking her guitar and put a hand on Erin's knee. "I don't think Jeremy would want us assigning blame. We have to stay as positive as we can. He's still alive, he's still fighting."

Erin didn't say anything in response.

I reached out and put my hand on Erin's other knee. I knew I had to be strong for her, even though I didn't feel anywhere near strong myself. That's the thing about loving someone; you had to be strong for them even when you were at your weakest. You had to maintain wholeness even when you felt yourself cracking.

"It will be okay. Jeremy's going to make it. We have to believe."

"It's hard to believe when you see no hope."

My heart bled for her, and I loved her all the more.

And yes, I said *love*.

***

When ten o'clock rolled around, the waiting room's population thinned out. Jeremy's relatives left either for their homes or for their hotel rooms. When people started dispersing I felt like I could finally take a deep breath. It had been a long forty-eight hours, and I felt like a tank had run over my face and then reversed and run over it again. I popped my meds like it was nobody's business and wondered when I would have to face Jeremy's parents. They had yet to make an appearance in the waiting room, rather opting to stay with Jeremy in hopes of his miraculous recovery. I dreaded having to face them, yet I knew it was necessary. I had made the biggest mistake of my life when I had picked Jeremy up from the community theater, and I had to look his parents in the eye and tell them I was sorry—a thousand, million times sorry.

My mom spent a good fifteen minutes trying to convince me that I needed to go back to Infinity with her, that I was in too bad shape to camp out in the waiting room all night. Her words fell on deaf ears. There was no way I was leaving the waiting room, no way I was going home to a comfortable bed and the heartening smells and familiarity of home when Jeremy couldn't.

I'm not leaving until Jeremy wakes up.

I was grateful that my father took my side, telling my mother I needed to stay with Jeremy and my friends and that she could sleep in the spare bedroom at his and Karen's house since they lived only ten minutes from the hospital. I could tell my mother liked that idea about as much as a glutton likes salad, but she finally relented and agreed to stay at my father's house. Erin's parents saw the writing on the wall and agreed to allow her to stay the night as they drove back to Infinity. Officer Taylor had to work in the morning, while Erin's mother would make the trip back to Toledo tomorrow afternoon to retrieve her daughter.

"I think it's time to put this away," Hannah said, tapping the body of her guitar. She reached for her guitar case and slid it across the tiled floor. After tucking her beloved Martin into its case, she held up her left hand to show indented string-mark calluses on her fingertips. "I think my fingers need a break. I'm gonna step into the hallway to call my mom." She stood and walked out the waiting room's double doors.

"How'd you guys get here?" I asked Timothy and Bertrand. In the emotional chaos I had forgotten that Toledo was sixty miles west of Infinity and my friends couldn't drive.

"My mom brought us yesterday. A nurse said we could use one of the staff's showers if we wanted to stay. We have toiletries and a few changes of clothes in the nurse's locker room."

"Good deal," Erin said "I'm going to be scuzzy until my parents bring me some clothes and stuff."

"I'm right there with you," I said. I glanced at the clock on the wall. "I have to take my pain pills. Drinking fountain's around the corner, right?"

"Yeah. You can't miss it," Timothy said as I stood up. I fished the two separate plastic bags of meds out of my pockets and walked through the heart of the room to get to the hallway. As I passed a frail elderly woman I assumed was Jeremy's grandmother, the woman smiled and whispered:

"I'm praying for you, Dakota."

I smiled back and nodded, partly because I was caught off guard by the old woman in my quest to cross the waiting room no-man's-land without drawing attention to myself, and partly because I didn't know how to respond.

Shouldn't you be praying for Jeremy? I'm the one who made this mess—I don't deserve your prayers!

I turned the corner and spotted the water fountain. I produced two pills from each plastic baggie and popped them into my mouth, their bitter tastes immediately assaulting my taste buds. I quickly thumbed the valve on the water fountain and stooped to get a drink. When I had successfully swallowed the pills and eradicated the goshawful aftertaste from my mouth, I turned around.

And ran right into Jeremy's mother.

chap·ter |'CHaptər|
noun
21

JEREMY

My blood froze. My breath caught in my throat. I knew I'd have to face Jeremy's parents sometime, but I hadn't wanted it to happen like this. I was caught unawares, so completely blindsided by the presence of Jeremy's mother that my bruised brain emptied of all logical thought. I had been rehearsing what I wanted to say to the Stineses in my head for the past thirty hours, but as Mrs. Stines stood before me, her eyes red-rimmed from crying, a crumpled tissue in her hand, I couldn't even remember my name.

"Hello, Dakota." Jeremy's mother's voice was even and calm like the undisturbed surface of a lake.

Say something, idiot! Speak! She's talking to you!

"I—I--" And then I lost it. My eyes became geysers of tears, my lips blubbering elastic bands attached to my face. My voice broke, and all I could muster were inhuman groans and desperately apologetic incoherent babbles.

I can't do this! I can't face her! Not like this!

What Jeremy's mother did next surprised me. Not waiting for me to form words, she wrapped her arms around me and hugged me in an intimate desperation I know I will never experience again. In her hug I felt her every doubting thought, her every vulnerable emotion seep into my pores and flow to my heart. I felt her urgency, her *need* to impart to her son things she'd yet to speak, her fleeting anger at God—at me—at herself, her maternal helplessness. In that hug I felt the depth of her love for her son, her unwavering devotion to motherhood, her willingness to sacrifice herself in an instant if only Jeremy could live. As she broke into sobs, I knew my role at this precise moment was not to be a blubbering, apologetic fool, but to be a pillar of strength for a grieving mother. My need to make my conscience right was secondary; my role now was to hug Jeremy's mother as though I were Jeremy himself.

"Would you like to see him?" Mrs. Stines asked when we pulled away. I swiped my nose and looked at her through a film of tears.

Aren't you mad at me? Don't you want to hit me—slap me—something?!

"I—I'm sorry—I--" I felt the tears threatening to burst forth again. I willed a dam of stoic emotion to keep them at bay. I *wanted* her to hit me, I *wanted* her to take her anger out on me without my crying like a baby.

"Sshh," Mrs. Stines held up a finger. "We're not going to do this. Not here, not now. What matters is not who's to blame, but that Jeremy knows you're here for him."

I swallowed a ball of something mucusy that had lodged in my throat as I wondered what Mrs. Stines had meant by her comment. Did she blame me? Was she mad at me? How could she not want to erase me from the face of the earth at this very moment?

What matters is Jeremy.

"Are you ready to see him?" Mrs. Stines asked, wiping a tear from her right cheek. She swallowed, and her jaw muscles twitched a few times as she tried to regain her composure.

I nodded, even though I knew there was no way I could ever

be ready for what I was about to see. How does one prepare himself for seeing one of his best friends hanging in the balance between life and death?

Mrs. Stines put a hand on the small of my back.

"He's this way."

***

As I walked into Jeremy's darkened room, my body trembled. When I saw his father sitting on a foldout chair, his head in his hands, fingers working through his hair, I shook all the more. The unfiltered despair of the father as he watched over his only son was almost unbearable. But it was when I saw Jeremy that my knees nearly gave out.

"It's okay. You can go to him," Mrs. Stines whispered, nudging me toward Jeremy's bed. Jeremy's father stood and nodded his head at me and wiped his hands on his jeans.

"I think I'm going to step out for some coffee," he said. As he passed me he patted my shoulder. I swallowed hard and trembled all the more.

I slowly made my way to where Jeremy lay hooked up to a ventilator and completely at the mercy of his warring body. His head was shaved, his skull wrapped in a large strips of gauze and bandages. His arms were in casts, and I knew that if I were to pull back his covers, his legs would be, too.

Dear God, what have I done?

I swallowed back the emotions rising in my throat and pulled a chair up to his bed.

He looks dead. He looks like he'll never open his eyes again.

"Jeremy?" I whispered. I was afraid to touch him, that if I so much as brushed a fingertip across the back of his hand the machines would scream out his death. Behind me I heard Jeremy's mother grab a tissue from a sightless box.

"Jeremy—I—I'm sorry. I never wanted this to happen. We

never should've—*I* never should've picked you up from the theater."

I could no longer hold back my emotions. The tears came in rivers, my body rocked with sobs.

"You have to live! You have to get up from that bed and *live*!"

That was all I could say before I was overcome again. I felt a hand on my shoulder. Here I was, a sobbing Judas, as Mrs. Stines was comforting *me*!

"It's okay, Dakota. Jeremy will fight this."

I turned to her, saw her through my bleary tears.

"I should be lying there! That should be me—not him!"

I was surprised when Jeremy's mother's voice took on a sharp tone.

"Stop! Stop that right now! What you did was foolish, but it is just as much my son's fault as it is yours, Dakota! I am not going to let you blame yourself. You'll never be able to forgive yourself if you do. Why don't you redirect you feelings of blame to prayers for Jeremy's recovery? I don't blame you, Dakota. It's not worth the hassle and it's just not merited."

I swallowed and sucked in air, unable to say anything.

"Why don't you collect yourself and go back into the waiting room with your friends," Mrs. Stines said, her voice softening. "Tell them they can see Jeremy tomorrow. You're the only non-family member we've allowed back here."

I sniffled. "Why?"

Mrs. Stines managed a weak smile. "Because when I saw you at the drinking fountain—when we hugged—I knew you needed to see him. You more than the others needed to see him."

I stood and hugged her again, knowing she was more right about my needing to see Jeremy than she could possibly realize. When I hugged her, something strange happened. I realized she hadn't just been saying words I wanted or needed to hear, but that she actually meant what she had told me about not loading the blame onto my shoulders. As I had hugged her at the drinking fountain and gave her a fresh dose of comfort and hope, she was now paying it forward. I knew she didn't blame me—that Mr. Stines didn't blame me--and with that knowledge, I felt a huge burden lifted from my spindly body.

Maybe there's hope, after all.

chapter |CH aptər|
noun

22

THREE WEEKS LATER

I grimaced as I pulled a soggy hamburger bun from the bottom of the bin. There were some things I'd never get used to, and grabbing backwash-sodden bread with my bare hand was one of them.

"You handle those hamburger buns like they're hand grenades," Pop said, walking into the dishwashing room, AKA my sanctuary to rehash horrific memories of the accident and worry about Jeremy's critical state.

"Yeah, I guess I just imagine how many germs are swimming in that nasty bin-bottom water." I hosed out the bin and set it on the countertop.

Pop wiped his hands on a dishrag and threw it next to the bin. He nodded toward the kitchen with his chin. "We're pretty slow right now. Thought I'd come back to see how your're doing."

"This is the last bin. All the rest are empty--"

Pop put up his bear paw of a hand.

"I'm not talking about the bins, Dakota. I meant how are *you* doing? How're you holding up these days?"

I took a deep breath and let it out slowly. Good question, Pop, how *was* I doing? Jeremy had yet to come out of his coma, and Erin had sunk into herself over the course of the last three weeks, hanging out by herself at lunch and sometimes not even responding to my texts.

"I guess I'm doing about as well as I can do. I'm back on probation, as you know, for three more months. That's why I asked to be put on the schedule more; the judge gave me work and school release, and that's it. After six p.m., my butt's at home if I'm not at work."

Pop nodded and scratched his hairy arm. "And your license?"

"Let's just say I won't be sitting behind the wheel of any motor vehicle until I turn eighteen."

"You know you can wheel your bike into the back room so you don't have to keep it outside. It must be freezing riding that thing in January."

It was. Along with the painful reminders I had of the accident every time I straddled my trusty Schwinn, I risked frostbite and my face falling off every time I rode to work. Also, no one ever tells you how a bike tire slips on ice patches. I nearly re-broke my face last week turning onto Carter Street from Primrose. But what could I do? My mother wasn't home from her rounds at the hospital before I needed to be to the diner, and I sure as sunshine on my shoulder wasn't walking two miles to my dishwashing job.

"Thanks," I said, grabbing the bin and making to take it back to the waitress's station. But when Pop didn't move his massive body from my path, I knew our conversation wasn't over.

"And how's that girlfriend of yours—what's her name—Evelyn?"

"Erin," I said, a lump of sadness rising to my throat.

Pop folded his python arms over his armoire chest. "Yeah, Erin. Sandy said she's a nice girl. How's she holding up?"

I wished I could tell him she was holding up well, but I

couldn't. In reality, I had started to become concerned about Erin over the course of the last two weeks. She had stopped painting altogether, her half-finished self-portrait frozen on the easel in her garage/studio. What had been most unsettling to me was that a week after the accident she had withdrawn her entry in the state art competition. That one had shocked me to the core because it was so unlike Erin, especially when a win or even placing second or third would bolster her college applications and make the art schools in New York City take notice. At school, she was a shell of her former self, not speaking until she was spoken to and sometimes answering with nothing but a shrug. Her beautiful eyes had lost their light, and as I watched my girlfriend slowly sinking under the murky waters of depression, I could do nothing for her but tell her everything was going to be okay.

But is it going to be okay?

"She's taking it hard," I answered. It was the most politically correct thing to say, given the circumstance. I just wanted Pop to go back to slapping heart attack patties on the grill so I could be alone with my thoughts.

"Has she been talking to anyone? I mean anyone professional?"

"I think her parents are looking into it," I said with a sigh. "Listen, Pop, I don't want to speak for Erin or her parents, so I think I shouldn't say much more."

I surprised myself with my own frankness. I guess tragedy has a way of stripping away frivolous niceties; and when it came to Erin, I was all about protecting her best interests, even if it meant I had to say so to my boss. I had no doubt that Pop had the best of intentions, but everyone deserved a modicum of privacy.

Pop put both of his big mitts up in a pose of respectful surrender. "I understand, Dakota. And I commend your wanting to protect Erin. That's admirable. Real mature. Sandy was right about you. You're a good kid."

If I was that good of a kid I wouldn't be on probation for the second straight year and Jeremy would be sitting in one of the diner's booths, flipping his hair and talking about theater mumbo jumbo.

I could only nod and swallow back my rebuttal. I couldn't consider myself "a good kid," but I could at least appreciate Pop's attempt at being a psychologist. He was only trying to help me breathe a little and put things into perspective, and I couldn't fault him for that. But when the world seemed to be crumbling around you, every day a new piece falling from the sky and shattering at your feet like a clay pigeon, it was difficult to see beyond the pain.

"I'll let you get back to work," Pop said, slapping me on the back. "You're a good kid. Don't forget that."

As Pop walked out of the room and I waited for the automatic dishwasher to finish its cycle, my mind drifted over the wreckage of the past three weeks. Sleep had eluded me, and I found myself constantly feeling like I had been run over by a charter bus during my waking hours. At one of my three doctor's visits, my mother had asked Dr. Steiner to consider writing me a prescription for some drugs that would help me sleep. He did just that, and I was sleeping better, but the pills could do nothing for the dreams that haunted me on a nightly basis. My brain was forever scarred by images of Jeremy's bloody, mangled body lying helplessly in the snow-laden field, of Erin's delirious state, her forehead gushing blood and her eyes frantic from shock. I dreamt I was back in my Daytona dangling upside down in the crumpled wreckage and unable to extricate myself from the seat. They were awful dreams, downright horrific dreams, and every night I prayed to a God I hoped was listening for Him to keep them at bay.

The dishwasher's cycle ended, and I raised the stainless steel lid and allowed a puff of soap-scented steam to plume into the room. Wanting the dishes to cool before I handled them, I grabbed the empty bus bin and walked it out to the waitress' station and came back to man my post as dish-wiper extraordinaire. As I toweled off the cheap dinnerware, I felt the press of hopelessness upon my chest.

Will things ever get better? Can things ever get better?

The fact that the accident happened over the Christmas holiday had been devastating. For the first time in my life, I had felt no homey warm fuzzies on Christmas morning, no church and happy-Jesus songs to rekindle my hope in mankind. Instead, I had spent Christmas morning in the hospital with Jeremy's parents, watching with a leaden heart and tear-streaked cheeks as Jeremy's parents unwrapped the gifts they had purchased for him, holding each gift to his lifeless hand in hopes that he would wake from his deep coma and take hold of the proffered gift with a strong sign of life. It was one of the most heartbreaking scenes I had ever seen, one that I refuse to expound upon further. Some things are too sacred for trifling words.

Going back to school after the Christmas break from hell had been awful. Infinity is a small town with a weekly small town newspaper full of hard news (gossip) and reliable information (hearsay). Of course, our accident dominated the front page headlines for two consecutive weeks. The issue the week after the accident showed a black and white picture of my crumpled Daytona underneath the headline: Reckless Joyride Lands Teen In Coma. I wanted to walk into the newspaper building on Main Street and sock someone in the kisser after that little number, the insensitive jerks. Suffice it to say, Erin and I were the buzz of the school for all the wrong reasons. It was as if the story of the wreck being the paper made it okay for anyone to come up and ask us questions about the accident, when all we really wanted—Erin in particular—was to be left alone.

I had been summoned to court one week after the accident. My punishment was swift and just, as I had already stood before Judge Hasslemeyer the year before, making me a repeat offender. Erin's hearing took longer than mine, and she had the added stigma of being the delinquent daughter of an Infinity police officer. The newspaper pounced on this tasty twist of irony two weeks after the accident with the headline: Cop's Daughter Gets Probation. Again, it made me want to rage on someone.

As if all of this wasn't enough, the Infinity school board had decided to drop a few a-bombs during Christmas break. The basketball and wrestling teams were told to fork over three hundred dollars immediately for each participant, or their programs would be effectively cut and the remaining games on their schedules forfeited. In a bad economy, asking parents to piece together three hundred dollars at the drop of a hat was ludicrous, and both the boys and girls basketball teams lost a substantial number of players, while the wrestling program folded completely. Students were livid, parents were peeved and the school board was sitting easier now that their little scheme to suck funds from anywhere they could procure them had worked.

I finished drying all the dinnerware and started gathering the plates to put them in their necessary cupboard. As I was just finishing my second stack of five, Pop came back and threw a thumb over his shoulder.

"There's a kid out front who says he needs to see you. Says it's urgent. His name's Tommy or Timothy or something."

My heart dropped to the pit of my stomach. What would Timothy be doing here? And what could be so urgent as to call me away from work?

Jeremy!

I felt bitter bile rise in the back of my throat as I wasted no time in brushing past Pop and making my way to the big window cutout that separated the kitchen from the diner. When I saw Timothy, my brain nearly exploded in panic. He was crying, his eyes red, his Adam's apple working up and down.

"What? What is it? Is something wrong with--?"

"They cut the music program!" Timothy seethed, trying hard to fight back the tears.

It's not Jeremy! He's okay!

My heart rate decelerated and my brain cleared of panic. I felt a stab of guilt when I thanked God that it was the music program and not Jeremy.

"Take it easy for a second, man," I said, putting my hands up. I looked out into the diner, saw it populated by no one but Sandra, the new middle-aged waitress Pops had just hired, and then back at Timothy. "How do you know?"

"I got a text from Sarah Matthews. Her dad's brother is on the school board. She said the choir and band will find out tomorrow."

I shook my head. Nothing like pouring salt onto an incredibly festering wound. The student body was already reeling from the previous cuts, and now this?

Timothy's eyes pleaded with me as his jaw muscles clenched and unclenched.

"Dakota, you have to do something."

I looked at him like he had fourteen eyeballs. "What? What can I do?"

Timothy sighed. "Craig Henderson—you know, the farmer kid—he said Mr. Dennis asked you to--"

I threw up my hands and adamantly shook my head.

"No. Not a chance. There's no way I'm about to stick my nose where it doesn't belong. Besides, I'm not a leader. No one would listen to me."

"Come on, Dakota! You know that's not true. Look what you did last year when you gave that speech--"

"That was last year," I interrupted, "and, if I can be honest with you, I can't believe you would bring this up, given the circumstances."

"What would Jeremy want you to do?" Timothy asked.

Ouch. That one got me. I knew Timothy had just thrown up a Hail Mary pass to the end zone with the statement, but it had hit home.

How can you know what Jeremy would want? That's ridiculous!

But as I looked at Timothy, saw him swallow back his tears, I knew Jeremy would want me to fight the school board. And at that moment, I knew I *should* go along with the whole thing because I *knew* it was right. But I was scared of failing the student body as I had failed Erin and Jeremy. So instead of capitulating, I redirected my feelings of vulnerability and exposure to defensiveness. Defensiveness was easier, more tidy. You couldn't fail yourself and your friends by getting defensive.

"How can you even say that?" I asked, feigning shock. "Our best friend is lying in a coma in a hospital bed, and *you* want to prostitute his name to get what you want?"

Timothy looked genuinely hurt and I felt terrible.

"You're twisting my words, Dakota. All I'm saying is that Jeremy would be proud to have someone standing up for him. Especially if it's you."

Stop! This hurts too much!

I softened my tone. "Look, I'm just as upset as you are about all this. But if Mr. Dennis wants someone to stand up to the school board, he'll have to find someone else."

Timothy shook his head and swallowed back tears.

"That's a cop-out and you know it, D.L. You could really do something good here, and you're just gonna let the opportunity slip by because you're too--"

Now my hackles really did rise. "Too what? Say it!"

"You're too much of a chicken," Timothy said, slapping his open palm on the countertop. "There, I said it!" With that he

Dakota Defined

stormed away.

I stood watching him go, a sadness I felt to the bone sweeping over my entire body. Timothy was right—I knew he was right—it was just—

What is it? What are you so afraid of? Excuses are easy to make.

"Tough break, kid." Pop's voice startled me from my thoughts. When I turned I saw him wiping down a counter, the muscles under his hairy arm twitching and dancing.

How long has been standing there?

"Long enough to hear the whole exchange," Pop said, freakishly reading my mind. "You want my two cents?"

I knew the question was rhetorical; I would receive his two cents even if I was allergic to pennies. I sighed and nodded, feeling more than defeated and even more bone tired. Pop threw down his rag and crossed his arms over his chest.

"Well, I'm gonna say my piece even if you don't want to hear it. Sandy's been keeping me posted about the goings-on at your school, and, quite frankly, what they're doing to you kids smells worse than cow pies, if you get my drift."

I got his drift.

"I think what Tommy said to you is right."

"Timothy. His name's Timothy."

"Same thing. You know what I mean, Dakota. Bright kid like you—you could really do some good for your fellow man, ya know?"

Great. Life lessons from Professor Hairy Arms!

Pop continued, uncouthly scratching his backside. No wonder his burgers had a funny taste.

"I know you're going through a lot right now. Heck, I lost a friend right after graduation. Was drunk and he wrapped his Camaro around a telephone pole. Real messy stuff. Anyway, I wish I could've had the opportunity you have to make a bad situation a little bit better."

I sighed again. "But I'm nobody. And I don't even know how to get something like this started. There have to be procedures and red tape to work through when you're dealing with the school board."

One of Pop's bushy eyebrows shot into his forehead. "You're nobody, huh? First that Dennis guy thinks you can get something cooking, and then Sandy concurs. And I take what Sandy says as straight truth, Dakota. She's not one to throw compliments around. As far as the school board procedure mumbo-jumbo goes, that's an excuse and you know it."

I stammered, unable to form a well-phrased rebuttal.

Pop smiled. "And you know what they say about excuses, right? Excuses are like backsides, everybody has one and they all stink."

I smiled with my mouth but I knew my eyes betrayed me.

Pop picked up his towel again and started applying elbow grease to the countertop.

"You'll figure it out, kid. You're too smart not to."

If only I could believe that!

chap·ter |ᴄʜ aptər|
noun

23

Erin's Evasion

"How are you feeling this morning?" I asked Erin as she put her books back into her locker. When she didn't answer, I tried again.

"You coming to lunch today? It's tuna noodle casserole; who could pass that up?"

She closed her locker and sighed. When she looked at me, the mirth was gone from her dark chocolate eyes, the little sparkle that was Erin hiding behind a spreading sadness that made my heart ache.

"I think I'm just going to go to the gym," Erin answered, taking her iPod from her pocket. "I'm not hungry."

She started on her way and I quickly caught up to her. "You have to eat, Erin. Even if the food might taste like a foot, you have to eat."

"I said I'm not hungry," she replied, defiantly putting her earbuds into her ears.

"But this is the third time in four days you haven't been hungry," I said, noticing my voice had taking on a pleading, almost whining tone.

She stopped and turned to look me square in the eye. "I said I'm not hungry, Dakota. What are you going to do, force-feed me?"

I grinned. "Maybe. Or I'll pretend I'm a momma bird and I'll regurgitate my casserole into your mouth."

Erin didn't even fake a smile. "That's gross, Dakota. Just—just let me be by myself for awhile, okay? I have a lot on my mind." She turned to leave and I grabbed her elbow.

"It's Jeremy, isn't it? You know it's not your fault. You know it's--"

She wrenched her elbow from my grasp and thumbed her iPod to PLAY. When I heard the burst of electric guitars coming from her earbuds, I knew the conversation was over.

"Please stop being my mother. You don't need to diagnose me."

With that, she turned the corner into the junior hallway and proceeded to the gymnasium, leaving me standing with my heart in my stomach in her wake.

★★★

"She's not coming to lunch? Again?" Hannah asked, spooning some tuna noodle casserole and grimacing as she tasted it. She immediately spat it out into a napkin. "I guess I can see why."

I poked at my dinner roll and shook my head. "I don't know what to do for her. It's like she's pulling away from the world—from me."

"Maybe you need to talk to her parents," Timothy said, biting into an apple. "Maybe she needs to have some extra sessions with her therapist."

I looked up from my tray. Timothy may have been mad at me last night, but after I had texted him and apologized for my reactions to his prodding, he was quick to forgive me. Now, I was more than happy to hear what he had to say on the subject of the despondent Erin.

"I can't talk to Officer Taylor," I sighed, "it's a miracle that he's even letting Erin and me see each other."

"So your cowardliness trumps what's best for Erin?" Timothy raised his eyebrows in an I-know-I'm-right way. And he was right. So right. He was two for two including last night.

Drat his intuition!

"It's not that—well—yeah, it's that," I said, surprised at my own honesty. "Maybe I should talk to her parents, I don't know. But first I want to talk to Erin. I mean, she's been pulling away from me since she got to see Jeremy for the first time."

"She thinks it's her fault," Hannah said. "She's internalizing it all. She has to realize no one is blaming her."

"It's more than that," Timothy said. "It doesn't matter if others don't blame her when she blames herself, you know? That's why I think she might need more help than any of us can provide. Think about it; she saw some pretty awful things that night."

I sighed. "Believe me, I know. I was there."

Hannah reached over and put her hand over mind. "All I know is that she needs you more than ever right now. If she pulls, you need to push—but gently. Don't let her sever your relationship. If she loses you, Dakota, she loses herself."

Wow. Profound words from the new girl from Defiance County. If what Hannah said was true, the weight of our relationship and Erin's well-being was on my shoulders. I had to be her constant, her rock in this turbulent time.

But can I be what she needs? I'm no therapist—I could mess this up big time. Why me? Why now?

"This is the third time in four days Erin has neglected to sit at our table of intellectual and social misfits," Bertrand said, scribbling madly on his notepad.

"Welcome to the conversation," I muttered. I didn't want to deal with deciphering Bertrand's high-nerd speak, nor could I deal with his stupid scribbling in his stupid notebook. I decided to ignore him rather than explode.

"I have been here the entire time," Bertrand blinked.

I shook my head. At least some things never changed.

***

"How is he doing today?" I asked, taking a seat beside Jeremy's bed.

"No change from yesterday," his mother said, taking a sip from a mug of steaming green tea.

"How are you holding up?"

Jeremy's mother sighed, and Mr. Stines stood over her chair and massaged her shoulders.

"We're doing as well as we can right now. Mark is going to go back to work tomorrow, and I'm going to have to start thinking about making the transition back to work, too."

I felt my stomach roil. It was amazing how one bad decision could have such a devastating effect on so many people.

It's not my fault—but I feel like it is.

"At any rate," Mark Stines said, "we're glad you're here, Dakota."

This had become my routine on days I wasn't scheduled at the diner. My mother, God bless her soul, had worked it out with the King County Health Center to take the hours from three in the afternoon to six in the evening off to take me to Toledo on my non-working days. Of course, I had to be back inside my house in Infinity by six, per my probation. That meant I had an hour to spend with Jeremy and his parents before I had to hightail it home.

"Your mom can come in, too," Debbie Stines said, taking another sip from her mug.

"She doesn't want to get in the way," I said, my eyes sweeping over Jeremy's broken body.

"She wouldn't be in the way," Debbie said. "Why don't you go out and get her after a bit."

I agreed and focused my attention on Jeremy. I had taken to talking to him about happenings at school, movie trailers that looked interesting, even what I ate for lunch. I wanted him to hear me—I prayed he could hear me. I wanted him to absorb every bit of information I rattled off to him so that when he popped out of his coma he could amaze the doctors when he regaled them with my arbitrary chatter. Stuff like that happened in the movies, and I was pulling for a movie-type awakening.

"They cut the music department. Timothy's pretty bent out of shape, and I get that. It's sad how much the school board is taking away from us. I wonder how many kids will transfer to Clearton or somewhere else? I can see the athletes doing it, especially. Open enrollment makes it real easy to go where you want. What do you think? You gonna stick around Infinity High if there's no theater department next year?"

I knew he couldn't answer me, but it felt good asking him questions. It made him feel alive and present instead of teetering on the brink of life and death and distant.

"Bertrand still writes in his stupid notebook. I don't get why he does it, it's like…"

And I went on talking about the mundane happenings of the day, not because I wanted to say them, but because I wanted Jeremy to hear my voice and know how sorry I was. I knew I could never make everything right again, but I could do my part in making his recovery easier.

I texted Erin four times as my mother drove home from

the hospital. She didn't respond once, and as we pulled into our driveway, I felt a wave of sorrow wash over me. I was slowly losing her to herself, and I wondered if it was too late to get her back.

shat·ter \ˈsha-tər\

VERB: To dash one's heart to pieces

chap·ter 24
noun

OVER

"What's that supposed to mean?" I asked, my blood beating in my temples.

"It's what it sounds like," Erin said from the other end of the line, "I don't want to hang out."

I gripped my cell phone tighter and swallowed a lump of foreboding/anger/complete bewilderment. I had called Erin because she hadn't responded to any of my texts—and I had sent more than plenty for her to have responded to at least *one*. She also hadn't been answering her cell, screening my calls like I was some stalker, or something. To be honest, it cheesed me off something fierce. It was after she had let my fourth call trickle to voicemail that I had waited half an hour and called the Taylor home phone. After battling for a good ten seconds with her mother about taking my call, (I heard their muffled voices in the background and it felt like my heart was being stomped on by a sumo wrestler wearing baseball spikes), she had finally grabbed the receiver and mumbled her greeting.

I plopped onto my bed and sighed. "What's the deal, Erin? What did I do? If I did something to tick you off, please tell me. Otherwise, what's going on?"

I heard Erin exhale on the other end of the line, and I imagined she was raking her hand through her hair as she did when she was exasperated or in a conundrum.

"You didn't do anything, Dakota. It's just—I—I don't know if--"

My heart thundered in my chest, my ears turning hot as the blood coursed through them. I felt a terrible ache in the pit of my stomach, felt the out-of-body rush of a thousand emotions running over me. This wasn't good. Not good at all.

"Don't know if what?" I demanded. "Say it. You don't know if what?"

I was met with silence from the other end of the line. I heard my mother drop a pan in the kitchen, her muffled mild curse float upstairs and into my bedroom. But I didn't hear Erin, and for an awful second I thought she had actually hung up on me.

"Erin? What's the deal? You don't know if what?"

I heard her exhale again, and when her voice caught in her throat I knew she was on the verge of tears. My brain exploded in panic.

"I don't know if—if—we can be together anymore, Dakota."

I nearly dropped the phone. I surely hadn't heard her right. Did she just break up with me? My face tingled, my extremities felt like gelatin. It took me a moment to find my voice.

"What? What are you—did you dad say we couldn't date anymore?"

If there was any kind of bright spot in this awful line of conversation it would be if Officer Taylor had forced Erin to end our relationship. If all this was real and I wasn't just under the influence of some really strong pain medication, I hoped Erin's statement to me had been her father's doing and not her own. But I couldn't see Officer Taylor forcing Erin and me to separate. If he'd wanted that to happen, he would've put an end to the relationship right after the accident. No, this wasn't

Officer Taylor's doing. This was Erin speaking for herself.

"No, it's not my dad. It's—it's—*complicated.*"

And then I lost it. All my pent up frustrations about the accident, about being on probation, about the uncertainty of Jeremy's condition, about Erin's slipping away from me, about Bertrand and his stupid notebook, came out in an avalanche of fierce emotion.

"Are you kidding me, Erin? It's *complicated!?!?* That's all you've got? This isn't a flippin' Facebook relationship status, this is *us*—this is *me!*"

I heard Erin's voice break, and I knew she was crying.

"Dakota—please--"

I wanted none of it. I had been betrayed by the person—the friend—I loved the most.

"Don't you *please* me! Don't talk down to me like you're my mother! I can't believe you're doing this *over the phone!* Do you realize how terrible this feels? Do you realize how I thought I knew you? First, you don't return my texts or my calls, and now you break up with me *over the phone?!?!*"

"Dakota, you don't understand--"

"Stop patronizing me, Erin! I understand! I'm not stupid! You don't want to be with me anymore, I get it!"

I wanted to hurl my phone across the room, wanted to see it shatter against the wall like my heart had just shattered in my chest cavity.

"It's not that I don't—"

I was done with this conversation. I wanted to leave, to get out, to be anywhere but in my bedroom, where the shrapnel of my heart reminded me of what I had just lost.

"Just stop! I get it! We're done! I hope you have a great flippin' life!"

I ended the call and raised my arm to hurl my iPhone through my bedroom window. At the last moment, I thought better of it, and instead tossed it onto my bed.

Dakota Defined

What just happened? How could she? Why would she just end it all now—especially now?

I crumpled onto my bed, the first waves of emptiness rushing over me. I sucked in a sob, and then exploded into a mess of tears and snot. Grabbing my pillow, I pressed it over my face and screamed as loudly as I could. When that didn't empty me of the hurt and anger, I did it again.

As I cried into my pillow, I felt the entire world crumpling in on me. First Jeremy, and now this. Things couldn't get any worse—this was the lowest of the low.

Through bleary tears I looked at my iPhone and willed it to signal an incoming text or jangle an incoming call. I stared at it for ten minutes—an hour—an eternity—who knew? The longer it sat silent, the closer the poison of solitude and hopelessness inched to my shattered heart. Evening turned to night and night turned to morning, and Erin hadn't texted or called.

It was over.

chap·ter | ˈCHaptər | 25
noun

AWAKE

I awoke the next morning, Saturday, with a feeling of hollowness pervading my entire being. Rolling onto my back, I studied the ceiling and thought of all I was losing. I wasn't foolish enough to think my friendship with Erin would revert back to pre-relationship days; things didn't work like that. There are some thresholds in life that, if you cross, you can't go back through, no matter how hard you want to. At twenty-eight after nine o'clock on the morning of January eleventh, I knew I had lost all of Erin and not just the parts that had constituted our more-than-friends relationship.

But why? Why now?

I knew I shouldn't have lashed out at her like I had. It had been foolish, a moment when I had lost my head and my cool as my already janked-up emotions melted into one. But hadn't I deserved more than a phone call? Hadn't I ranked higher than the method of a junior high break-up?

I looked to my iPhone on my bed stand. It hadn't made a peep in over ten hours. If Erin really had cared about my feelings, she would've called me back. I reached for my phone, knowing it was hopeless. When I picked it up and thumbed at the screen, I realized it was turned off.

What?! It's been off this entire time?!

I quickly booted up the phone, cursing myself for my stupidity. It must've turned off when I had tossed it onto the bed. And since Mom had disconnected the home phone line after we had both picked up iPhones, the only way Erin could've contacted me was via cell phone. And since it was four o'clock when I had called her to see if she wanted to hang out, she couldn't come over for fear of violating her probation.

She might have called! She might have texted!

As my phone blipped to life, I nearly wept when I saw I had twenty-seven texts, nine voicemails and twelve missed calls. They were all from Erin. She had been trying to contact me five minutes after I had ended our conversation all the way until three fourteen in the morning.

I felt hope well in my chest. I had to go over to her house, had to speak to her face-to-face. Maybe there was hope, after all. Maybe our relationship wasn't over.

But then my heart sank again. Noticing I had over forty Facebook posts to my wall, I quickly accessed my account.

What?! No!?

I scrolled through post after post of 'sorry dude' and 'I thought you guys were gonna get married.' Fearing the worst, I thumbed to Erin's page and felt the muscles in my chest tighten.

No! Why did you—

At three eighteen in the morning, four minutes after Erin had written me her last text, she had changed her relationship status to single. I felt like throwing up. I had missed her calls and texts and she had thought I was just ignoring her. Tossing my phone onto my bed, I quickly stripped and ran to the shower. I had to get over to Erin's ASAP. She had to know I still loved her.

And, yes, I said love.

***

I had just turned off the shower, steam thick in the small upstairs bathroom, when I heard my mother knock on the bathroom door.

"Dakota?" She wiggled the doorknob and I heard the old hinges squeak as she cracked the door. I quickly grabbed my towel and held the shower curtain firmly against the shower wall.

"Mom! What are you doing? I'm kind of naked, here!"

She didn't even register I had said anything, instead, she threw open the door all the way.

"Get your clothes on quick! We have to get to the hospital."

My heart began to thunder in my chest. What now? What more could go wrong?

"Why? What happened? Is Jeremy--"

"He's awake!" My mother shouted. "He's out of his coma! Let's go, let's go, let's go!"

"Wait—what—how is he? Does he remember anything about--"

"I don't have any particulars, honey. You now know as much as I do. Debbie Stines called and specifically asked if you could come the hospital, and I came up here to get you. Come on, Dakota! Hurry!"

I didn't have to think twice. I quickly toweled myself off as my mother pounded out of the bathroom. Making up with Erin could wait. Besides, if Jeremy was awake, she would be at the hospital, too.

***

I hadn't bothered to read Erin's text messages, nor had I listened to her voicemail messages. After I had seen she had changed her Facebook relationship status, they had become irrelevant. But after I called Pop and told him I wouldn't be in to work because I was going to the hospital, I thumbed a quick text to Erin:

Sorry about not answering your texts/calls. Phone was off. I'll explain later. See you at the hospital.

chapter 26

Return of Stupid Hair Jokes

We arrived at the hospital a little less than an hour later. My mother's hair was still wet, as she had jumped into the downstairs shower after she had taken Debbie Stines's phone call. That explained why the water had been so flippin' cold. As we took the elevator to the third floor, my stomach turned over, both in anticipation of seeing Jeremy and in fear of seeing Erin.

I feel like I'm going through menopause!

"You okay?" my mother asked as the elevator doors opened onto Jeremy's floor.

No.

"Just a little excited and nervous to see Jeremy."

My mother put her arm around my shoulder. "It's going to be okay. Be happy—he's awake!"

I mumbled an 'I'm happy' or something of that nature as we walked into the waiting room. To my surprise, no one was sitting in the uncomfortable seats.

"Um—you did say he's awake, right?" I asked my mother. "You didn't just dream you took the phone call?"

"Stop it, Dakota. I took the call."

"Then where is everybody? I expected there to be people here--"

"You were one of the first people we called," a voice behind me said. I turned and saw a beaming Debbie Stines. She looked ten years younger than she had a few days ago, the worry lines on her face erased by a large smile. Even her eyes had lost their hangdog appearance, and for the first time since the accident, a fierce hope replaced the dread. She crossed the sterile waiting room and wrapped her arms around me in a tight hug.

"This is a big day," she whispered in my ear. "We wanted you to be one of the first people to see him."

I didn't want to waste any more time. Pulling away, I looked toward Jeremy's room.

"Can we go back now?"

"Let's go."

Debbie Stines took my hand and began talking a mile a minute as we turned the corner and headed for Jeremy's room.

"He woke up at four twelve this morning. The doctor said not to let the news out until he had a chance to check Jeremy out. Right now, Jeremy's pretty tired. He doesn't remember anything about the accident; the last thing he can recall is putting on his makeup before *The Christmas Carol* performance. His prognosis is a little unclear at this point, but the fact that he's awake is the biggest blessing. There could be some brain damage, but we'll know more when all the testing is done and the results come in."

"Can he—will he walk?"

Jeremy's mother took a deep breath and let it out slowly.

"That's not something we're really thinking about right now. The short answer to your question is probably not. He was given less than a one percent chance. But we can't focus on what he won't be able to do. We need to be happy for the miracle his being awake truly is."

Josh Clark

I couldn't agree more, though in the back of my mind I kept seeing a strobing 1%--1%--1%...

Ignore it. This is a day to celebrate, not focus on what you can't control.

We made it to Jeremy's room and Debbie Stines reached to push the cracked door open. Before she could, I grabbed her wrist.

"What does he know? I mean—about the accident?"

"We were honest and straightforward with him. He knows the truth, Dakota."

My stomach churned as I realized what knowing the truth could mean.

"Is he mad at me? I mean—does he blame me? Erin?"

Debbie Stines patted my back. "He asked to see you. And Erin, too. He understands his role in the accident. We made it very clear that he is just as responsible for what happened as you and Erin. Don't worry, Dakota. He can't wait to see you."

Jeremy's mother pushed the door open, and when I saw Jeremy in the bed, his eyelids blinking with life, I all but wept. Here he was, out of his coma and ready to begin the healing process. It truly was a miracle.

"Is he here?" Jeremy said, his voice weary and rough. He didn't move his head to see who had just come through his door; he couldn't if he wanted to, what with all the machines and spine-aligning devices he was hooked up to.

"It's Dakota, honey," Debbie said, nudging me toward the bed. My heart machine-gunned in my chest cavity, my palms going slicker than an out-of-water trout. When I got to his bedside and stood over him, he looked up at me with a tired smile.

"Hey, D.L."

I didn't know what to say. For one of the only times in my life, I was absolutely, one hundred percent at a loss for words. What came out of my mouth was purely accidental, but, in retrospect, one of the most perfect things I could've possible said.

"You finally cut your hair, I see."

What?! Really?! That's the best you can do?! Your friend just came out a coma, for cheese sake!

Jeremy's smile widened. "I didn't do it. I never would've done it. I guess they had to save my brain and all."

"How're you feeling?" I asked, finally finding words suitable for the occasion.

"Like I've been in a car wreck and in a coma for three and a half weeks."

I laughed, unable to hide the tears that glazed my eyes.

"I see they didn't take away your sense of humor."

"If anything, brain surgery helped it."

A brief silence settled between us. I knew what I wanted to say to fill it, but I didn't know how to adequately express myself. How do you apologize for paralyzing someone? For putting one of your best friends into a coma? Can words possibly suffice when your stupid decision has completely altered lives, racked up insane amounts of medical debt and completely shattered the hopes and dreams of someone you love?

"Jeremy—I don't know how to say it. And I know words will never be enough to--"

"Can it, D.L.," Jeremy said. "No apologies, please. What happened happened. It wasn't anyone's fault."

"But it was my car. I picked you up from the theater. I sat in the back seat and let you have the front when I never should've let you get into the car in the first place."

"And I don't remember any of it," Jeremy said. "I'm not interested in playing the blame game. Nobody wins when that happens. I'm just happy I'm alive. But, to tell you the truth, I'm ready to poop on my own."

I couldn't help but burst into laughter. Maybe brain surgery really did give Jeremy a better sense of humor.

"Is Erin here?" Jeremy asked when I finally stopped laughing.

Josh Clark

The mention of Erin's name caused a wad of something gross to lodge itself in my throat.

"She wasn't when I got here. She's probably here now. Want me to get her?"

"We're only allowed to have one non-family member in here at a time," Jeremy's father said. His voice startled me; I hadn't even realized he was in the room.

"Really? That's dumb," Jeremy snorted.

"Rules are rules," I said, shrugging. "I'll be here all day. We'll see more of each other." I turned to go, but stopped when I was overcome with emotion. I had one more thing to say. Gently grabbing Jeremy's hand, I looked him in the eyes, my own bleary with tears.

"I love you, man. It's good to have you back."

***

Erin was the first person I saw when I walked back into the waiting room. The rest of the Hodgepodgers had arrived in the time I was with Jeremy, but somehow they all faded into the background. Erin was the only person I could see.

Erin saw me, too. Without hesitation, she ran to me and wrapped her arms around my neck. Stunned, I held her tight as she breathed into my neck.

"We need to talk."

"Later," I whispered back, kissing her on the cheek. "Jeremy wants to see you."

Erin pulled away as if she had been struck by lightning.

"He wants to see—is he mad? Does he blame me?"

I shook my head and rubbed her shoulder. "No. He's not blaming anybody. But he is waiting to see you."

Erin took a deep breath and looked over her shoulder at her mother and father. Officer Taylor nodded once, and Erin's jaw twitched twice. She nodded.

"Okay," she said, resolutely.

I squeezed her shoulder. "He won't bite you, I promise."

Erin smiled weakly and walked past me toward Jeremy's room.

As I watched her go, I felt my spirit praying for two miracles in the same day.

chap·ter |CH aptər|
noun

27

"Us"

"It stinks that we have to talk this way," I said, flopping onto my bed. I threw my pillow to the foot of the bed, opting for a back-of-the-head-to-mattress approach to this going-to-be-an-uncomfortable conversation.

"Probation stinks," Erin said softly. Silence filled the line. Awful, abysmal, reach-for-the-Pepto-Bismol, silence.

That's it? That's all you have to say?

We had both stayed at the hospital until five o'clock. Jeremy's relatives had flooded the waiting room like Hebrews out of Egypt, and the rest of the Hodgepodge clan had shown up an hour or so after my mother and I had arrived. Because of the chaos of the waiting room, and because the site of Jeremy's miraculous resurgence to life was not the place for a lengthy conversation about the state of our floundering relationship, Erin and I hadn't said a word to each other since she had been called to Jeremy's hospital room. I was eager to hear what her experience at Jeremy's beside had been, but the selfish part of me wanted to get down to the nitty-gritty of our fractured relationship.

"How are you doing?" I asked, figuring this was as good a place as any to start. My heart pounded, and somewhere in the

Dakota Defined

back of my mind the terrible realization that our relationship might really be over sizzled like bacon in a skillet.

Erin sighed and took a moment before answering.

"I've been better, Dakota." Silence.

"What do you mean? Jeremy's awake—he's going to be okay--"

"He'll never walk again. I don't call that okay."

I ran my fingers through my dirty-blonde hair.

"The doctor said he has a chance."

"One percent isn't a chance, Dakota, and you know it. It's a lifelong sentence to a wheelchair."

"You don't know that--"

"What is there to know?" Erin exploded. "I flipped your car and got Jeremy paralyzed! He'll never walk again—and it's *my fault!* *I* put him in a wheelchair! *I'm* the one who should be hooked up to all those machines! Not him!"

A flare of panic ignited in my stomach. Erin's funk went far beyond our relationship; it was deeply rooted in guilt and self-loathing. Here I was trying to sew a patch onto the frayed fabric of our relationship when Erin's mind couldn't be farther from keeping us together. She was just trying to keep *herself* together.

"Erin, it's not your fault. You can't blame yourself."

Erin snorted. "Yeah. Right. That's what my therapist said, too. Anything else you want to add, Dr. Lester?"

I was blown away by Erin's tone with me. To say it wasn't like her would be the understatement of the century.

Stay calm, Dakota. It's not about you, it's about Erin.

"All I know is you have to stop blaming yourself for what happened. Jeremy's parents don't blame you, I don't blame you and *you* can't blame you."

Erin sighed. I could practically feel all the fight go out of her from the other end of the line.

"I don't deserve to be alive. That's the thing. It isn't

enough that Jeremy's awake. His way of life as he knows it is changed forever."

"Erin, you can't do this. Please don't."

I could tell Erin was crying and that she was trying to stifle her sniffles. My heart tore in two for her. You can't wrap your arms around someone over the phone, and what she needed the most right now was for me to hold her.

"I wish I could hug you," I said, putting my thoughts to words.

"I'm nothing to waste pity on, Dakota."

"It's not pity, it's--"

The word *love* was on the tip of my tongue. I knew I should say it, knew if I did I meant it without a doubt. But something kept the word inside my mouth, made it dissolve on my tongue and, thus, dissolve from my initial sentence.

"It's that I need you, Erin," I said instead. "*I* need *you* to stay strong. *I* need *you*, Erin. We have to be strong for each other. That's what people do when they're in relationships."

I added the last part despite my better judgment. I didn't know what I expected her to say, but I did know I had to know where we stood as a couple.

If we are a couple...

A painful silence fell over the line, and I immediately assumed the worst. Erin was an intuitive girl; I knew she had caught the last part of my statement even in her guilt-ridden state. The ball was in her court. I just hoped it wasn't deflated.

"Dakota—do you really think we can be together after all this?"

Of course. She threw the ball right back into my court. And my court was full of a thousand different kinds of worry-snakes. Super.

"I don't see why not. If anything, we need each other to stay sane." I swallowed and sighed. "And I need you because I like having you around. And because you're pretty darn cute."

I was surprised when Erin laughed lightly.

"But I'm going to fail you sometimes, Dakota. Just like I failed Jeremy. I'm not the perfect girlfriend you think I am."

"I don't need perfect. I just need Erin. Besides, I screw up for the both of us."

Another silence took over the line. I felt my heart beating through my chest, heard it pulsing in my ears. Whatever Erin said next was crucial. She would either make or break us with her next statement.

"I think I would die without you, Dakota," Erin finally said. "I don't think I could face all this. I'd want to end it."

I felt a sailor's knot cinch in my stomach. Somewhere in the back of my mind, warning sirens started to scream. What Erin had said threw me off. I liked what she had said but not how she had said it. I didn't know which aspect of her statement to address, the fact that she still wanted to be with me or the creepy suicidal undertone of her comment.

Shake it off. Stay positive. She still wants to be with you. Work with that and forget the rest. She didn't mean it.

"So we're still us?" I asked, knowing as the words came out of my mouth that they sounded straight from a cheesy romance movie starring some nameless British actor.

I could hear the smile in Erin's voice. It was one of the best things I had ever heard.

"We're still us."

I fist pumped and nodded to myself.

"Just the way I like it. Just the way it's supposed to be."

chap·ter 28
noun

Adios, Wayne

Monday morning saw more dismantling of the Infinity High School student body's morale. I coasted into the metal bike rack, my cheeks numb and my forehead burning, and realized with only mild despair that I was the only idiot still riding bike to school. I didn't have any alternative, though. My upperclassman friend base was non-existent, and my mother had to be to the hospital for her rounds by six o'clock. I would rather have French kissed a blender than straddle my Schwinn in the frigid northwest Ohio mid-January weather, but my options were a little on the limited side. Plus, there was no way I was riding the bus with a bunch of first and second graders. I didn't particularly enjoy cruising to school with crusted boogers pasted onto the seat in front of me. Kind of ruins the appetite for a few days.

When I entered the school, I knew something was amiss. Upperclassmen and underclassmen alike whispered to each other in the hallways as they clustered into their little groups of exclusivity. As I turned into the freshman hallway, my fellow classmates cast furtive glances toward the junior hallway as though they expected a hideous creature to come bounding around the corner. It was too quiet, the sounds of slamming locker doors and muffled music from blaring iPods not present as they always were in the morning. Something was up, and I immediately sensed I wasn't going to like it.

I opened my locker with silent reverence. I wasn't going to be the one to puncture the void of sound, and, anyway, human nature dictates that one should observe the pre-established ambience of a given setting. Until I knew what was up, I wasn't going to rock the boat.

I felt a tap on my shoulder, and when I turned around, Timothy was standing behind me.

"Dude," Timothy whispered, "did you hear?"

I gently pulled my books from my locker and slowly closed the door so that I didn't break the code of silence.

"What's going on? Is this a Quaker meeting or something?"

Timothy's eyes grew wide as he stepped closer.

"Dennis got canned this morning."

I nearly dropped my books. Had I heard him correctly? Did he just say Mr. Dennis had been *fired*?

"What? What happened?"

Timothy spoke with his hands as he regaled the story as he'd heard it.

"So, you know how Mr. Dennis is here at the butt crack of dawn, right? Well, I guess Principal Stemwalter and Superintendent Carlson were waiting for him."

"Why? What did Dennis do?"

"What Todd Lawrence told me—you know his dad's on the school board—was that Mr. Dennis has been really flapping his gums about all the cuts the board is making. Todd says his dad is always the only 'nay' vote when it comes to the cuts, but that's beside the point. What happened is Stemwalter and Carlson tag-teamed Dennis in Dennis's room this morning. Probably telling Mr. Dennis to back off with his anti-board talk."

"And they fired him?" I asked incredulously.

"I don't think they had any want or need to fire him until the fireworks started."

"Oh, no."

Timothy shook his head. "Oh, yes. I got here when the shouting was at its worst. You could hear it clear in the senior hallway, and that's even with Mr. Dennis's door closed. I guess Mr. Dennis went ballistic on Stemwalter and Carlson and Stemwalter and Carlson went ballistic back. Mr. Dennis stormed out of the building about five minutes before you got here. His face was all red and that big vein in his forehead was sticking out like five feet."

I took a deep breath. "I can't believe this. How can they can Dennis? He's the best teacher Infinity High School has. He's won the teacher of the year award like nine years in a row."

Timothy shrugged. "It just shows how money talks."

"And how corrupt our school board is," I added.

"Makes you want to do something about it?" Timothy asked, stepping even closer.

"If that's a question with a direct implication, then no," I said, a wave of heat sweeping over my face.

"Dakota, you were Dennis's pick to stand up to the board. I mean, look at everybody." Timothy swept his open hand over the freshman hallway and beyond. Timothy was right; they all looked like beaten puppies. Mr. Dennis was the most liked teacher in the district. The student body had weathered the cuts and had taken the school board's political abuse in stride. But what would they do now that their mouthpiece for reform had been fired? How would they cope now that the administration was sending a very clear message: he who speaks out against the great and terrible school board will be metaphorically executed.

"If there ever was a time to do something about all this, it's now," Timothy said, putting a hand on my shoulder. "It's not like we don't all know you were Dennis's hand-chosen man for the job."

"It's not a job I want," I said, shrugging Timothy's hand off my shoulder. "I never asked to be Dennis's man or whatever."

"Does anyone ask to be a revolutionist leader?"

"Okay. Enough with the dramatic crap. You're turning into Jeremy by the day." My stomach tightened when I mentioned Jeremy's name. It was an old habit; whenever someone said something overly dramatic I would drop Jeremy's name. But now his name felt sacred, and as I used it against Timothy, I couldn't help but feel as though I had said something dirty. What is more, I could already anticipate Timothy's next line. I had all but walked into it.

"What do you think Jeremy would want you to do?"

I began to walk away. "Stop talking about him like he's past tense."

"You know what you need to do, Dakota. You're just afraid of the putting yourself out there," Timothy whisper-called.

I snorted.

Just leave me alone about all this! I have other things to worry about!

But as I headed to my first period class, woefully early and my homework woefully incomplete, I couldn't help but think Timothy was right.

★★★

"You gonna do something about it now?" Craig Henderson asked. He hooked his thumbs into two of the front loops of his jeans and stood glaring at me like the farmer he was.

I slammed my locker shut and prepared to head to the cafeteria for lunch. Craig was only making a miserable day worse.

"What, Craig? What is it I can do that you can't do?"

Craig blocked my path and leaned one flannel-clad arm against a locker.

"You were the guy Dennis wanted. You were the guy he talked to me about."

"You still didn't answer my question," I said, calmly. "What can I do that you can't?"

Craig shook his head and raked his free hand through his straw-blonde hair.

"All I know is I want the agriculture program back and I'm not a public speaker. We all saw what you did last year—how you spilled your guts in front of the student body. That's what I'm saying. That's what we need."

I smiled ever-so-slightly. "You want a martyr. Someone who will take all the bullets so you can have your program back."

I saw on his face that Craig didn't know how to respond.

"We just want to get our stuff back."

"Then you better get a bulletproof vest," I said, stepping around him.

For the second time that day I felt the weight of responsibility on my shoulders as I walked away from a petitioner.

This is crazy. Leave me alone!

✶✶✶

"Where's Erin?" Hannah asked, spreading a napkin onto her lap.

"Absent," I said, not really in the mood to talk but knowing I'd have to. Too much was going on these days with Jeremy and the collapse of Infinity High School as we knew it to play the silent card.

"Is she sick?" Timothy asked, slathering butter onto a piece of white bread.

"Not sure. She didn't text me or anything. And she's not responding to any of mine."

Which is weird. Normally she texts me to let me know when she's not going to be at school.

Dakota Defined

I tried not to invent theories as to why Erin wasn't in school or why she wasn't texting me back. I was going to pedal my Schwinn over to her place after school let out to make sure she was okay, but something about her being gone and not telling me about it scratched at the back of my mind.

"There is a strong outbreak of influenza going around," Bertrand said, scribbling into his open pad of paper. "My mother has been devastated by influenza for going on three days."

We all ignored Bertrand. If he was hurt by our not acknowledging him, he didn't show it. Instead, he kept scribbling into his note pad and squinting his eyes open and shut in typical Bertrand fashion.

"You going to see Jeremy tonight?" Hannah asked.

I shook my head. "Can't. I have to work at five. You going?"

Hannah nodded. "Yeah, I'm going. Jeremy's mom said the doctor is going to talk to them sometime this afternoon about possible rehabilitation facilities."

"To try to get him on his feet again?" Timothy asked, taking a bite out of his bread.

Hannah nodded. "Yeah. I guess there are some really great facilities around here that might give him a fighting chance to walk again."

"I wouldn't call one percent a fighting chance," I said, immediately regretting the words as they came out of my mouth. I still felt guilty about Jeremy's paralysis, and the comment was meant as a slight on myself, not Jeremy. But, of course, the others wouldn't see it that way.

I put my hands up. "That came out wrong. I guess what I mean is that Jeremy's going to need to go to a top-notch facility if he has a chance to walk again."

"I wonder what a facility like that costs?" Timothy asked, mercifully ignoring my previous comment.

"And if their insurance will cover any of the cost," Hannah continued.

I sighed and shook my head. If only I could rewind the clock and make all this disappear. This wasn't a conversation teenagers were supposed to have at lunch. We were supposed to talk about movies and the latest gossip, not about a friend's odds to walk again.

This is a miserable day.

When I looked up from my tray I saw Craig Henderson looking at me from two tables over. I quickly looked away.

A truly miserable day.

ra·zor \ˈrā-zər\

NOUN: A nasty, sharp, vicious, awful instrument used to divide things.

chapter 29
noun

GROSS-OUT CENTRAL

When the bell sounded to end the school day, I was out of the school in less than two minutes. I didn't want to talk to anybody, I most certainly didn't want to run into Craig Henderson again and I wanted to forget that the day had happened at all. But as I pedaled my Schwinn to Erin's house, all I could think about was Mr. Dennis having to tell his wife he had been fired from the institution he had devoted his life to.

I pulled into Erin's driveway and jumped off my bike. The sky was a miserable grey, the temperature just frigid enough to make my nose run and my cheeks burn. I leaned my bike against the iron pole of a long unused basketball goal and hurried up the Taylors' front walk, peeling my gloves and stocking cap off in the process. Officer Taylor's police cruiser wasn't parked in the driveway, and I knew that Erin's mother wouldn't be home from her insurance-selling job until around five, so I had some much-needed alone time with Erin, should she be well enough to want me to stick around.

I knocked on the front door and tried the knob. Finding it unlocked, I decided to let myself in. If Erin was sleeping in bed or on the couch, there was no need for her to get up to let me in. Opening the door, I stepped inside the Taylors's warm living room and quickly shut the door behind me so as to not let the heat out. Erin wasn't sleeping on the couch, but a crumpled sheet and an Erin's-head-indented pillow showed she had been at some point. I looked around for any tell-tale signs of the flu—a box of tissues, an old soup bowl—but I could find nothing that indicated Erin had contracted the influenza Bertrand's mother had been suffering from for the past three days. I threw my gloves and hat on the recliner and took my coat off and draped it over the arm of the couch.

"Erin?" I called softly. I didn't want to scare the biscuits out of her, but I didn't want to walk in on her if she was sleeping. I had done that once and she had adamantly insisted I never do such a thing again, saying she was an ugly sleeper, whatever that meant.

"Erin? How are you feeling?" I called again. I heard a loud thump and an un-Erin-like muffled curse come from the bathroom.

"Dakota?" Erin called from behind the closed door. "What are you doing here?"

"I just came to see if you're okay. When you didn't reply to my texts, I thought I'd stop over to see how you're doing."

I heard the unmistakable sound of the medicine cabinet closing, and, a moment later, Erin stepped out of the bathroom.

"Hey, Dakota."

My first instinct was that she was nervous to see me. She kept looking behind her into the bathroom and then back at me, her dark eyes definitely distracted and antsy.

"Hey. How're you feeling?"

Erin glanced behind her one more time and then crossed the living room and pushed the crumpled sheet onto the floor. Her movements were short and abrupt, and she made no move to sit down on the couch.

"I—I'm doing fine. I was just feeling a little under the weather this morning."

I decided not to draw attention to her nervousness. Maybe she had just finished pooping and was worrying about the smell lingering into the living room. Girls were weird when it came to poop.

Erin pulled her hair back into a pony tail. She was wearing a navy blue hoodie and light, slim-fitting jeans. Her bare feet sunk into the white carpet, and if I didn't know any better, I would've thought she looked as healthy and un-sick as I had seen her in weeks.

"Something big happened today," I said, sitting down on the recliner. Erin's eyes darted from me to the front door and then back to me.

"What's that?" She still made no move to sit down, and, for the first time, I got the feeling she didn't want me here.

"Dennis was fired today." I proceeded to tell her the whole story. While she was shocked and asked a few questions, I couldn't shake the feeling she was trying to get rid of me.

"Erin? What's wrong?" I finally asked. I could take it no longer. If she didn't want me around, she needed to tell me. Besides, I could go home and enjoy some quiet time before I had to be at the diner.

"What do you mean? I'm fine."

"No you're not. You're acting like you don't want me— Erin, what's that?"

I was shocked to see a thin line of blood soaking through her jeans just inside the crook of her upper thigh.

"What are you talking about--" Erin looked down and saw the blood, looked up at me and then covered the area with her hand.

"You need to leave, Dakota," Erin said, her face a deep red. She began to inch toward the bathroom, her hand still over the wound.

"What? How can I just leave? You're bleeding! What happened? Are you okay?"

Erin continued toward the bathroom, shooing me off with her free hand.

"It's nothing, Dakota. I'm just—I'm just on my period."

Oh.

I didn't know how to respond. She'd said the "p" word and it had shaken all the rebuttals from my brain. I felt my face go hot.

Okay, idiot. Now you have to leave. This is awkward.

"Uh—okay—uh--" I stammered as Erin backed into the bathroom door.

"I'm sorry, Dakota. Now can you see why I was nervous? Just—can you please go? I'll text you later, okay?"

She didn't have to ask me twice. Not when the "p" word was involved. I gathered my coat and winter accessories and made for the front door.

"I—uh—I guess I'll talk to you later."

"Okay," Erin called as I opened the door and the biting January wind nipped at my face. I quickly walked to my bike, throwing my coat on in the process, stuffing my hands into my gloves after I had finally conquered my fumble-fingers where my zipper was concerned. Throwing my leg over the seat of my Schwinn, I was out of Erin's driveway and down the street in less than thirty seconds. My mind alternated between two thoughts:

That was more than embarrassing—how can I face her again?

And:

Gross! Gross! Gross! Gross!

***

It wasn't until I was punching my time card at the diner, when my brain chilled from its embarrassment/revulsion at what I had experienced at Erin's house, that I clearly thought back on the moment.

Wait a minute…

I pulled an apron from a nail on the wall and tied it.

I'm not an expert on periods, but I doubt you bleed in a straight line.

I threw a wave to Pop, who was hunched over the grill, and walked into the dishwashing room.

No. She wasn't on her period. It was something else…

A chill tickled my spine, and as I reached for the handle of the stainless steel dishwashing machine, I kept coming to the same conclusion that a menstrual cycle didn't bleed like that. The line of blood was too straight, too precise. Kind of like…

A cut from a razor blade.

***

It was late when I got home from work. I was only supposed to work until nine-thirty, but a party of twenty had decided to pop into Pop's at nine-fifteen. Along with getting initiated into food preparation at Pop's Diner, I also got the "privilege" to work an extra hour and a half. Super.

I hadn't had the chance to check my phone during work, so when I clocked out and saw I had a text from Erin, the realization about the bleeding cut on her leg reentered the forefront of my mind. I knew it hadn't been her period as she had claimed. She had only used the "p" word to get me out of the house. I had clearly walked in on her doing something sinister to herself, and as I thumbed up Erin's text, I didn't want to believe she had resorted to self-mutilation.

I'm OK. Thanks for checking on me. You're the best.—Erin

Her text was a simple, straightforward lie. She was not okay. She was not happy I had checked on her. I had walked in on her cutting herself in the bathroom, and she had panicked, hence the swear word and the loud thump I had heard upon entering the Taylor residence. That had to have been what the blood was all about.

But I could be jumping to conclusions. There could be a logical explanation for her leg to be bleeding. Maybe she really had cut herself with a razorblade, except inadvertently. She could have been shaving, you dolt, have you thought of that?

As I showered off the smell of Pop's Diner from my skin, I couldn't help but feel weighed down by the situation. As the hot water created a muggy steam, I knew I would have to confront Erin about what I had seen. But should I go to her parents?

Not yet. If you're jumping to conclusions, going to her parents can backfire. You need to confront her first.

I turned the shower off and stood still, allowing the water to bead off my scrawny body. How did I get myself into these kinds of situations? Last school year it had been Blake Blanton, and this year it was something far worse. Not only was Jeremy's road to full recovery all but impossible, but my girlfriend was potentially delving into some very dangerous territory.

And it's my job to make sure she doesn't hurt herself.

Peeling back the shower curtain, I grabbed my towel and buried my face in its Downy fresh scent. How many hard conversations was I going to have with Erin this week?

As many as it takes. You love her, don't you?

Love her? Yes, I loved her.

Then do what it takes.

As I toweled myself off, I hated myself for my own advice.

chapter 30

PROMISES

The next morning brought with it a new sense of foreboding. I hadn't worked up the courage to talk to Erin, so instead of being proactive my suspicions, I let them marinate in my brain all night. Suffice it to say, when I pedaled my Schwinn to school in the morning, all I could think about was what kind of damage Erin could have done to herself last night. How many times had she cut herself? Was this an isolated incident? Would she even talk to me about it? I realized that by confronting her with my suspicions I would be skiing on a very slippery slope. And I had never skied before.

When I turned into the freshman hallway, my heart nearly pounded out of my chest when I saw Erin sitting against the wall across from my locker with her iPod ear buds jammed into her ears. When I reached my locker, she looked up and smiled.

"Hey, there."

Erin couldn't fool me. Her smile didn't reach her eyes. Instead of seeing the dancing sparkle of the old Erin, I saw the pain and desperation of the new one. My heart couldn't bear to see her this way.

"Hey."

Erin dropped her feigned smile and sighed.

"Look, about what happened yesterday. It was embarrassing for both of us. I know guys hate it when girls talk about their periods, but--"

"Erin, look at me," I said, gently grasping her shoulders and turning her body so she stood directly in front of me. "Are you really on your period?"

Erin's eyes darted to the right and then back to me. She scrunched her nose and squinted like what I was asking her was ridiculous.

"What are you asking me that for, Dakota? I don't mean to get all gross, but you saw the blood--"

"And you're not lying to me at all?"

Erin shrugged my hands off her shoulders. "Dakota, what's the matter with you? Why are you being this way? I know you're grossed out and all--"

"I'm not grossed out," I said resolutely. I never took my eyes off hers. "I think you're lying to me."

"Lying to you?"

"I think you cut yourself."

An uncomfortable silence settled between us as I watched Erin decide what she wanted to say next. I prayed she wouldn't make this hard on me, that she wouldn't try to lie her way out of it. To my surprise, her face dropped, and when she raised it again I saw her eyes were glazed over with tears.

"It was just that one time," Erin said. "It was just once."

I heard my heartbeat in my ears. As much as I was certain I knew what Erin had done to herself, everything within me had been pulling for her to be telling the truth and for me to be the dunce who had walked into an extremely embarrassing misunderstanding. But no dice. I had been dead on, and now Erin was telling me so.

"Erin—what were you thinking? You can't just hurt yourself like that. We have to tell your parents--"

Erin grabbed my shoulder hard.

"No! You can't tell my parents! They'll think I'm crazy."

"But you could hurt yourself--"

Erin's eyes were wild. "It was just that one time, I told you. Please—you can't say anything. I promise it'll never happen again."

I studied her for a moment. "But why? Why would you even--"

"Because it was a release, okay? Because I'm having trouble dealing with this whole Jeremy thing. But you don't have to worry about me anymore, okay? It was one time. That's it. I promise. Just—please don't tell my parents."

I sighed and shook my head. Her chocolate eyes were begging me, pleading with me to keep her trust. How could I tell her no?

"Okay. Fine. I won't say anything to your parents. But if I find out it happens again--"

"It *won't* happen again. I already told you that."

"Okay, then. It was just one and done."

Even as I said it, I wanted to take it back. I couldn't help but feel I was making a mistake by staying quiet about Erin's cutting herself. But what could I do? She was my girlfriend and she was telling me she was done with the whole business of cutting herself. I had to believe her. It was my duty to believe her.

"Just one and done," Erin said, "and you won't say a word about it?"

"No."

"Promise?"

I swallowed and sighed again. "I promise."

She kissed my cheek, her eyes not displaying affection for me but an unmistakable relief that I had promised to keep the incident a secret.

I couldn't help but feel I had made the wrong decision.

rev·o·lu·tion·ist \ˌre-və-ˈlü-sh(ə-)nist\

NOUN: Me, apparently

chap·ter 31
noun

THE REVOLUTIONARY

The fallout from Mr. Dennis' firing gained momentum. By lunchtime, numerous false reports about Principal Stemwalter stepping down in shame and Superintendent Carlson getting punched in the gut by a disgruntled Mrs. Dennis had swept the school like wildfire. As much as we all wanted the reports to be true, they had ended up being nothing more than myths perpetuated by cheesed-off students.

"This place is like a pressure cooker," Timothy said at lunch. "I heard some guys talking about breaking into the school tonight and spray painting 'we want Dennis back' on the wall outside Stemwalter's office door.

"Breaking into the school isn't the way to solve all this," Hannah said.

Timothy snorted. "Yeah, how did breaking into the school last year work out for you, D.L.?"

I glared at Timothy and said nothing. I was more concerned about Erin. She had declined to eat in the cafeteria, opting once again to sit on the top row of the gymnasium bleachers with her iPod ear buds jammed into her ears. She also hadn't turned in any of her homework in the three classes we had together, which was not like Erin. As I absently moved my tater tots around on my tray with my fork, I couldn't help but think my promise to not tell anyone about her cutting herself was the worst decision I could possibly have made.

"Earth to D.L.," Timothy was saying. He threw a tater tot at me and missed badly. He was a choir boy, after all. An athlete he was not.

"Huh?" I snapped out of my funk and swiped Timothy's errant tater tot off the floor.

"I asked if you're going to see Jeremy tonight."

"I have to work at five, so I might just call and talk to him."

"I am going to visit Jeremy and inquire about his prognosis for rehabilitation," Bertrand said, squinting behind his glasses.

"Good for you," I said, not because I was being mean, but because I really hadn't understood what he had said.

"When I was there last night, Jeremy wondered if anybody is going to step up and rally the student body to take on the school board," Hannah said, pretending not to direct the comment in my direction.

"Really?" Timothy asked, suddenly very interested. "And you said?"

Now Hannah looked up at me, her acorn-brown eyes smiling.

"I said Mr. Dennis asked D.L. to head something up."

I rolled my eyes. "And what did Jeremy say?"

Hannah didn't waver. "He said Mr. Dennis knows what he's talking about."

I took a deep breath and let it out slowly. I didn't want to deal with this today—I didn't want to deal with this ever. Why couldn't people understand that I didn't want to be their leader?

"How's about it, D.L.? Even Jeremy thinks you're the guy for the job," Timothy said.

"I think Jeremy's been away too long to fully understand the climate here," I said, grasping at straws.

"You could always form an exploratory committee," Bertrand said, opening his notepad.

"What are you talking about?" I looked to Bertrand and realized Blake Blanton might have been right about what he had said about the poor kid last year; Bertrand really might be from planet redheaded stepchild.

Bertrand looked up from his notepad. "You can form an exploratory committee, a coalition of the willing, if you will. You will purposefully choose the most influential students from every social group Infinity High School has to offer. You will conference with them to see what the best course of action should be. This should be your first step, and I am volunteering to be a part of this noble endeavor."

I saw Timothy nodding.

"Yeah—yeah, D.L. I think Bertrand's on to something."

"It's a great idea," Hannah offered. "You get a bunch of the most influential people from each social group together and see what they want to do about this. It takes a lot of the burden off you, D.L. You don't have to be a one-man wrecking crew that way."

I shook my head. "Guys, I'm telling you—I don't *want* to be the guy to--"

Timothy slapped me on the shoulder. "I don't think you have a choice, D.L. Some things are bigger than you. I'll talk to Erin about making up some flyers."

I shrugged his hand off my shoulder. "Flyers? What are you--"

"For the meeting of the minds," Timothy responded with a smile. "The coalition of the willing, as Bertrand called it."

"I believe George W. was the first to use the term, but that's beside the point," I said, still shaking my head. "Guys—this—I—*no!*"

"You better help us pick a day," Timothy said, "because it's your name going on the flyers. And you don't want to let us all down."

"So you're guilting me into this?"

Timothy laughed. "Call it what you want. Shaming—guilting—either way, I know you. And I know you'll do what's best for your fellow man."

Are you kidding me?!?!

"Fine. One meeting. That's all I'm agreeing to."

"Done," Timothy said, all smiles. "I knew you'd come through, D.L. It just took a little cattle prodding."

I looked around the table, saw three smiling faces looking back at me. Shaking my head again, I sighed.

"You know I hate all of you right now, don't you?"

***

"Missed you at lunch," I said as Erin pulled her books for seventh period out of her locker. She shrugged.

"Just wanted to be on my own I guess." She shut her locker and turned to face me, her dark eyes heavy with a sadness I wished I could absorb from her into my own being so she wouldn't have to feel tormented by guilt any longer. She brushed a strand of hair behind her ear and swallowed.

"I never got to tell you how sorry I am."

I shot my eyebrows up. "Sorry?"

"For putting you in a weird situation. I had some time to think on it, and I realized if I found out you were cutting yourself, I'd threaten to tell your mom, too."

"Erin, I—"

"No. Please. Let me say this." She reached out and touched my cheek right there in the sophomore-clogged hallway. "You mean so much to me, and I haven't been showing it lately. I'm sorry. I promise I won't put you in that kind of situation again."

I reached up and took her hand from my cheek. Feeling its soft warmth against my skin recalibrated the rightness of our relationship. We were still us despite all the doubts that had been invading my mind like a swarm of ticked-off hornets.

"You know I'll always be there for you," I said. "No matter what."

Erin smiled, and this time it even reached her beautiful chocolate eyes.

"I know, Dakota." We started down the hallway together a little way before she nudged my arm.

"And I'm proud of you for *agreeing* to rally the student body against the school board. You really are amazing, you know that?"

I came to a dead stop. "What? How did you--"

Erin laughed. "Timothy already has me signed on to make the flyers."

I shook my head. "There's really no getting out of it, then, huh?"

Erin smirked and her eyes twinkled. At that moment, I would have rallied the student body and sat through a school board meeting wearing nothing but a thong and a cheesy smile if it only meant Erin would smile like that at me again.

Don't ever lose her, Dakota. If you did, it would be the stupidest thing you've ever done.

"You're stuck, kid. But look on the bright side: you have me to make sure you don't screw anything up."

"I guess there's a perk to every horrible situation."

Erin winked. She drove me wild.

"Call me 'perk.'"

★★★

"It sounds like a noble thing to do, Dakota."

Super. Great. Weren't parents supposed to talk you out of rebelling against the system instead of encouraging it?

As my father continued, I overheard Ethan squealing gleefully in the background.

"There are times when you have to stand up for what you think is right. Since I'm not paying taxes into your school district and, therefore, have an outsider's perspective on the entire issue, I think what the school board is doing is deplorable. They should be stopped before there is a mass exodus to other districts."

"There's already rumblings of an exodus," I said, playing with a plastic pear my mother used to accessorize the centerpiece and insisted added to the homey feel of our kitchen.

"Really?"

"Can you blame them? I mean, the school board has taken everything. I'm worried Erin will decide to go to Clearton. They have a great art program there."

"You seem pretty worked up about the whole thing," my father said.

"I am."

"So, there you go. Use that passion to fuel your resistance movement."

I sighed. I really *did* feel like the students of Infinity High School were getting hosed. But did I feel strongly enough to put my neck on the line?

"It's ultimately your decision," my father continued, "but it sounds pretty legit to me. You have my support."

"Thanks, Dad."

"And Dakota?"

"Yeah?"

"I'm proud of you."

***

I picked up my iPhone, sure this was the moment I had finally steeled my resolve to punch the necessary numbers that would start the revolution. My hands shook, my heart pounded. I had just got off the phone with Jeremy, and he'd said exactly what Hannah had; I was the guy to unite the student body if there ever was one. That was all the confirmation I needed. In reality, I had secretly wished Jeremy would have told me I, and everybody else who thought I had the knowhow to go against the school board, was absolutely cuckoo. But in the end, he'd said he believed in me, and I had teared up like a flippin' girl. How was it that everybody else could believe in me but me?

What are you made of, Dakota? What do you want your legacy to be? The guy who got in trouble with the law two years in a row? The guy who inadvertently paralyzed his best friend? Who are you?

I swallowed hard and gripped my phone so tight all the blood vacated my fingertips, leaving them ghost-white.

It's now or never, chum.

I punched in the numbers slowly and listened as the other party's phone rang three times. When the person picked up after the fourth ring, my stomach fell to my feet and my brow broke out in sweat.

"Hi, Mr. Dennis? This is Dakota Lester. I'm ready to help you get your job back."

chap·ter | ˈCHaptər |
noun
32

COURTING ADDIE

The following day saw Erin back to her old funk. As the conversation I had had with Mr. Dennis the previous night was still fresh and—yes, admittedly inspiring—in my mind, Erin began to slide into social isolation again. She hadn't met me at my locker before school, nor had she chatted with me in the hallways between classes. In fact, Erin didn't even come to school until lunch period, and when she did arrive, she took her place at the top of the gym bleachers, a statue of solitude amongst the sea of teenage humanity.

All day I was a conflicted being. On one hand I wanted to figure Erin out, to really get to the root of her up-and-down mood swings. I knew it had to deal with Jeremy and his paralysis—she's said as much—but I wanted to make sure she knew I'd always be there for her. I also wanted to make sure she was sticking to her promise about not cutting herself anymore.

And then there was the whole stick-it-to-the-school-board thing. I was excited for the first time about the possibilities. Nervous I was, but excitement at the prospect of helping to give the student body back all they had lost outweighed the nervousness—at least at this point.

Mr. Dennis had been expecting my call. At least he said he

had been. With all the extra time on his hands that getting fired had afforded him, he had taken to building model airplanes and contemplating revolutions. You know, stuff everybody thinks about. He had reiterated that he believed I was the young man for the job, and had admitted to having Craig Henderson hound me about joining the just cause. He had also classily admitted he couldn't care less if he got his job back—besides, he would get snatched up by any school district in the county (my words, not his)—as long as the student body got back what was rightfully theirs. My admiration for him had grown immensely, and as we talked strategies for unifying the student body under one banner, I knew I would be contacting him throughout the duration of the Infinity High School Revolution. He would mentor me, and I would try not to screw up beyond belief. At the end of the conversation, we had agreed that I would outline the strategy at the first meeting of student leaders, scheduled to take place next Monday after school. At lunch, Timothy had said Erin had already submitted her flier sketch to him—news to me—and he would show me the final product when he had written the text. All in all, I felt overwhelmed/eager/petrified/hopeful about what was going to go down. If all things went according to the strategy Mr. Dennis had outlined, I didn't see how any board member with a heart could refuse to give us our programs and extra-curriculars back. But Infinity school board members had already proved their hearts pumped formaldehyde instead of compassionate lifeblood, so this was truly going to be a game of Russian Roulette.

Game on.

★★★

"You've *got* to be kidding me!" Timothy said as we walked together toward the school's glass front doors.

"Not kidding in the slightest. Mr. Dennis was supposed to call her today."

Dakota Defined

Timothy readjusted his backpack on his shoulder and looked at me with his mouth agape.

"Addie Wilkins is going to come back to face the school board." The way he said it wasn't a question, more like an awe-inspired statement. And why wouldn't Timothy be struck with awe? Addie Wilkins had been worshipped by students and teachers alike, had walked through the hallways being ogled by boys with raging hormones and praised by teachers who thought of her as the epitome of all things education. When she had graduated last year, Infinity High School had all but garbed itself in black and declared underclassmen exam week a period of mourning. If there was anyone who was the embodiment of Infinity High School, it was Addie Wilkins. And her long—oh, so long—legs and brilliant mind were possibly going to come back to take on the school board. How poetic.

Refresher for those seriously slipping on their Addie Wilkins knowledge: Addie Wilkins was the senior uber-beauty I used to get all hot and bothered by last year. The mere sight of her made my palms sweat an ocean and my hormones burst out into big band music. Addie Wilkins was everything it meant to be a high school goddess, and more. So, for her to potentially to leave Ohio State for an evening to faceoff against the student body was more than epic. It was--uh--whatever is better than epic.

"Dude, this is awesome," Timothy said as he opened the glass front doors. We were immediately blasted by Arctic northwest Ohio wind, but Timothy didn't seem to notice. He was too dumbstruck by the concept of Addie Wilkins coming back to Infinity High.

We walked to the bike rack where my trusty Schwinn waited for me like a lonely puppy wanting to be played with. Poor Mr. Schwinn. Soon spring would come and he would be able to chill with the other bikes, but, for now, he was riding solo.

"It'll be awesome if it pans out," I cautioned, unwilling to get overly optimistic. "She could nix the idea."

"I'm not going to focus on that," Timothy said, pulling his stocking cap down tighter. "I'm just going to pretend we have this whole thing in the bag already."

***

"She's distant again, huh?" Jeremy asked, reaching for the television remote. "I can't watch another rerun of *The King of Queens*. Kevin James is only funny in small doses." He flipped the televsion off and gave me his full attention.

"Yeah, she's distant. I thought she'd be okay after we talked, but--I don't know--she seems to be getting the opposite of better."

Jeremy sighed and looked out the hospital room's window. Outside, the wind was blowing a few dandruff snowflakes over the hospital roof, AKA Jeremy's scenic bedside view.

"I tried to tell her I'm going to beat this thing. I told her I'm going to walk again."

"I know. It's just--it's the process she's depressed about. Or, better yet, it's the fact that you even have to go through all this in the first place."

Jeremy swallowed and reached for his cup of ice water from his retractable bed stand.

"I'm out of here in a few days. Once I get the all clear, it's on to rehab. Maybe when she sees me outside of this room it'll be better."

Now it was my turn to sigh.

"I hope so. I'm just not used to her being like this."

"And I'm not used to having someone helping me pee," Jeremy said, "but I'm getting used to the changes."

I shot my eyebrows up. "And where are you going with the whole peeing thing?"

"My point is that you start to get used to the reality of things. For Erin, it's tough seeing me cooped up in this room watching *The King of Queens* reruns. But maybe when I'm out and about, she'll be able to see that being paralyzed isn't a death sentence."

I shook my head and cracked a half smile. "How do you do it, man? How do you stay so positive?"

Jeremy considered my question for a moment before responding.

"It all comes down to hope. I hope to someday walk again; it's something I hope for. Without something to hope for, I'd be done."

"Maybe that's what Erin needs to hear."

"She'll be able to see it soon. And seeing me walk is better than hearing about hope, because it's hope in action."

I patted his shoulder. "Just promise me one thing, okay?"

"What's that?"

"When you're up and walking again that you don't grow your flippin' hair out again."

Jeremy and I laughed until we were both crying.

chap·ter |ˈCHaptər|
noun
33

BROKEN PROMISES

Erin broke her promise. And the thing is, she didn't even seem to care.

"How could you cut yourself again? After what you said--after you apologized to me for putting me in that kind of situation--you do it *again?*"

Erin crossed her arms, the cotton pad she had placed over the seeping cut on her inner forearm nearly soaked through.

"So, it's about you, Dakota?"

I was astonished/confused/utterly mind-blown. I hadn't expected to be put in this situation again. Stupid me for believing Erin and her promise to never again take a razorblade to her flesh. How could I have been such a dunce (sarcasm intended).

"It's not about me--it's about you not doing this to yourself anymore!"

Erin sighed. She looked tired, her dark eyes heavy with the weight of her own guilt. If she didn't get out from under it, it might bury her. A corpse-cold chill shook my body.

Dear God, make her stop!

"So, what? You're going to tell my parents? Is that what you're going to do?"

"I think it's time they know what's going on. You skipped

school today for the second time in a week--"

"I don't need you to be my mother, Dakota. Besides, she called in for me, so it's an excused absence."

I jumped up from the sofa. "Then what am I supposed to be? You tell me, Erin. I'm two for two in catching you mutilating your body! Do you want me to believe that you've only cut yourself twice? Do you want me to believe the only time you cut yourself is when you skip school?"

Erin stood from the loveseat and pressed the cotton pad to her forearm. The blood that seeped through the pad was bright red. Just seeing it made me want to throw something. Or throw up. "Dakota--calm down!"

I ran my hand through my hair. "You really don't get it, do you? I can't calm down, Erin! I care about you too much to calm down! I'm going to tell your dad when he gets home--"

Erin's eyes went wide. For the first time since I had walked in on her slicing her forearm with a razorblade she showed more than nonchalant emotion.

"Dakota--you can't tell my parents!"

"Watch me!"

Erin burst into tears and crumpled back onto the loveseat. "Do you want to make things worse? Do you want to make me do it?"

My blood froze. My heart pounded in my chest, in my temples.

Do it? Do what?

I walked over to Erin and knelt down in front of the loveseat. I reached out and touched her head, ran my fingers through her hair. I calculated what I said next, weighed it on the scales of my ability to cope with whatever it was she would say. I didn't want to hear it, but I knew what it would be. My whole body trembled, my voice coming in a whisper.

"Do what? What are you talking about, Erin?"

Erin looked up at me through eyes full of tears. Deep

within my chest, I heard my vital organs ripping and tearing to shreds. The pain came a second later, delayed, but no less cruel and hope-sucking.

"I can't live like this anymore! I can't stand it that I *paralyzed* my friend! I can't live anymore!"

My vision began to pulse, the room began to spin. My stomach lurched and I thought I was going to be sick all over the carpet.

"Erin--what are you saying?"

Erin exploded into a torrent of tears.

"What does it sound like? I want to die! I want to take all those pills and never wake up! I just want to be rid of this guilt!"

I grabbed Erin's face with both hands and forced her to look me in the eye.

"Erin, I need you to listen to me, okay? What pills?"

"No--never mind--"

"*What pills?!*"

Erin's shoulders sagged, her body shutting down. She collapsed forward into my shoulder and sobbed on my neck.

Dear, Jesus--God--if you're listening--help!

"The pain pills they gave me after the accident. There's a whole bottle of them--"

"Where are they?"

Erin's tears ran down the neck of my shirt. They felt like hot lava oozing over my skin.

"In my bed stand," she said softly. She sighed deeply as if exhaling the universe's burdens into the family room.

I gently pushed her off my shoulder and leaned her back onto the loveseat.

"Wait here, okay?"

Springing up from my kneeling position, I quickly made my way to Erin's bedroom. Making a beeline to her bed stand, I threw the small drawer open and found an orange bottle of prescription medication. Judging by its heft, the bottle was nearly full. I quickly made my way back into the living room where Erin still sat sobbing on the loveseat.

"Are these the pills you're talking about?" I held the bottle out in front of me as though it was a live grenade.

"What are you going to do--"

"*Are these the pills?*"

Erin could only nod as she was overcome by another wave of sobs. Without hesitating, I quickly crossed the living room to the bathroom. Throwing on the lights and clanking the toilet seat up, I unscrewed the bottle's plastic cap and proceeded to dump all the pills down the toilet. When the last blue capsule had plunked into the water, I flushed the toilet once, waited for the bowl to fill up, and flushed the toilet again. When I was satisfied the pills were now the village of Infinity's problem, I pocketed the bottle and made my way back to Erin.

"They're gone," I said as I knelt down beside her again. I rubbed her back as she cried.

"I'm so messed up, right? Finally fulfilling the emo stereotype."

I took a deep breath and prayed for the right words to say. I felt the empty pill bottle in my pocket and realized I was holding the container that had held death in pill form. I shuddered and vowed to speak to Officer Taylor and Erin's mother tonight.

"It's a tough time. But Jeremy insists he'll walk again. You're not messed up, just hurting."

Erin snorted through her tears.

"What does Jeremy know? Is he a doctor?"

"No, but he's got the will to walk again."

Erin swallowed and looked at me with her dark, desperate eyes.

"You can't tell my parents."

I brushed a strand of hair off her forehead. "You know I

have to."

She grabbed my hand and held it firmly. "You don't have to do anything. We can forget this ever happened--"

I shook my head. "Not this time. This time I have to talk to your parents. You've cut yourself at least twice, and you said you were going to kill yourself by ingesting pills--"

"I never said that! All I said was--"

"It doesn't matter how you said it. I know what you meant. This isn't a cheesy movie on the *Lifetime* network, it's your life, Erin. I'm not going to play dumb."

Erin scooted forward and pleaded with me. "You don't know what they'll do to me! They'll put me on suicide watch or something--maybe even keep me home from school! I'm not going to be humiliated like that--"

"You don't have a choice," I said firmly.

Erin studied me for a moment before swallowing. Her jaw twitched as she mustered her next words.

"If you tell my parents, we're through. I would never rat you out."

It felt like an arrow had pierced my lungs. For a moment, the world spun and I couldn't breathe.

Is this really happening? Is she really doing this to me?

I took a deep breath and warred with myself. To keep a girlfriend and lose her life or lose a girlfriend and keep her alive?

How much do you love her, Dakota? Enough to let her kill herself? Or enough to sacrifice your relationship to save her.

My eyes filled with tears, my throat clamping shut.

"I guess we're through. Because I'm calling your dad right now," I managed.

Erin's face went blank for a moment, my words sinking into her guilt-damaged brain. I'd called her bluff and now she had no idea what to say.

"I'll never forgive you for this," she said, finally. "If you call my dad we'll never talk again."

Hot tears ran down my cheeks as I dug my phone out of my jeans pocket.

"I'm sorry, Erin. I have to."

chapter 34

SEVERED

Officer Taylor wasted no time in getting home. On patrol three blocks from the Taylor residence, he pulled into his driveway no more than two minutes after I called him. Although he had responded quickly, it had been the longest two minutes of my life. True to her word, Erin didn't speak to me. Instead, she crossed her arms over her chest and curled her knees up under her body and glared at me through vicious tears. Her father's presence, usually an intimidating, imposing force, was a relief beyond words.

"Tell me what happened from the beginning," Officer Taylor said, sitting down on the couch. He asked the question like the cop he was, as though Erin and I were ruffians plucked from the street and plopped into an interrogation room. It took me a moment to realize he was talking solely to me and not his daughter.

I looked at Erin and felt her deep brown eyes boring holes into my forehead. The minute I opened my mouth and spilled the whole ordeal, our relationship was over. Over like Bambi's mother. Over like the dude who got frozen to the door in *Titanic*. I knew I still had time to back out, still had time to say 'oops! I made a mistake! I guess it was a false alarm!' But I knew I had to tell Officer Taylor the truth, knew I had to spill everything. If I wanted to retain some shred of human decency, not to mention a conscience, I had to rat Erin out. And it was going to be the hardest thing I had ever done; harder, even, then admitting to wrongs and getting myself arrested last year.

I love you! Know that I am doing this because I love you!

I looked at Erin one last time, felt my heart rip in two. I took a deep breath and ended our relationship forever.

"Here's what happened…"

chap·ter 35

Greater Love

Some people say teenagers can't possibly understand love, they are too young to appreciate its intricate moving parts, to fully comprehend the intimacy of being emotionally captive to another human being. Some people say teenage 'love' is really lust in disguise, that two barely-pubescent hormonally-charged neophytes mistake the chemical reactions in their brains for adult love and devotion.

'*Some people*' are idiots.

I spent the night staring at my darkened ceiling, the blessed anesthetic of sleep eluding me when I yearned for it the most. My head swirled with memories of Erin—snapshots and still frames of her that threatened to make my heart stop beating out of the agony of losing her. I had crossed a threshold and I could never go back. Her eyes had told me that much. As I had spilled my guts to Officer Taylor, Erin had abhorred me, loathed me, hated me. She had said all she needed to say with her piercing brown eyes. I was now dead to her.

What bubbled in my chest was that I hadn't told her how I really felt about her. I hadn't said the three words that truly expressed who and what she was to me. The urgency I felt as I stared up at my ceiling, the immediacy of the need to make her understand I had only told her father out of my pure and honest love for her, all but killed me. If she didn't know now, would she ever know? Next year—five years from now—thirty years from now—would she look back on today and see it as a day of salvation? Would she realize my love for her had possibly saved her life? That I had sacrificed everything so she wouldn't continue down her path of destruction?

My eyes leaked hot tears. They rolled off my cheeks and soaked my pillow as I tried to find some solace in the darkness. There was none. Could solace be found in loss? Could hope be found in hopelessness?

After a time, I rolled to my side and let the salty tears flow over my lips and bead on the tip of my nose. Why couldn't everything be normal again? Why couldn't things be the way they were? One decision had changed everything. If I had never allowed Jeremy to get into my car, this never would have happened. *All* of this never would have happened.

Why, God? Why did this happen?

I listened for God's answer, pleaded for Him to put all the pieces back together. But He remained as silent as the winter night. The burn in my heart for an answer, my yearning for all things to be right again, would not be satiated.

So, You are going to be silent, huh? I thought You're God! I thought You were in the business of making things new!

Through the darkness and the tears that distorted my vision, my bookshelf loomed large against my bedroom wall. My eyes felt compelled to look at one book, drawn to the spine with the silver letters. Despite my better judgment, I kicked the covers off my legs and trudged to the bookshelf. Taking the bulky book off the shelf, I sat back down on my bed and flipped on my bedside lamp.

The Bible was brand new in the sense that it'd never been opened and old in the sense that I'd had it for going on three years. My grandmother had given it to me one Christmas, and as I sat on the edge of my bed with tears rolling down my cheeks, a wave of guilt swept over me for ignoring it for so long. A thin layer of dust had settled on the spine and the silver-edged pages, and as I opened the Bible the leather of the spine cracked.

What am I doing with this?

I thumbed through a few pages, not knowing what I was expecting. A lightning bolt of revelation? A booming voice from heaven telling me how to make everything better? Fat chance. In my personal experience, God didn't speak that way. In fact, He didn't really speak to me at all. Why would He start now?

Some God You are...

When I got to the book of Ezekiel, I snapped the Bible shut. What I was doing felt beyond hopeless, like a desperation heave into the end zone at the end of a football game. Besides, I didn't deserve to have God answer my prayers. I hadn't shown an interest in Him for so long, and He sure as sunshine hadn't shown an interest in me. Shaking my head, I tossed the Bible to the floor. It spilled open atop the carpet as I buried my head in my hands.

How do I make this hurt go away? How do I make Erin's *hurt go away.*

Through my tears, I saw the Bible on the floor. I snorted.

Some God You are! Some help!

I reached down to pick up the Bible from the floor, my intention to hurl it across the room. Why not? God had abandoned me. He was silent, and I was alone. Wasn't He supposed to save you when you needed to be saved? Wasn't He supposed to swing low in a chariot or something?

I brought the book to my lap, saw it was opened to the book of John. I ground my molars together, ready to whip the holy book across the room. But then my eye was drawn to the lower right page. I sniffled, wiped the tears from my eyes and read the words written in red:

"There is no greater love than to lay one's life down for one's friend."

The verse was simple and straightforward, not flowery and churchy like some were. And it pierced me to the core, plunged a hot blade into my heart and defined who I was to be in relation to Erin—what I was supposed to be for her.

I have to lay down my life for her—I have to give up the concept of "us" so that she might get better.

I closed the Bible and swallowed hard.

Love? Is this what it is? Is it possible to love someone so much you'd kill off a part of you so they can live?

I ran my thumb over the Bible's leather cover.

Apparently yes. But—can I give myself up for her? Can I forget about us as a couple and love her beyond what I even understand?

That was the question. But as I walked the Bible back to the bookshelf, I was bound and determined to find the answer.

For Erin. And for me.

chap·ter 36

Battle Plans, Hairy Philosophers and Door Slams

"Addie said she's on our side," Mr. Dennis said, taking a sip of his instant coffee. Anita Dennis set a plate of oven-warm chocolate chip cookies in the middle of the table. Score.

"That's huge for us," I said, taking a cookie. Mrs. Dennis asked if I wanted a glass of milk and I accepted. I'm not one to turn down free dairy products offered by the wife of my former teacher.

"Yes, getting her on board is a big deal. We both know she was a very influential student during her tenure at IHS," Mr. Dennis leaned forward, "and I'll bet she'll pull out all the stops for us."

That was good. Addie on our side was more than a plus, it was a plus to the fourth power. Thinking about the implications of Addie's being pro-Infinity High temporarily blocked the feelings of awkwardness I had about being in Mr. Dennis's kitchen on a Saturday afternoon. That and his pukish lime green and orange argyle sweater.

"When is she able to come?" I asked, savoring the cookie as it melted in my mouth. After the long night where I'd warred with myself about what to do concerning Erin, a chocolate chip cookie was a welcome mini-pleasure.

Mr. Dennis scratched the back of his head. "Well, that's the thing. Addie is booked pretty solid at college. The quickest she can make it to a Monday night school board meeting is April."

I glanced at the small calendar dangling from a magnet on the refrigerator. It was February second; we had two months to plan our take-back-Infinity movement.

"I guess that's okay. It gives us time to get our ducks in order."

Mr. Dennis arched his eyebrows. "You realize the *we* you are talking about is *you*, right? I can only do so much from my end. The teacher's union is fighting for me, wrongful termination and all that, but they are fighting for quite a few IHS teachers right now. And, to tell you the truth, I don't really want the entire town of Infinity knowing I am mentoring your 'revolution,' as you call it. You're the inside man, Dakota. You and your—what did you call it?"

"Coalition of the willing," I said, proudly. "We kind of stole that from George W. Bush."

"As long as you don't steal his public speaking skills, I think you guys are going to be surprised at how your collective voices can have a major impact. When is the first meeting of the minds?"

"This Tuesday. There are flyers, too. I didn't bring one, but it's a drawing of my face in Uncle Sam's garb. You know, the old 'Uncle Sam Wants You' thing?"

Mr. Dennis smiled. "I *am* a history teacher." He sighed. "At least I used to be."

I snagged another cookie. "You will be again. Trust me. The state of our union will be strong again."

Mr. Dennis laughed. "Now you're going a little overboard with the political stuff. But I like your optimism. So, meeting Tuesday. And after that?"

"After that we start moving."

Mr. Dennis nodded thoughtfully. "April will be here before you know it. Addie going before the school board will be a great final explosion, but what we need is a few early strikes."

"Early strikes?"

"Something to let the suits know we're serious—*you're* serious."

I leaned forward as Mr. Dennis reached to the kitchen island for a tattered red notebook.

"What are you thinking?" I asked, suddenly invigorated by the whole thing.

"This," Mr. Dennis said, opening the notebook.

***

"You slap two squares of cheese on the meat and give 'er a squirt of mayo—just like that. And that's how you make a Pop's Roast Beef Hoagie." Pop slammed down the squirt bottle of mayonnaise and folded his hairy arms over his grease-stained apron. "Just that simple, kid."

"Uh—okay. I think I got it." I picked up the sandwich, put it into a hoagie tin and popped it into the conveyer oven.

"Two minutes and she comes out golden brown," Pop said, wiping his sausage fingers on his apron. "You can eat that one when it comes out. You look like you could use some meat on your bones."

I wiped down the counter while I waited for my hoagie to brown. I wouldn't be manning the dishwashing station tonight, as Pop had called me to the front to learn the ins and outs of the greasy spoon diner. And that was okay with me. Anything to keep my mind from wandering to Erin was a welcome distraction. I would make fifteen thousand hoagies if it meant I wouldn't have to think about how Erin no longer wanted me as her boyfriend, and what I had to do—knew I had to do--about the whole situation.

Dakota Defined

"You okay, kid?" Pop asked from the grill. He flipped over a thick slab of meat as his brow dripped sweat onto the grill face.

"Uh—yeah. I'm fine," I answered. I checked on my hoagie as Pop raised his caterpillar eyebrows.

"You don't fool me, kid. Something's eating you."

I sighed. As much as I wanted to unleash my Erin problems on the world, I didn't want to have the conversation with Pop. Not that Pop wasn't an empathetic guy or anything; it was just that the whole thing was a little sensitive. Erin had had thoughts of suicide, after all. And saying as much to Pop—or to anyone else, for that matter—might prod them to try to help, which could very well muddle the whole situation.

"You know, kid, when I was your age, I had all kinds of problems. And I'm not just talking about the girl kind," Pop said, flipping a burger. The grilled hissed like a cobra. "I was higher than a kite half the time. Drugs, I mean. It was the early Seventies—not that I'm making any excuses. I was smoking pot, dropped acid a time or two. And you know where it got me?"

The question was rhetorical, so I waited out the pause.

"Right here behind this grill," Pop said, stabbing the air with his spatula in my general direction.

"I wanted to be an a lawyer—I can argue with the best of them," Pop continued, seeming to gaze beyond the diner's wall. "Heck, yeah, I would've made a daggum good lawyer. But I was stupid. Too doped up to go to college, too independent and stubborn to listen to my folks telling me I was wasting time—wasting life."

Pop sighed and smiled wistfully, his bushy mustache hiding his upper lip. "I guess what I'm saying is you never know what kind of time you're wasting until it's too late. Sandy went off to college, got a job at the high school, and I was stoned in my parents' basement." Pop turned from the grill to look me in the

Josh Clark

eye. "Get what I'm saying, kid? You gotta be proactive about life. You gotta seize it by the horns and wrestle it into submission. Sure, you'll lose sometimes. But it's the wrestling that matters, kid. It's the blood, sweat and tears you put into the fight that counts the most."

A lump rose in my throat as I listened to Pop philosophize. How could he have known this is what I needed to hear right now? How could he possibly have read me so well?

Pop smiled. "What it all boils down to is what you're made of. What you stand for. Who you really are. Are you defined by your weaknesses, by what you're scared of? Or are you defined by the amount of love you pour into this silly bag of tricks called life?"

Pop waved a big hand and flipped a burger with the other. "Look at me. Standing over this grill and lecturing you like I got it all figured out. I don't. Not in the slightest. But I do know I wake up every morning wondering 'what if?' You don't want that, kid. You don't want to be my age asking yourself those kinds of questions."

My hoagie was waiting for me at the end of the oven's conveyer belt. I put on an oven mitt and took it off the belt. Pop flipped a patty onto an open sesame seed bun and smiled at me.

"I don't know why I said all that. Guess I just felt like I was supposed to. I'll let you sort out the parts you can use."

I emptied my hoagie from the tin and smiled back at him, the lump still heavy in my throat.

"Thanks. I needed to hear that more than you know."

Pop shook his head and jabbed the spatula in my direction.

"Now, don't you go getting all sappy on me. I may look like a hairy linebacker, but I'm as tender as one of my meat patties. There's one rule I have in this kitchen: don't go crying on the merchandise."

I laughed and set my hoagie on a chipped plate.

***

"Leave."

Erin stood in the open doorway and glared at me. All of a sudden the Taylor's front porch seemed very small.

"Erin—look—you don't understand how much--"

"I told you to leave, Dakota. We're through, remember? Besides, I'm letting in cold air." Erin made to shut the door, but I stopped it with the heel of my hand.

"I care about you, Erin. I just want to know you're okay. We don't have to be a couple anymore, just--"

Erin sighed exasperatedly. "It's Sunday afternoon. I have homework, and my parents are watching my every move, thanks to you. I can't even go to the bathroom without them thinking I'm going to kill myself."

"Erin—I just want to tell you--"

"Goodbye, Dakota."

She slammed the door in my face before I could say anything else.

I'd be back tomorrow.

Josh Clark

co·a·li·tion \ˌkō-ə-ˈli-shən\

NOUN: A body formed to thwart the school board's tyrannical plans

chap·ter |ˈCHaptər| noun
37

The Coalition

"How many are in there?" I asked Timothy as I wiped my clammy hands on my jeans. My heart rate was elevated, and I felt as jittery as a caffeine addict without his morning fix of joe.

Timothy peeked into the room—Mr. Dennis's old classroom—through the glass slit in the door. "Quite a few, man. It's a great turnout."

"Is Erin here?" I asked. Just mentioning her name made sweat burst forth from my pores. She had turned me away two days in a row, but despite her steadfast resolve to basically hate me, I was going to show up at her door again today. I had to be a constant in her life, had to let her know that I loved her even though I'd never spoken the words.

"She's in there. Relax, D.L. You'll be great." Timothy patted me on the shoulder and smiled. "Do you know what the coolest thing is? We have Jeremy on the SMART Board via Skype. How cool is that? He's live from his house and he's representing the theater department."

"Oh, sweet. No pressure now," I said, the sarcasm in my voice as thick as maple syrup. When I was nervous, I tended to get sarcastic. And gassy.

"Well, you ready to go in? You can't hang out in the hallway the whole time." Timothy gently urged me forward with a hand to my back.

"I just puked in my mouth a little," I said as Timothy opened the door.

I walked in and all the chatter stopped. Someone had arranged Mr. Dennis's old room into two horizontal rows of desks, and with just a cursory glance I could tell a representative from every school-board oppressed group was present. It looked like a United Nations convention minus the mini flags and the obligatory borderline-terrorist dictators.

Oh, boy.

Erin sat in the second row, her dark eyes tired and distracted. Her cheeks seemed to sink in a little, and I was alarmed to see how much weight she had lost in the last few weeks. She didn't have weight to lose; her already slender frame needed every ounce of fat, and since she was losing said fat, the implications could be dangerous.

Jeremy's face was large on the SMART Board to my left, and even he was silent while he waited for me to officially start the revolution. Bertrand was front and center, his notebook open, pen ready to take notes as the unofficial secretary.

Here goes nothing.

I licked my lips, wiped my palms on my jeans one last time and started the meeting of the minds.

"Well, I guess the first thing to do is say hello and welcome to—uh—this meeting. I don't have to tell you all why we're here; your extra-curriculars being cut and or exploited for profit ticked you off enough to want to do something about it." Craig Henderson was nodding from the seat to Erin's left. His positive reinforcement squelched my nerves.

"Look, here's the deal," I continued, "we're going to have to work hard if we want to get our stuff back. That includes Mr. Dennis' job. I have been working on a plan that will culminate in all of us storming the April school board meeting, but it is what we do from now until then that will weaken the board's foundation. Exposing weaknesses should be our business. But we need to work together. I can only do so much by myself. To be honest, I'm still not quite sure why I'm the one standing up here when anyone of you is just as qualified to do it. I guess that's mu point; we need to be one body—one mass of disgruntled teenage humanity against the suits and good-old-boy community members. We have to stand together when it gets even tougher—and it will get tougher. The community will become aware of our little movement before you know it. We live in a small town where even the trees seem to have eyes. I want to know right now who is with me." I pointed at Bertrand. "Take their names down as they call them out, will you?"

Darren Osterman, a junior football captain, raised his hand. Beside him, Todd Lawrence, a sophomore whose own father was on the school board, raised his, too.

"Me and Todd will represent the football team." Bertrand scribbled their names down as more hands shot up.

"I'll represent the choir," Timothy said. More hands went up.

"I'll do what I can for the theater department," Jeremy said from the SMART Board.

Erin raised her hand. "I'll represent the art department," she said softly. I smiled at her, but she went back to closing herself off from the world.

When Bertrand had recorded all the names—twenty-four in all—it was apparent our little band of rebels had the potential to make some noise. Representatives from every oppressed group had pledged their loyalty to the cause, and when I told them Addie Wilkins would be making an appearance at the April school board meeting, a murmur worked its way throughout the room. Todd Lawrence raised his hand.

"Uh—it's a little awkward for me to be here, because my dad is on the school board. I just want to let everybody know that he has never voted in favor of cutting funds to any of the programs represented here. In fact, he is going to be resigning from the board effective tomorrow morning." Another murmur worked through the room. Todd held up his hand.

"I'm only telling you this to let you know he is on our side. He's not very popular with the rest of the board members for his opinion on things, but he can't see how slashing funds and cutting programs is a good idea. I just thought everyone would like to know that."

A question niggled at the back of my mind.

"How do they find a replacement for him? Do they go to the public and have an election?"

Todd raised his eyebrows and gave a half smile. "Well, that's the thing. It could be quite a process. First, the public is notified of the resignation. In the same letter there is an invitation to run for the board. The school board will take the names of those interested and must come to a unanimous decision about whom to choose for the open spot. If they aren't unanimous, the decision goes to a county judge, and then he or she will appoint the new board member."

I sighed. "So, if I hear you correctly, your father's resignation could have an even worse impact on the school. What if one of the good-old-boys from the community runs and then the suits unanimously vote him onto the school board? We're worse off than we were when your dad was still on the board."

Todd's smile widened. "What the rest of the board doesn't know is that Frank Thompson is starting to see things my dad's way. He told my dad he's sick of voting against the school's best interests."

"So, what you're saying is this Thompson guy is on our side?" Timothy asked.

Todd shrugged. "I guess that's what I'm saying. Basically,

if one of the school board's community cronies throws his hat in the ring, Thompson will make sure there's not a unanimous vote."

"So, we can push for one of our own candidates since we know the school board won't have a five to zero unanimous vote," I said, thinking out loud.

"You have somebody in mind?" Craig Henderson asked.

I couldn't contain my smile. "I just might"

★★★

"You want me to what?" my mother asked as she stirred the ground beef she was browning atop the stove.

"I want you to put your name in for the open spot on the school board," I said, reaching into the cupboard and producing two plates.

"And why would I want to do that? Besides, didn't we just elect a new member last November?"

I walked the plates over to the table and came back to the kitchen island for silverware.

"Mom, what I am about to tell you is top secret to the fourteenth power, okay?"

My mother stopped stirring the ground beef and it sizzled its pleasure from the cast iron skillet. She put a hand on her hip and gave me the Look. "Okay, what kind of clandestine operation are you into now? Please tell me the Blanton boy isn't back in town."

I set a fork beside my mother's plate and shook my head. "Mom, Blake's locked up. And besides, give me some credit. I'm talking about Bill Lawrence stepping down from the board."

I proceeded to tell her the whole thing, from the first rumbling of the revolution to today's first coalition of the willing meeting. I hadn't told her before because I thought she'd blow a gasket about the whole thing. Kind of like a my-baby-shouldn't-be-involved-in-local-politics sort of thing. To my surprise, her response was the exact opposite of what I had been expecting.

"I think what the board is doing is deplorable. And you're sure Bill Lawrence is stepping down and Mr. Thompson is switching sides?"

I nodded. "As far as I can tell. Todd is a pretty reliable source, I'd say."

"Come here and hold the strainer," my mother said. I dutifully obliged as she dumped the skillet of ground beef over the strainer as I held it over the sink.

"Mom? What are you thinking?" I asked through a plume of steam.

My mother took the strainer from me and dumped the ground beef back into the skillet. Setting it on top of the stove, she wiped her hands on a dishtowel and put one hand on her hip.

"I'm thinking how proud I am of you."

I think I might have even blushed a little.

"And that I'm in," my mother said. She saluted. "Lisa Lester, reporting for duty"

***

I only had an hour until I had to be back home per my probation. As I stood on the Taylor's front porch looking at Erin as she held the door in a way I knew meant she was about to slam it shut, the old familiar lump in my throat was back. I loved this girl--loved her down to the tips of my toes. Why did things have to be this way?

Erin sighed, her exasperation nearly palpable. "You know the drill, Dakota. Go away. Leave. I don't have anything to say to you."

"If you could just give me a minute to--"

She slammed the door in my face for the third day in a row.

The chill wind assaulted my cheeks, my nose.

"I love you," I said to the closed door. "I'll be back tomorrow."

chapter 38
noun

OF BOYCOTTING AND BOYFRIENDS

The Coalition put its first plan into motion the last week of February. Each member rallied his or her respective club members and athletes to boycott the cafeteria until further notice. I was apprehensive the first day, to say the least. Would students actually follow through? Would my peers who weren't involved in clubs and extracurricular activities join the side of the cause and boycott by our sides?

"Would you look at that," Hannah said as she sat down at the Hodgepodge table and opened her packed lunch. She wasn't a part of any IHS clubs yet, as she had moved into the district when the clubs and programs were being slashed left and right. But she was an adamant supporter of all things Coalition, and she did her part in helping to raise awareness about the boycott.

I looked around the cafeteria and smiled.

It's working!

As I scanned the cafeteria, the round tables were filled with students who were either brown-bagging it or had dug deep in the bowels of their closets for their old elementary lunch boxes and bags. Athletes and geeks alike were taking up the cause, and when I looked toward the lunch line all I saw was a thin trickle of confused students who made their way through the line to get their cafeteria slop. Some might not have heard about the boycott, and others would probably be peer-pressured into packing their own lunches tomorrow. A few disgruntled lunch ladies ladled soup and casserole onto empty trays, but most were whispering to each other and shaking their heads. Day one was going swimmingly.

"This is incredible, D.L.," Timothy said, biting into a peanut butter and jelly sandwich, "And I forgot how much I like PB and J!"

"Although my mother's leftover casserole is bland and lackluster, I will eat it willingly for the sake of the cause," Bertrand said, forking a bite of his mother's admittedly gross-looking vegetable chicken concoction.

"I wonder how much money the school will lose in a week," Hannah said, "I mean, we're not buying anything from the drink machines, either. They'll have to be hurting."

"Here's hoping we can make this last more that a week," I said. "My only fear is that the boycott with have the opposite effect from what we're hoping for. What if they start cutting more teachers?"

"Who are they going to cut?" Timothy said. "We're down to bare necessities the way it is. There's no one left to cut. All the arts teachers have been axed, all the assistant coaches and non-district program advisors. The teachers who are left teach core subjects, and I hear they're trying to get rid of Mrs. Denny because she's been here for about a thousand years and her salary is as high as it can go."

"I believe he is correct," Bertrand said, squinting through his enormous lenses, "the student population dictates the retention of the remainder of the teaching staff. Our refusal to partake of the institution's provisions can only positively impact our noble interests."

"So, this boycott is a good thing," Hannah said, putting a period on the topic.

Dakota Defined

"I hope so, because it's working," I said, feeling the hope swell in my chest. But when I looked to my right and saw Erin's empty chair, the hope became liquid poison in my stomach. She hadn't eaten at the Hodgepodge table since I had ratted her out to her father. The other Hodgepodgers didn't know the truth of her absence, and I had kept them at bay by telling them we were having some disagreements. But my lies could only last so long. Pretty soon I would have to admit to the others--maybe even admit to myself--that we were truly done as a couple. But what Pop had said stuck to my mind:

'Sometimes you gotta seize life by the horns and wrestle it into submission.'

But what happened when a circumstance was wrestling *you* into submission?

"You miss her, huh?" Hannah said, obviously noticing the change in my facial expression.

I sighed. Might as well tell the others now.

"Guys--Erin and me--I think--I think we're through."

Timothy actually dropped his fork. "D.L.--are you serious? What happened? I thought your fighting was just teenage drama."

I would love for it to just be teenage drama...

I held up my hands. "Look, I don't really want to talk about it. It's--kinda personal."

Hannah reached over and touched my shoulder while Timothy shook his head. Bertrand flipped open his notebook and scribbled something onto the paper.

"If you ever need to talk, I'm here. You know that, right?"

Thanks--but I can't talk about this.

"Thanks. I appreciate it, I really do. I'd also appreciate if you guys wouldn't hound Erin about it."

Timothy was still shaking his head. "Things are gonna get weird. This is why we never should have allowed fellow Hodgepodgers to date."

Josh Clark

"At least Hannah and Jeremy are still going strong," I said, trying to deflect the focus of the conversation.

Timothy was still shaking his head. "Never should have allowed dating among friends."

★★★

"I wrote a few monologues some of the theater people can read at lunch or wherever," Jeremy said as I sat across from him in the Stines's living room. He was in an adjustable bed situated where the couch used to be. I sat on a loveseat where the television used to be. I guess after tragedy strikes, family time starts to mean more. The Stines family had thrown out their forty-eight-inch flat screen to make Jeremy's bed fit into the living room, and they vowed they'd never sit for hours in front of any boob tube again. If there was one bright spot in the aftermath of the accident, the Stines family "getting it" when it came to the importance of family relationships was one.

"That's great, man," I said. "What are they about?"

"Oh, just about standing up to The Man and not being sheep led to slaughter. That sort of thing. They're on that stand right there," Jeremy said, pointing to the end table to my right. "Don't forget them when you leave."

"I won't. I'm sure they'll be great for the cause."

Jeremy only smiled. "How's Erin? She doing any better? She hasn't stopped by in a few weeks."

The familiar stone-sized lump lodged itself in my throat.

"Uh, she's--well--we're not really together anymore."

Jeremy's eyebrows shot up. He hadn't lost his theatrical flair. "What? Why? What happened?"

I swallowed and looked at the ceiling. I felt like I had to tell someone the truth. I couldn't keep it bottled up inside me where it would only putrefy and rot as time went on. I hadn't told anybody the truth--not even my mother. I told her we were taking a break and she nearly cried. As I looked across the room at Jeremy, I decided I'd tell him everything. He was my friend and I desperately needed to unleash some of the pent up emotions that swirled within me.

So I told him.

Everything.

It felt so refreshing to get it all off my chest. Sometimes sharing your pain with a friend is the most therapeutic thing you can do.

"Wow, man, that's tough," Jeremy said when I had finished.

"Yeah. It really stinks, and it hurts something fierce," I said, unashamed at the tears rolling down my cheeks. I wiped them away with the back of my hand.

"I wish she'd come talk to me," Jeremy said. "I wish I could convince her that I don't blame her. You know, tell her it's not her fault."

"But Erin blames Erin. We're always hardest on ourselves," I sighed. "I just have to keep telling myself its not about how much it hurts me but about Erin getting through this."

Jeremy smiled. "You know, D.L., you're a straight up good guy. Better than I would be in this situation."

I brushed off his compliment. "Well, it's not like I have a choice. I have to let her go."

"That's the thing, D.L. You *do* have a choice. You've been dealt a bad hand and you are choosing to do the noble thing and honor a girl you are head over heels in love with by letting her get well. Even if it means you have to lose her in the process. That's true love, man."

I started to rebut, but Jeremy stopped me.

"You love her and you know it, D.L. We all know it--Timothy, Hannah, probably even Bertrand. Have you told her?"

I stammered out a no and Jeremy narrowed his eyes at me.

"You have to tell her. She has to know how much she means to you. And you know what, D.L.? I know something else: she feels the exact same way about you. She just might not realize it through the fog of her guilt."

Jeremy's words struck me to the core. I had never really thought the feelings I had for Erin could be reciprocal, that she could actually feel them about me.

Jeremy studied the ceiling. "Then again, maybe your actions are speaking louder than your words ever could." He looked at me and smiled again. "All I know is that you're a good man, D.L. Erin will see that sooner or later."

I hope you're right…

***

Erin slammed the door in my face again. Only this time she didn't even speak to me.

***

"Well, I did it," my mother said, setting her purse on the kitchen table. She threw her keys down beside it and kicked off her comfortable white nursing shoes. "I officially sent my name to the school board to be considered for the open position."

I set my mechanical pencil down atop the pre-calculus homework I was working on. Okay, more like doodling on. I had a lot on my mind, so sue me.

"That's great, Mom! Did they give you any idea how long it would be until they made a decision?"

My mother walked the fridge and took out the pitcher of sweet tea. "They said they are open to name submissions until the end of next week, and then they will go into executive session to vote on a new board member."

I smiled as my mother poured herself a glass of tea. "Well, well, well. It looks like I'm not the only politician in the family!"

She took a drink and then set her glass down on the kitchen island. She looked at me with a face as serious as a don't-do-drugs assembly.

"I have no idea what I'm doing. What if I win?"

I couldn't help but laugh.

Josh Clark

numb \ˈnəm\

NOUN: Devoid of feeling; the sensation of hopelessness beyond repair

chapter 39

When Everything Falls Apart II

A week later, the school board was at an impasse. Todd Lawrence, who got his information from his father, who got his information from our mole, Frank Thompson, said two viable candidates for the open board position were presented. One was Cal Stevenson, a personal finance consultant and full time tool shed. Without Frank's abstaining vote, Cal would most certainly waltz onto the board with his just-rolled-in-a-pile-of-cheddar-cheese-Doritos spray tan and pearly white teeth. The other candidate was my mother.

"They like her because they don't know about the resistance coalition and because she has what is considered an upstanding job in the community," Todd had explained. "My gut says this thing's going to the county court. My dad says the board is stubborn like that."

So it was a waiting game. For me, it was a waiting game on two levels. I was fighting two resistance movements, one against the school board and one against Erin's resolve. Another week of showing up on her front porch had proved futile. She had taken to having her mother come to the door for her, and every time Mrs. Taylor said Erin didn't want to see me I could tell it pained the mother to turn me away. It pained me more, believe you me. Erin had blocked my number on her cell phone and unfriended me on Facebook. She'd even stopped following me on Twitter, even though I seldom logged on to my account. It was as if she was sweeping up all the crumbs from our used-to-be relationship and trying to forget we'd ever been us. And it hurt more than I ever imagined it could. Still, I knew I had to keep trying to reach out to her. She had to know I loved her and that I wanted her to get better. I hoped she was spending time with her therapist, hoped her parents were giving her the adequate support she needed.

And I hoped upon hope that she wouldn't forget what it felt like to love me back.

***

It was a Sunday afternoon like any other. My mother and I had come home from church and I was helping her prepare our lunch of baked chicken, green bean casserole and apple pie. My mother had just opened the oven to peek underneath the aluminum foil to see if the chicken was close to being ready. I had just poured a glass of iced tea for myself and had reached for another glass to pour one for my mother when the telephone rang. I wiped my hands on a towel and walked to the wall cutout to answer the phone.

"Hello?"

I heard heavy breathing on the other end of the line, commotion in the background, elevated voices that conveyed a sense of urgency.

"Dakota—it's Officer Taylor."

All the blood rushed from my face. I immediately felt faint, and I pawed at the wall to keep my balance.

"What—is everything okay?" I stammered, my tongue feeling thick and sluggish in my mouth. My heart was racing, my palms and forehead slicking with clammy sweat.

Officer Taylor sighed hard. "No. It's Erin—she—they're transporting her to the emergency room."

Emergency room?!

I swallowed, willing my muddled brain to form coherent words.

"What—what happened? What's wrong?"

More voices in the background. A woman crying.

"She tried to kill herself, Dakota. Please come to the emergency room. We can talk there. I have to go."

"But—how—why--"

But the line went dead. And so did my hope that everything was going to be okay.

THE ATTEMPT

The doctors pumped the thirty-eight ibuprofen tablets from Erin's stomach as my mother and I waited with the Taylors in the too-clean waiting room. None of us had said anything for over ten minutes. We all stared silently at the gleaming tiled floor or the pile of dog-eared magazines on the circular coffee table in the middle of the room as we waited to hear from the doctor.

I took a deep breath and tried to compose my thoughts. In reality, my brain was screaming, reeling from the awfulness of the situation. How many hospitals was I to visit this year? For how many friends was I to wait in an uncomfortable waiting room, hoping good news would come in the form of a doctor through big swinging double doors?

How had I let this happen? How did it come to this?

Erin's mother had found Erin sprawled atop her sheet-less mattress, an empty bottle of ibuprofen by her head. Mrs. Taylor had immediately called nine-one-one, and Erin had been transported to the emergency room less than ten minutes after her mother had found her unconscious atop her bed. She'd left no note. Erin had been rushed to the emergency room, and my mother and I had arrived as they were wheeling her in. A nurse told us it was a good thing Erin arrived when she did, any longer and Erin's life might have been forfeit. The nurse said that, unfortunately, stomach pumping associated with suicide attempts was becoming more and more common, and she expected Erin to make a full recovery since the Taylors had been quick about calling an ambulance. Now it was just a waiting game.

"Dakota?" Mrs. Taylor's voice pierced the silence of the waiting room. I looked up from the floor and into her red-rimmed, dark brown eyes. Erin had her mother's eyes.

"You need to know that despite what is going on between you and Erin, we will never be able to thank you enough for coming to us when you did." She nodded at Officer Taylor, who sat with his big hands on his knees in the chair across from me.

I swallowed. "But it wasn't enough. It didn't stop this from happening."

"You can't blame yourself, Dakota. You did all you could. This is not your doing," Erin's mother said. My own mother put her hand on my arm. I wished I was five years old again so I could crawl into her lap and cry my eyes out.

Officer Taylor rubbed his hands together. "She thinks the world of you, Dakota. Erin, I mean. She's just confused about a lot of things right now." He looked at his wife and sighed. "And so are we."

I guess we all are...

***

I don't know how long we waited for the doctor to come out and tell us how Erin was doing. An hour? Five hours? Three days? All I know is that when the silver-headed fifty-something doctor came out and told us Erin would make a full recovery, I felt like I could breathe again.

"What now?" Erin's mother asked the doctor.

"Well, now we let her rest a bit," the doctor said. "We are going to call First Call for Help, the mental health crisis service for our four-county area. A trained professional will come here and conduct a psychological assessment to see what we are dealing with."

"What we're dealing with?" I jumped in. So sue me if I wasn't a family member. I loved this girl.

The doctor eyed me for a moment before deciding I was safe to talk to.

"The mental health professional will assess how serious Erin's attempt was and determine the likelihood of her doing it again. If Erin is deemed to be a "cry for help" case and her physical condition is suitable, she may be sent home. If the assessor believes Erin is a danger to herself or others, other options will be explored. It's really not my place to speak for the assessor, so I will allow him or her to answer any questions you may have when he or she gets here."

Officer Taylor nodded and rubbed the stubble on his chin. He'd obviously been around this kind of thing before, being a police officer.

"Thanks, Doctor. May we see her?"

"Let's let her rest a little bit longer. In another hour she may feel ready for visitors," the doctor said. "We can round up some coffee for you folks in the meantime."

chap·ter |ˈCHaptər|
noun
41

DEAD TO HER

An hour and a half later, after Erin's parents had a chance to talk to their daughter, the Taylors allowed me some time alone with Erin. To say I wasn't nervous would be a blatant lie. I was petrified of this encounter to the point of nausea. What would she say? What would *I* say? Now wasn't the time to profess my undying love for her. So what was it?

'Greater love,' Dakota. Be there for her and forget yourself.

I walked into Erin's room and was immediately surprised by how dark it was. The window blinds had been pulled, the overhead lights off. The only slab of light came from the half-open bathroom door and it cast its yellow light over half of Erin's face. I pulled up a chair, well aware that Erin was staring at me the whole time. Sitting down and swallowing back my nervousness, I prepared for whatever the encounter would bring.

Erin looked me directly in the eyes, her dark brown ones tired and aching from her inner torment.

"You think I'm crazy, don't you?"

I smiled weakly and tried to feign calm while my heart machine-gunned in my chest.

"You know I don't think you're crazy."

Erin looked away from me and stared up at the ceiling. "Ibuprofen. I'd be dead right now if you hadn't dumped the stronger stuff down the toilet."

"Is that what you want? To be dead?"

Erin's eyes moved as though she was reading something written on the ceiling.

"Sometimes I want to be dead. Like when I took those stupid pills. When I did it I wanted to end it all—just get away from everything for good. But ten minutes after I swallowed them, I started to get all panicky. Like I knew I had made a mistake I couldn't undo unless I made myself puke them all out."

"So why didn't you puke them all out?" I asked gently.

Erin was silent for a moment. "I guess to punish myself for being so stupid."

"You understand how your logic sounds flawed to me, right?" I asked. When she didn't say anything, I continued. "Erin, you have so much to live for it's not even funny. You're going to go to an art school and do what you love for the rest of your life. You're going to get married, have babies and be the best mama ever. And—*I* need you. Because I lo--"

Erin snapped her head back to me. "This doesn't change anything between us, Dakota. We're still not going to be together."

My heart felt like it had been stomped on. She had cut me off right when I was about to tell her I loved her. The moment had felt right. And now I felt like I had been set aflame on the inside, like my vital organs were sizzling where I sat.

"Erin—I--"

Erin sighed and looked back to the ceiling. I saw a tear trickle from the corner of her eye.

"You don't get it, Dakota. I'm no good for you. It's not about my hating you for ratting me out to my parents—it might have been at first—but it's not that. It's—I just—you deserve so much better than me."

I reached out and grabbed her hand. It stayed lifeless as a dead fish.

"What are you saying? Erin—*I'm* the one who doesn't deserve *you*!"

Either Erin hadn't heard me, or she pretended not to.

"It would've been easier with a gun. Except Dad has his handgun locked inside an old school locker in the garage. It would have been better than this."

Erin—no…

"If you keep talking like that, they're going to ship you to a psych ward. You don't mean that—you can't possibly mean that."

Erin looked at me again, tears dribbling down both cheeks. "I think you should go, Dakota."

"But—Erin—I---" But I knew it was useless. She closed her eyes and I was dead to her. I waited a full minute before I stood and moved away from the bed. As I walked out of her room, the sense of hopelessness washed over me like a tidal wave.

And there was nothing I could do not to drown.

★★★

A marshmallow-thighed mental health professional named Wilma Cunningham assessed Erin to be mentally stable enough to go home. Ms. Cunningham made Erin an appointment to meet with Dr. Bowerman, a psychiatrist who practiced close to the Swirley Freeze in Clearton. Even though Erin was already seeing a therapist, Ms. Cunningham insisted that Dr. Bowerman was the right psychiatrist for Erin, as he specialized in teen suicide cases. Ms. Cunningham's work done, she waddled out as the Taylors discussed Erin's prognosis with the doctor. She would be wheeled over to King County Health

Center, where she would stay the night and be discharged in the early afternoon.

I couldn't stay any longer. Not after Erin had sliced the jugular of our relationship. It was too hard to hold to hope, too hard to pretend everything was going to get better, when deep down I knew things would never be the same. Maybe I had known all along; maybe I had seen the writing on the wall but hadn't recognized the script. The bottom line was that Erin didn't want me near her. Regardless of her reasoning, I needed to respect that if she had any hope of getting better.

"Mom—it's time to go home."

Chapter 42

THE MONTH THAT FOLLOWED

There is nothing to say about the month that followed. It was the starkest time of my life, void of anything that could be construed as happiness and/or mirth. I was a hollow being, a husk of myself. I lost weight I didn't have to lose and sleep I desperately needed. Pop, God bless him, tried to stuff potato skins and bacon cheeseburgers down my gullet to fend off the gauntness that had taken over my cheeks and eye sockets. He said I was beginning to look like a prisoner of war. Suffice it to say, I started to hate the taste of red meat and fried-to-within-an-inch-of-their-lives potatoes.

Mom won the empty school board seat when Judge Harry Steinberger appointed her to the position. The school board's impasse hadn't been able to be reconciled, and the King County court system had made the final call. The word on the street was that Judge Steinberger chose my mother because he viewed her job as a nurse as upstanding, and because he owed a favor to King County Health Center for successfully keeping his ticker beating when he had suffered a massive heart attack in the summer of 2010.

The only thing that kept me from delving into the same despair Erin wallowed in was the revolution. Without it, I wouldn't have been able to function. Erin no longer showed up to the coalition meetings, and Samantha Harris had taken her position as the art club representative. Seeing Samantha at the meetings instead of Erin drove the stake further into my heart, but I knew I had to keep on keeping on. This stand against the school board was bigger than my feelings, and morale at I wasn't getting any better.

The cafeteria boycott was still going strong—a greater success than any of us could have imagined. The school board members had to be sweating bullets as they watched the revenue from the cafeteria plummet. We had also adopted a dress code to show solidarity against the board. Every day we wore plain white t-shirts and khaki pants. The white symbolized the purity of the cause, and the khakis were just something Mike Freeman, the basketball team representative, suggested. The dress code caught on with the student body, and it became rare to sit in a classroom where ninety-five percent of the students didn't wear the colors of the cause. Former band members also began playing their instruments outside Superintendent Carlson's office at six-thirty in the morning. Trumpets blared, percussionists hammered away, and since the school day hadn't officially started, and since Carlson arrived precisely at six-fifteen, and since his office was at the far west side of the high school building and school property fifteen feet from the outside of the building, he could do nothing about it. He had tried to get the police involved, saying that the band members were disturbing the peace, but the officer who took the call, the one and only Officer Taylor, told Carlson to get earmuffs and to stop calling the station. So, the band played on.

I stopped showing up at Erin's house. What was the point? She had nailed the coffin shut from her hospital bed, successfully closing the lid on any hope I had of us being us again. I found my head swimming with conflicting emotions of deep sadness and rage. In the end, I knew it wasn't worth it to hate

Erin, but I desperately wanted to blame someone for the horrifically debilitating emotions that sliced through my heart like a hot knife through butter. They killed my appetite, lowered my grades and gave me an overall feeling of numbness I had never felt before. Even the abhorrence and emptiness I had felt toward my father for so long couldn't compare to my feelings surrounding Erin. At least I had known my father was willing to reconcile, should I want to mend fences. But Erin didn't seem to be in the business of mending fences. I hadn't spoken to her in over thirty days, and she hadn't sat with the Hodgepodge table in nearly fifty. Like a spot of moisture on a hot slab of cement, Erin was slowly evaporating from all our lives.

And there was nothing we could do but hope she would get better soon.

chap·ter |CH aptər|
noun

43

THE IDES OF MARCH PLUS THIRTEEN

March fifteenth plus thirteen days. In reality, it felt like the Ides of March. Not only was it the day Julius Caesar got knifed by his BFFs, it also was the day I officially got off probation.

Yippee cakes.

Although my probation's ending afforded me opportunities outside of the house after six o'clock, I didn't have anywhere to go outside the house after six o'clock, save work. And I was already allowed to go to work, so, without Erin in my life and Jeremy bedridden, I had no reason to celebrate. Of course, my family made a big deal of it. My mother invited Dad, Karen and Ethan over the night before my official "release date" and we had lasagna and garlic bread and a nauseating load of conversation about child-rearing and frozen food coupons. I could have done without the hoopla, but, to my family's credit, no one mentioned Erin. And that was good. Because I might have burst into tears and/or put my fork through my eyeball. Life had to get back to normal soon, right? It's always darkest before dawn and all that really cliché and vomit-inducing jazz.

March twenty-eighth found me peddling my trusty Schwinn to school and wishing upon a star that I could be anywhere but Infinity High School. My freedom from probation seemed to bring with it more responsibility, as the day of reckoning was drawing nigh. Addie Wilkins would be crashing the April school board meeting in t-minus two and a half weeks, and the coalition had a lot to do to prepare for its time to shine. A presentation had to be made, all our ducks had to be in line and I had a speech to write that would bring down the house. No pressure or anything.

I was deep inside my woeful thoughts when I pulled open IHS's glass front doors and made my way to the sophomore hallway. They say that more and more people were walking into traffic because they were texting or too absorbed in the music blaring from their iPods to realize they were about to walk in front of a bus. As I turned the corner that led into the sophomore hallway, I walked into a bus named Erin.

"Oh--" I managed, stumbling backwards as though I had walked into a Venus Fly Trap instead of a beautiful girl whom I loved beyond words. I was shocked/nervous/more nervous and it showed.

One of Erin's iPod earbuds fell out of her ear, the white cord dangling from her shoulder like a sliced wire. She thumbed her iPod off and looked at the ground. She made no attempt to move around me. I realized I had caught her off guard as much as she had caught me unawares.

"Hey, Erin," I said, feeling as dopey as Forrest Gump when he had said the same thing to his friend Bubba after the latter had been shot in Vietnam.

Erin said nothing, moved nothing. It was as if roots had sprouted from her red Converses and had taken hold underneath the tiled floor. My heart hammered, all parts of me sweated profusely, but I knew I had to use this awkward, unplanned moment for good. I had to find the diamonds in the dross and all that jazz.

"I—uh—it's been awhile," I stammered. I cleared my

Dakota Defined

throat. "How are you—how are you doing?"

Erin took a deep breath and looked up at me for the first time. When she did, I nearly gasped. It was her eyes that did it to me; they were dead. Long dead. As the familiar lump of hopelessness lodged in my throat, I knew beyond a shadow of a doubt that Erin was not getting better. Her lifeless eyes told me she was getting far, far worse.

"Don't," Erin whispered. "Just don't. Please."

She still made no move to leave. When I stepped forward and touched her shoulder, she flinched away from me.

"Erin, I—I miss you more than you can understand." I paused, hoping she would tell me she did understand, that she did know what it felt to mourn the loss of love. She said nothing.

"We miss you at the coalition meetings. The dress code—it's catching on. We'd love to have you join us by wearing white and--"

"Save it, Dakota. Just save it. I'm biding my time here. I'm enrolling at Clearton next year."

I felt like I had just taken a shotgun blast to the chest.

What? Clearton?

"But why--"

"I have to get away from here," Erin said, her eyes looking beyond me. "I just—I have to get away." She took a step forward and I blocked her way.

"You're telling me like this? We've been friends since the sandbox and you're telling me like this?" It was all I could come up with. I had thought Erin couldn't hurt me any more than she had, but when you give your heart to someone, love and loss come with extreme emotions.

"Just—you can't understand, Dakota."

"Then make me understand! *Talk* to me about it!" I said, realizing my voice had raised in volume and octave.

Erin sighed, and for a brief moment I thought she was going

to spell it out for me. But then she somehow closed herself off to me again, flipped a switch in her mind and completely killed any of the remaining life in her eyes. And there hadn't been much light, if any, to start.

"Let me go, Dakota," Erin said softly. I didn't know if she was talking about letting her pass so she could leave the conversation or letting her go altogether, releasing her to her world of pain and guilt and torment. And Clearton. I couldn't forget Clearton.

"It doesn't have to be this way," I said, coming closer. "We can go back to the way things were."

"You wouldn't want that. I'm a nut job, remember? Just ask anyone in this stupid school," she swept her arm around the now bustling sophomore hallway.

"Erin, don't talk like that," I said, "you know that's not true."

She took another deep breath and shook her head.

"You'll never understand. You wouldn't want me."

"But how can you--"

She took another step to get around me, and this time I let her go. As I watched her walk away, I felt my breakfast roiling in my stomach. For an awful second I thought I was going to be sick in the hallway.

You're just going to let her walk away? You're just going to let her up and enroll at Clearton? What happened to 'greater love?' Why aren't you going after her?

"I can't," I said out loud. "I just can't."

***

"We have seventeen days until the April school board meeting," I said, surveying the room. "It's time to turn up the heat."

In the front row, Bertrand scribbled into his notebook. Behind him, Craig Henderson raised his hand.

"If you want, I can let loose some chickens in the hallways.

Dakota Defined

That'll get 'em riled."

I raised my hands. "Let's keep the poultry parked for now."

"Okay, but my coop is your coop," Craig said, throwing his manure-caked boots atop the desk in front of him. Sierra Malachi, the unfortunate patron of the desk beside Craig's boots, scooted one desk to her left.

A soft laughed filtered through the room. I looked to Hannah, who sat beside Timothy on the right side of the room.

"Any ideas from the indie rock artist?"

Hannah put up two fingers. "One, I don't play rock. Two, I'm fresh out of ideas."

"What if we walked out of our practices?" Todd Lawrence said from the back of the room.

Bertrand turned around and squinted at him. "Please elaborate on what you have just stated."

Todd couldn't help but grin. I didn't blame him. Bertrand was quite possibly from another planet.

"I'm saying all the spring athletes could show up to practice, and then walk out."

I narrowed my brow in thought. "And what purpose will that serve? Correct me if I'm wrong, but spring sports don't generate as much funding as fall and winter sports."

"You're right," Todd continued, "but they generate enough for people to take notice."

"Wait, wait, wait," Timothy said, "you're talking about practice. Practice doesn't generate any money."

Todd nodded. "I see what you're saying. So, maybe we wait for our first games." He looked to Amy Watkins, a skinny redhead with a runner's build who represented the interests of the track team. "When's your first meet?"

"March twenty-first. At Lewiston."

Todd grinned. "And that's the day we have our first game here against Redemption." He looked to Lexi Randolph. "What about softball?"

"Same day. Here against Redemption, too."

Todd slapped his desktop. "There you have it. The baseball and softball teams will wait until the third inning—when they know all the parents and fans are sure to be there. The track team waits until about an hour into the meet and then---"

"A walk-out," I said for him. I felt myself grinning ear to ear. "It's not so much about revenue, initially. It's about parents and fans getting ticked off enough to badger the school board."

"There you go," Todd said, smiling. "I like it."

"But it won't work without one hundred percent buy-in from the rest of your teams," Hannah said. "They all have to walk out, or this thing fails."

Todd looked at Amy and Lexi. "I don't think we'll have to worry about that. They all wear the colors of the cause."

"There has to be one more element added to the mix," I said. "The fans have to know why their beloved sons and daughters are walking out of a sporting event." I looked at Bertrand. "Make a note. We need three bullhorns."

An excited murmur worked the room.

"We need three volunteers. The instant the walk out begins, the bullhorns are up to your mouths and you're letting the people know what's going on."

Craig Henderson shrugged and stomped his feet to the floor. Caked manure crumbled to the carpet, but at this point, everyone was too excited to notice.

"Count me in. If I can't release the chickens, I'll release my voice. I'll do the softball game."

"I'll do the track meet," Hannah volunteered.

"And I'll do the baseball game," Todd said. "I'll hide the bullhorn in my baseball bag and get it out when the walk-out begins."

I nodded, the smile still wide on my face. After what had happened with Erin, I desperately needed to smile.

"I like it. Let's do it."

***

"I'm not gonna lie, I'm nervous," Jeremy said as I thumbed through the rehabilitation center's pamphlet.

"This looks amazing, man," I said, throwing the pamphlet down on the coffee table. "State of the art amazing. You'll be walking across a stage before you know it."

"I hope so," Jeremy said, his eyes scanning the living room ceiling. "We leave for Columbus at six o'clock tomorrow morning. I have consultations at ten. After that, I think we jump right into training."

As Jeremy continued to scan the ceiling, I couldn't help but feel a wave of guilt wash over me. If he'd never been invited into my car, he would not being leaving at the butt crack of dawn tomorrow to go to a rehabilitation consultation in Columbus. Even though I had been forgiven by all the people I needed to be forgiven by, I couldn't help but think 'what if' sometimes. I could only imagine in part what kind of torment Erin felt.

"So, you'll be living down there, then?" I asked.

"Yeah. Mom's work is giving her insane leeway with all of this. She's taking three months off to stay with me in an apartment in Columbus. Dad was able to take vacation days Thursdays and Fridays for the next three months, so he'll come down Wednesday nights and drive back to Infinity Sunday nights."

"Apartment nice?"

"I haven't seen it, but I think so. It's not a swanky loft or anything, but it'll do for Mom and me."

I pointed to the pamphlet on the coffee table. "That place looks amazing. Since I'm off probation now, I can come and visit some weekends."

"That'd be cool," Jeremy said, "so I can own you at *Call*

of Duty."

"I think you'll walk before you're able to own me at *Call of Duty*," I answered. We both laughed. "You're coming back for the board meeting, right?"

Jeremy raised his eyebrows. "You think I'd miss that? Especially with *the* Addie Wilkins coming back to town?"

"Easy, Matthew Broderick. You have a girlfriend, remember?"

"You know what I mean," Jeremy said, a mischievous grin on his face. I definitely knew what he meant. Addie Wilkins was hot to the fortieth power. I could lie and say I wasn't a little bit jazzed to see her. And her legs, if we're being honest.

"I just hope we're able to pull this thing off," I said, changing the subject back to the cause.

"I hope so, too," Jeremy said.

Maybe if we can pull it off, Erin won't open enroll at Clearton...

chapter 44
noun

NEVER FAILING

"They will not bully me!" my mother said, slamming down her glass of ice water. "I don't care if I'm the greenest school board member--I'm not stupid!" She speared some green beans with her fork and huffed as she brought them to her mouth.

"It's because of me, Mom," I said, feeling my blood simmering in my forehead. "They're all over you because the cat's out of the bag about who the leader of the coalition is. And it happens to be me."

"I hope they know all the threatening emails and phone calls will only serve to make me dig my heels in more," my mother said, wiping her mouth with her napkin. And I don't care if the leader of the coalition is Joe Piscopo, grown men don't need to be telling me how to vote by means of underhanded threats."

"Who the heck is Joe Piscopo?" I asked. "Never mind. I'll Google him. You can't let them get to you, Mom. They're only trying to rile you to rile me."

My mother sighed. I saw the tired lines at the corners of her eyes, the slightly puffy bags that pillowed beneath her baby blues. I silently wondered if I had done the right thing in asking my mother to run for the open school board seat. What they were doing to her cheesed me off something fierce. Every son wanted to protect his momma just like every momma wanted to protect her son. But I knew the best thing I could do was stay the course with the cause. I'd hurt the stupidly-tanned and Just-For-Men-ed-to heck suits by keeping on keeping on.

My mother waved her hand as she sipped from her water glass. "Enough of this school board talk. Just thinking about it is giving me an ulcer. What about Erin? How is she doing?"

I felt rejection's stinger plunge into my heart. Every time I thought about Erin I felt a part of me die, just crumble off and evaporate away like it hadn't been a vital piece of my existence.

"I--I don't think she's doing well," I managed. I swirled my water in my glass, the ice cubes clinking their discontent.

My mother raised her eyebrows. "And? Why do you think that?"

Did I really want to get into this? Wasn't it easier to pretend the wound was scabbed, even though it seeped blood despite my ignoring it? Sure, my mother had consoled me when Erin had attempted suicide, but I hadn't told her about the cutting. She didn't know the whole story, and I worried that if I ventured onto these turbulent waters, I would burst forth with the full truth. In way, the secrecy was all I had left of Erin. Protecting her honor was of utmost importance to me.

"It's just--I bumped into her at school yesterday and she looked--she looked terrible."

"Terrible?"

I shredded my napkin with my fingers as I remembered Erin's dead eyes, her weight loss, the bitterness she exuded when she talked about Infinity High School.

"She just wasn't herself. She's just not Erin." I tried to put a period on the conversation the way teenage sons do when they don't want to talk about tough issues anymore. Unfortunately, my mother wasn't about to let me off that easy.

Dakota Defined

"Dakota, I can't say I know exactly what you're going through, because I don't. I never had anyone I care about attempt suicide, so I'm not going to pretend to walk in your shoes. But I do know what it's like to feel lost at times. I know what it's like to love someone who doesn't know how to love you back." She reached over and took my hand. I didn't protest her hand, nor the lump that lodged itself in my throat.

"You love her, don't you, Dakota?"

My eyes welled with tears. How do moms always see through to the guise of stoic resolve?

"I do. I love her, Mom." The tears spilled down my cheeks as my mother stood from the table and embraced me where I sat.

"I know you do, honey. I've known for a long time."

I was sobbing--sixteen and sobbing in my mother's arms. But it felt so right, so necessary.

"What do I do? How do I--what can I do to let her know I love her?"

My mother rocked me in her arms. "You let her know by what you do. You let her see your love by how you respond to this situation, how you help to make it better."

"But what if it doesn't work? What if I can't do it?"

My mother kissed my forehead and whispered into my ear. "Love never fails, Dakota. It may be beaten, abused and left for dead, but it never fails. It's always right where you left it."

My mother rocked me some more, and I cried some more. It was good to cry, good to be held and good to know my mother believed love conquered all.

And maybe since my mother believed it, I could, too.

★★★

After supper I saddled up my Schwinn and peddled to Erin's house. What my mother had said about love never failing resonated with me. I had stopped displaying love to Erin the past month. I had given up, had allowed her feelings of guilt and pain push me away. But not anymore. It was time to be a persistent Pete again, to show up daily at her door and show her how much I cared. After all, actions spoke louder than words.

But when I arrived at the Taylor residence, no one was home, or at least it appeared that way. Officer Taylor's cruiser didn't occupy the empty spot by the basketball pole, and Erin's mother's car was gone, too. Maybe they had gone out to eat and weren't home yet. Maybe they were taking Erin to an appointment with her therapist. Whatever the case, when I knocked on the front door, no one answered. I was just turning to leave when the door squeaked open a bit Turning, I saw the seam of darkness coming through the yawn, thus confirming the Taylors were most certainly gone. They had probably forgotten to firmly shut the door, is all. The Taylor's front door was old and shut heavy, and I remember Erin always telling me that if you didn't give it an extra push it wouldn't shut the way it was supposed to. I reached for the knob to pull the door shut and then stopped.

No, you're crazy. Don't even think about it.

But I was thinking about it. Last summer I had walked into Erin's bedroom and found her writing in a journal. When I playfully asked to see her diary, she had socked me on the shoulder, eyes glinting mischief, and told me it was a *journal,* not a diary. She had quickly stuffed the journal between her mattress and box spring and told me she would let me read her journal over her dead body, that if anyone ever got a hold of the black spiral notebook they'd have access to all her secret thoughts and feelings. I had asked if my name ever showed up in her journal, and she had raised her eyebrows, pecked me on the cheek and whispered something to the effect of 'more than you will ever know.' As I stood on the Taylors' front porch, my hand on the door knob, I knew five minutes with that black spiral notebook would tell me all I needed to know about how Erin truly felt about me.

Don't. It's stupid. What if they come home?

I was willing to risk it. I had to know what Erin truly felt about me, felt about *us*. Pushing all naysaying thoughts aside, I opened the door a little more and slipped into the house. I was greeted with the familiar Taylor smell, and it made me nostalgic for better days, when Erin and I would watch movies on the couch or sit and talk about life at the kitchen table. But I didn't have time to get all sentimental. I was on a mission, and I was on the clock.

I passed through the living room and into the hallway that led to Erin's bedroom. Her door was open, and I saw crumpled clothes and books scattered on the floor. As I walked into the room, I grinned at the strewn clothing and the unmade bed. Artists: they could create emotionally captivating works on canvas, but they couldn't keep themselves organized for anything.

Get the journal, read it and get out!

I wasted no more time. Lifting the mattress ever-so-slightly, I jammed my hand into the crevice I made and felt for the notebook. I didn't have to feel around very long, as my fingers brushed against the metal spirals. I extricated the notebook and held it out in front of me. Here it was, all of Erin's secret emotions and thoughts written for me to read. All I had to do was flip open the black cover and find all the answers I so desperately craved.

What are you waiting for? Just do it, already!

But I couldn't. I was frozen in place, the journal in my hands nearly pulsing like a life source. All I had to do was open it, all I had to do was *read it*, for cheese sake. And I couldn't do it—*wouldn't* do it. If I opened Erin's journal I would violate her trust and expose her secret thoughts. I couldn't do that to her. Even if she never found out, I would know, and if I wanted to be a young man of integrity, I had to put the journal back where it belonged.

And hightail it out of here! Don't forget that little tidbit!

I didn't waste any time. Placing the journal back between the mattress and the box spring, I took one last look at Erin's room and smiled. I loved her, loved her untidiness, loved her secrets, loved everything about her.

I loved her so much I left the Taylor house, pulling the front door firmly shut behind me, and straddled my Schwinn without abating the torturous feelings of uncertainty that plagued me every second of every day.

Greater love, Dakota—that's what it is. Sacrificing your peace for her pursuit of wellness. Your love hasn't failed. Because love never fails.

chapter 45

Heating Up

The walk-outs were a smashing success. Every member of the softball, baseball and track teams followed through like champs and walked out of their respective sporting events. Todd Lawrence reported that the baseball fans were stunned at first, but when he got on the bullhorn and explained the reason for the walk-out, he got a standing ovation. Hannah reported an identical story in regards to the track meet. Midway through field events, the entire Infinity High School track team simply dropped their shots, discs, pole vault poles and other track paraphernalia and walked out of the stadium. The coaches, who were not informed of the walk-out, were a little more than peeved, but when Hannah took to the bullhorn, they applauded with the rest of the Infinity track fans, and some fans from other school districts.

Craig Henderson had not been as lucky. The softball team's walkout had been a success, but Craig's personal stake in it had not. The team had walked out after the third inning, and Craig had taken to the bullhorn as he was instructed to. Unfortunately for Craig, Principal Stemwalter had a niece who played shortstop for Redemption, and when Craig took to the

Josh Clark

bullhorn and the Infinity crowd had been successfully informed and riled by what Craig had to say about the school board and administration, Principal Stemwalter had tried to wrestle the bullhorn from Craig's hands. What ensued was an unfortunate but reportedly hilarious game of catch-me-if-you-can. Craig had yanked the bullhorn from Stemwalter, hopped the fence, and proceeded to continue his spiel from the pitcher's circle. Stemwalter, who refused to look like a dunce in front of the I and Redemption fans, hopped the fence and made his way to the pitcher's circle. Craig took off, and that's when the fun began. Ten minutes later, and only after Stemwalter had chased Craig all over the softball infield and outfield, and only after he had enlisted support from his relatives from Redemption, had Craig been tackled and the bullhorn ripped from his hands. The Infinity parents watched the whole spectacle, and when Craig was escorted off the field, Stemwalter was met with a chorus of boos. Craig had been marched into the high school office, his bullhorn confiscated, and written up for insubordination, a three day out-of-school suspension tacked on to the write-up. For the cause, Craig's suspension was a great thing, as it enforced to the public that the administration were nothing but bullies. For Craig, his suspension was a blessing in disguise. It gave him time to clean his chicken coop and catch up on his homework. Whatever the case, the walk-outs had been a huge success, so much so that walk-outs were planned for every game and meet on the respective schedules until the school board relented. Couple the success of the walk-outs with the success of the ongoing cafeteria boycott, and we were convinced our voices were being heard. The April school board meeting, now only ten days away, would be the icing on the cake.

"You guys are doing great," Mr. Dennis said after I had reported the outcomes of the walk-outs. "Better than I even thought possible."

Dakota Defined

We were sitting at his kitchen table, Anita Dennis fussing over a sink of dishes to our left. I had kept Mr. Dennis up to date about the goings-on surrounding the revolution, and he had fed me advice along the way. With the school board meeting ten days away, he was helping me with my speech and promising me Addie Wilkins would come through for us. He said there was also a surprise he couldn't tell me about, but when it went down, I'd be shocked like the rest of the school board.

"Why can't you tell me?"

Mr. Dennis smiled and sipped from a mug of coffee. "We need the effect of surprise. From everyone. If this thing goes the way I think it will, the school board will be floored. It just can't seem canned."

I eyed him skeptically. "You sure?"

Mr. Dennis smiled. "Trust me. I was right about you being the man to lead this whole thing, right?"

I didn't know how to respond to that, so I just kept quiet. Responding to compliments always made me feel awkward because I wasn't good at it.

"You don't have to say anything, Dakota. You're too humble. You've done a heckuva job. I'm proud of you."

Anita Dennis asked if we'd like a slice of chocolate peanut butter pie. We both voiced our affirmatives, and over pie and relatively nasty coffee, we continued to iron out my speech.

chapter 46

THE WAITER

"Oh, no. Don't look now, but Erin and her family just walked in," Timothy said, sipping his Mountain Dew.

Of course I looked. Whoever came up with the phrases 'don't look now' or 'heads up' when a ball or some other potentially hazardous object was hurdling toward your head was an idiot. Since we were in a booth along the wall and my back was to the door, I had to crane my neck to look. When I did, I caught Erin looking at me. She immediately dropped her eyes, and I felt my heart drop into my stomach.

"What are they doing here?" I whispered, trying to act as casual as possible.

"Well, since this *is* an eating establishment, I'm guessing they are going to order food," Timothy said. I could have poked him in the eyes.

"Save the sarcasm, okay?"

Timothy held up his hands. "Okay, okay. Easy, boy. She's just here with her family to get something to eat."

"But why here? They could've gone someplace else," I said. My heart hammered in my chest, and I wondered where they had seated themselves.

Dakota Defined

"Infinity isn't exactly God's gift to restaurants. It's either here or McDonalds. And the Chinese place is closed for renovations."

Timothy was right. Pop's Diner was the only logical place in Infinity for the locals to come to eat if they wanted sit-down instead of drive-thru cuisine. McDonald's was probably healthier, what with all the grease that grimed Pop's burgers and everything else. But the town loved Pop's Diner, and Pop's Diner loved the town. I just wished the Taylors had chosen McDonald's on this particular night. I was on break, and I had texted Timothy to come and have a burger with me while we hashed out plans for the school board meeting. Even though I desperately wanted to see Erin, I wanted it to be on my terms, when I had prepared my heart for possible rejection. Her showing up unannounced did great damage to my sophomore psyche.

"You're still crazy about her," Timothy said. It wasn't a question, but a statement.

"You have no idea," I said, stirring my Dr. Pepper with a straw.

"Lester!" Pop barked from the cutout that looked into the kitchen. I looked to where Pop stood with a metal spatula in his right hand, his hairy arm slicked with grease, his apron spotted with the stuff.

"Yeah?" I checked my cell phone to see if I had taken too long a break. According to the digital numbers, I still had ten minutes left.

"I want you to wait on table seventeen," Pop said, pointing.

"Wait on table seventeen--" I questioned, turning to see where table seventeen was located. I didn't know how the tables were numbered because I was little more than a busboy who sometimes helped Pop in the kitchen. When I saw where Pop was pointing, my mouth went dry as construction paper.

You can't be serious!

I turned back to Pop. The right side of his mustache was raised in a sly smile, and I knew there was no way I could tell him no. I had never waited a table before, and my first experience with it was going to be taking the orders of my estranged girlfriend and her family. Super.

"Good luck, man," Timothy said, patting me on the back as I stood from the booth. "Go get her."

"Shut it," I said, glaring at him. I walked to the kitchen cutout and gave a surprisingly wicked glare to my hairy boss. If Pop was upset at my attitude, he didn't show it. The grin never left his face.

"Do I need a notebook thing to take their order with?" I asked, trying seem more exasperated than I really was. What I really was was diarrhea-nervous.

"Naw, kid. You're a smart one. Your memory will serve you just fine." His grin widened into an all-out smile as I turned to make my way to the Taylors' table.

"Hey, kid?" Pop said. I turned back around. "Go get her." He winked, and although I wanted to, I didn't tell him to shut it as I had Timothy.

Stay calm. You're cool. Just stay calm.

"Well, well, well. Look who we have here," Officer Taylor said as I approached. My hands were clammy, and I had to swallow a ball bearing of fear before I could open my mouth to speak. Erin didn't look at me. Instead, she seemed to find all the typos on Pop's menu very interesting.

"Hi, Officer Taylor, Mrs. Taylor," I nodded to them both.

"It's been awhile," Officer Taylor said. "You been staying out of trouble?"

Somehow his asking me that question unnerved me. I could take it from my grandpa and even my dad, but from a police officer whose squad car I had seen the back of, it weirded me out.

"I've been okay," I said, thinking that I was lying out of my mouth. I had been miserable. Horrible. More than horrible.

More than more than horrible.

"What you are doing at the school is quite an accomplishment," Mrs. Taylor said as she spread a paper napkin atop her lap. "I've heard a lot of good things about the way you kids are conducting yourselves in the face of adversity. It's admirable the way you're taking a stand in a civil way."

"What she said," Officer Taylor said, throwing a thumb in his wife's direction.

"If we get our departments and extra-curriculars back, Erin could stay at Infinity instead of going to Clearton," I blurted. It had just come out, spewed forth like a burp you can't hold back. I wanted to shrink down to micro-Dakota size and hide under the mustard squeeze bottle.

Officer Taylor looked at Erin. She didn't look up from the menu. "We'll have to talk about that if you all are successful with your mission. Right, honey?"

Erin mumbled something close to 'right' and continued to "study" the menu. An awkward silence ensued.

"Okay," Officer Taylor said, slapping the table. His huge palms knocking the tabletop nearly made me fudge my Fruit of the Looms. "I think I'm ready to have a heart attack. How's 'bout a Pop's Burger with extra pickles, no onions?"

★★★

I was back at the dishwashing station after my initiation into the art of being a waiter by means of my ex-girlfriend's family. Pop had come to the station and patted my back as soon as I had come from walking over the searing coals of the Taylor family. Timothy left, seeing the writing on the wall a mile away. Now I was alone with my thoughts, alone with my feelings of *why?*

Why did it have to be this way?

Why couldn't I go back to the fateful night of the car accident and rearrange reality?

Why did Erin refuse to speak to me?

And why did I love her so much?

It would have been so much easier on me if I could just turn a valve and all the intense feelings of love and yearning I had for Erin would shut off. Instead, the lingering residue of a relationship—a friendship—long gone tormented my every thought. Why had God made love when He knew it had the potential to be followed by pain and suffering? Why had He, in His infinite wisdom and master plan, given man the ability to love and then *remember* the feeling associated with it after it had exploded into a million jagged pieces?

"Hey, kid. Somebody wants to talk to you. Out back," Pop said from the doorway. He wiped his meaty hands on his apron. "I'll spray this load. Nobody left in the diner."

I wiped my hands on a dry dishtowel and headed for the swinging door that fed into the hallway that served as the back entrance to the diner. Pushing the door open, I was surprised to see Officer Taylor waiting for me in the hallway.

"Hey, Dakota. Sorry to take you away from your work. Pop doesn't mind, he and I go way back." He worked a toothpick from the left side of his lips to the right side. What could he possible want to say to me?

"Listen, Erin and my wife are waiting for me in the car. I said I forgot my wallet and had to come back in, so I have to make this brief."

I nodded to show I was following, still unsure where this was going. Did he know I had been in his house?

"We don't know what to do with Erin," he started, his voice low and heavy with helplessness. "She's not getting any better. She's going to therapy, but it doesn't seem to be helping. We're spending every waking moment with her, afraid that if we leave her she'll try—you know—again."

My heart pounded in my chest cavity. "It's that bad?"

Officer Taylor sighed. "I think we have no choice but to

send her to an in-house facility, Dakota. She's been cutting herself—we took all her blades away from her, but she uses a bent paperclip."

I shuddered, trying not to visualize what Officer Taylor was saying. How could it have gotten this out of hand? How could Erin have spiraled so far as so fast?

"An in-house facility," I said, trying to process what he was saying, "you mean like rehab?"

"We feel it's the only way. We don't know what to do anymore."

My head spun, a weird buzzing sound messing with my ears. "Where? When? How long?"

"There's a great facility in southern Ohio, right inside Hocking County. The length of her stay will depend on her progress. She'll be leaving the day after the April school board meeting."

The day after the school board meeting...

"How does she feel about it?" I asked, my voice coming out strained and defeated. I felt helpless, completely incapable of doing anything to help make Erin better, and it was the most miserable feeling of my life.

Officer Taylor sighed and rubbed the back of his neck with his right palm. "She doesn't know yet. We're only going to give her a couple days' notice. We don't want to—trigger anything."

I matched Officer Taylor's sigh. "So--"

"My wife and I just wanted you to know. We know you won't say anything to Erin or anybody else. We just know how much you care for our daughter and—and we wanted to say thank you for all you've done. She'll get better someday. It's just not going to be as soon as we hoped."

I felt like I had been knifed in the chest, my beating heart ripped out and stomped upon.

"Thanks for telling me," I managed. I was fighting against

the explosion of tears that wanted to burst forth.

Officer Taylor stepped forward and wrapped his arms around me in a bear hug.

"You're a good kid, Dakota. The kind of guy I want dating my daughter." He let me go and turned to leave.

"Officer Taylor?" I called after him.

"Yeah?"

"Tell her I lo--" the words caught in my throat, and I could hold back my tears no longer. "Tell her I hope she feels better soon."

storm \\'stȯrm\\

VERB: To unleash fury against the school board

chap·ter |CH aptər|
noun 47

SMALL CAPS: STORM THE BOARD

April first: crash the school board day. To say I was nervous was an understatement. I was couldn't-eat, couldn't-sleep terrified, hadn't-had-a-solid-number-two-in-three-days petrified. Too much information, I know, but it conveys how freaked out to the twelfth power I was.

Erin had been on my mind for the past six days. The fact that she'd be leaving for Hocking County without any knowledge of what she was in for gave me conflicted feelings. I didn't like the fact she was going to be surprised by the rehabilitation stint, but, on the other hand, I knew there was no other alternative. I just wondered how she would react when she found out.

The board meeting started at six thirty, and it was to be held in the auditorium due to the number of the public who had attended the last few meetings when the board had started their budget slashing. My mother said they'd heard rumors that something big was supposed to go down at this particular meeting, but no substantial information had found its way to the board's ears, and for that I was more than thankful. Still, they were preparing for the worst, as they rightfully should be.

Dakota Defined

They had seen the public reaction to the athletic walk-outs, which were only gaining strength and momentum. Two television stations out of Toledo and one out of Lima had come to a track meet and a baseball game respectively, and the footage of the IHS athletes civilly walking out of their sporting events had hit the airwaves and Internet with a vengeance. The cafeteria boycott was still going strong, and the coalition strongly believed we were slowly choking the life out of the school board's stubborn resolve. We were terrified, but prepared to stand before the board.

But first we had to get through the Monday school day.

Erin was absent. The lack of her presence in the classes we shared only served to add to the weight of sorrow in my chest at her leaving for an indefinite amount of time. I tried to steel myself against such sorrow. I had the school board to think about, my speech and Addie Wilkins' push to topple the evil empire the board had created. But Erin's absence loomed large in my mind, and I wondered if the Taylors had told her and she was readying herself for the move.

Please, God, let this work for her...

As Ms. Ericson, my young sociology teacher fresh from college, (where she'd enjoyed herself a little *too* much, according to the pictures she'd been tagged in on Facebook—healthy digression: change your privacy settings, for cheese sake! You might not be friends with your students, but they sure-as-sunshine creep you on Facebook!), whom my male constituents thought was hot, droned on about mass hysteria and the Salem Witchcraft Trials, I mentally put all my ducks in order: Addie was meeting with Mr. and Mrs. Dennis at his house for a rundown of what she was going to say. I had to arrive at the school at six o'clock so I could reserve seats for the coalition and set up for my spiel to the board. The surprise Mr. Dennis had alluded to would follow my speech, and then the coalition would collectively make a final statement of resistance against the school board. Easy-peesy-lemon-squeesy. In theory, anyway. If only I and the anti-diarrhea tablets I had taken could conquer my boiling stomach.

That's the thing about theories versus reality: reality still gives you the runs.

★★★

Lunch; Hodgepodge table; T-minus six and a half hours until operation Storm the Board.

"I am beginning to feel the effects of nervousness on my body," Bertrand said as he scribbled into his notebook. He squinted his eyes open and shut as he wrote, and I found myself wondering what could possibly be so important for him to constantly be scribbling in his notebook. Some mysteries were unsolvable: Stonehenge, the pyramids, Bertrand.

"We've done all we can do. Now, we just rock the house," Hannah said, taking a bite of her turkey sandwich.

"I hope we've covered anything," I said, sipping from my bottled water. There was no way I was going to put any solid foods into my body just to have them pretend my intestines were water slides. No thanks. The school's toilet paper wasn't exactly bum-friendly.

"Relax, man," Timothy said, "you've done everything you can to make this thing work. I'm sure you have a killer speech, and I'm sure Addie Wilkins is going to be smokin' hot tonight."

Hannah raised an eyebrow. "And that's her only purpose tonight? To be 'smokin' hot'?"

Timothy raised his hands in surrender. "Easy, easy, easy. I'm just talking from a personal perspective. I like to look at her—a lot. But, seriously, she'll be one of the biggest factors in this thing. I hope she knocks 'em dead."

"I hope Addie Wilkins sends the school board into cardiac arrest," Bertrand said, squinting up from his notebook.

"Um—we're not talking *literally* dead, you know that,

right?" Timothy said, looking at Bertrand with warranted suspicion. You never really knew when it came to Bertrand.

Bertrand's Garfield hair blazed in the cafeteria lighting.

"I see my attempt at comedic genius was lost on you," Bertrand replied.

"Oh, you were making a funny," Timothy said. "The one time I understood what the heck you're saying and I think you're out for a body count."

We all laughed. It was good to laugh. It made me forget everything for a while, and temporarily forgetting my life was a premium these days.

***

"I'm so nervous my hands are shaking," my mother said as she attempted to secure an earring back onto her right earring. She wasn't lying; her tremulous hand prevented her from making any headway.

"At least we have something in common," I said, tugging the lapels of my suit coat. I had to say, even though I was nervous enough to projectile vomit all over the full-length mirror in my mother's bedroom, I was making nervous look good. I adjusted the knot on my mom-tied red tie. Had to wear the power color tonight. Goodness knows I needed all the power I could get.

My mother cursed under her breath, something she only did when she was extremely exasperated or I when I got arrested for breaking into the school and watching goons destroy county art projects. She held out the earring back to me.

"A little help here, Dakota?"

I took the earring back from my mother's shaking hand and secured it to her earring.

"I think we both need to chillax a little," I said, sitting down on her bed.

"Chillax? How am I supposed to chillax?" my mother said

in a mild-freak-out tone. "I'm going to a school board meeting where pert near all the members hate me, and my son and his coalition are planning a hostile takeover. What could I possibly be nervous about?"

"I'm gonna be honest with you, Mom, you're about to make me lose my cookies."

"Can't you at least give me a *hint* about what you and the others are going to be doing? I heard Jeremy will be there, and your father's coming. Does he know what's going on?"

I put up my hands in a don't-shoot-me surrender pose. "You know I can't give you a heads-up, Mom. Even though I'm pretty sure you're on our side, it wouldn't be ethical. We want to be as civil as possible. Think Ghandi and MLK here, Mom. And, no, Dad doesn't know anything. You are both delightfully ignorant tonight."

My mother put her hands on her hips and managed a nervous smile. "Whatever happens tonight, I'm proud of you. You know that, right?"

"You're getting all mushy, Mom."

"I know, I know. But you know what I mean."

I smiled and stood. I wrapped my arms around her and we hugged as utterly terrified mother and child.

"I know what you mean, Mom. And I'm proud of you, too."

★★★

"You got your speech?" Timothy asked, slowly pulling out of my driveway.

"Got the speech," I said, reaching into my suit coat pocket and fingering the three by five index cards.

"You know if Addie is all ready to go?" Timothy came to a stop at the stop sign at the end of my street. He had just received his license a little over a week ago, and I could already tell he was going to be one of those elderly knock-off drivers.

Dakota Defined

My mother and I had both agreed that showing up at the board meeting together wouldn't be in the best interest of the coalition or the school board, so I decided I'd ride with Timothy and she'd fly solo.

"Your questions are making me nervous, man. I haven't talked to Addie. I've let Mr. Dennis handle that and whatever surprise he has in store."

"I'm hoping Victoria Secret models and a cotton candy machine," Timothy said, grinning.

"Don't hold your breath," I said. "By the way, I like the suit."

"Thanks. You're pretty dapper yourself."

I swallowed as Timothy turned onto Main Street.

"I'm gonna need all the dapper I can get."

★★★

My cell phone vibrated in my suit pants pocket as I walked out of the restroom. I had successfully expelled the rest of the solid foods that hadn't been expelled the last fourteen times I had gone, and I was pretty sure I had nothing left to give to stall number three. Timothy was in the auditorium saving seats, and I had slipped out to do my business and to try to keep my head from spinning off my shoulders. I was nowhere near prepared for what I saw when I opened my phone:

I'm going away for a long time. Thanks for always being there for me. I've never
deserved you. Please remember the better times—Erin
P.S. Good luck tonight.

It wasn't that Erin's text had said anything profound; it was that it was the first piece of communication she had initiated in I don't know how long. I was immediately torn in two by the short text, half of me wanting to run out of the school and hijack Timothy's car so I could be with her. Her parents had most certainly just told her she would be entering an in-house rehabilitation center. They had waited until the day before they would drive her to southern Ohio to tell her. I didn't know if that was a good or bad thing, but my heart bled for her all the same. The other half of me was a little ticked she had waited until a half an hour before one of the biggest nights of my life to contact me. Remember the better times? The better times seemed like a lifetime ago. I was disconcerted by the conflicting emotions that swirled inside me. If I hadn't just given my all to stall number three, I might have taken a toilet timeout to sit and collect my thoughts before going back into the auditorium.

I felt an arm wrap around my shoulder. I looked to my right and saw Craig Henderson's big grinning farmer-face.

"Howdy, Dakota. Just saw Addie Wilkins. She's looking as hot as ever. How do you like my boots?" Craig lifted his left leg so I could take a gander at his expensive-looking black polished cowboy boots. They matched his suit perfectly.

"They're great, Craig," I said, trying to will my focus back to the task at hand.

But all I could think about was Erin.

★★★

Craig Henderson was right: Addie Wilkins was hotter than ever. I tried not to trip over my own tongue as I walked over to where she and Mr. Dennis stood. What can I say, a guy never really gets over his first crush.

"You all ready to go, Dakota?" Mr. Dennis asked. He extended his hand, and I gave him mine. The go-get-'em handshake.

I took a deep breath and looked around the choir room. The walls were bare and risers were folded against the back wall. Since the music department had been cut, the room had seen no use. Mr. Dennis had felt this was the perfect place to meet before addressing the school board, kind of a this-is-why-you're-doing-this thing. It was also the only room he could pay the night janitor five bucks to unlock, so that might have had something to do with the choice of meeting place.

"I think so. I mean, I've gone over my speech at least a million times. And we've all worked hard to get to this day," I said, looking around the room. The coalition, God bless them. They all looked great in their suits and dresses.

"You'll do great," Addie Wilkins said, extending her hand. When I took it, the old feelings of wanting to sweat out an ocean at her sheer beauty reemerged, but they resolved themselves like good little hormones within a few seconds.

"Thanks. I can't wait to see what you've got planned."

Addie touched my shoulder. "Your speech is the important one, Dakota. If it's anything like the one you gave in front of the student body last spring, you guys have this in the bag."

I smiled. The smile was probably dopey, but whatever. A guy couldn't think about not smiling like a doofus and standing up to the school board at the same time.

"We'll see how it goes," I said.

Just don't screw it up!

***

I was just about to walk into the auditorium to take my seat when I felt a tap on my shoulder. To my surprise, Officer Taylor grinned down at me.

"Just thought you might like to know that Erin's here. She wanted to come."

"She's here?" I felt my mouth go sandpaper-dry.

"In the auditorium all ready. I think the whole town's here."

I smiled back, the blood pounding in my temples.

Great. Both Erin AND the whole town are here. No pressure or anything.

chapter 48
noun

OPERATION MASS EXODUS

I took my aisle seat beside Timothy, my stomach churning like a sick-cycle washing machine. I had made the mistake of scanning the audience before I sat down. Oops. The place was packed, Officer Taylor's assessment correct: all of Infinity had indeed come out of the woodwork to see the show. I had no idea our cause's tentacles had had such far-reaching effects. Heck, I even saw a few farmer-billies from way out by County Road U. Farmer-billies didn't come out for anything except to check their crops and to do a number two in their outhouses.

And I saw Erin. She was nestled between her parents as though she had just escaped from Alcatraz. Her dark hair was pulled back, her skin pale and sallow. Her eyes, once pools of milk chocolate, were now black holes in her face. This I could tell from over forty feet away; I was in the fifth row of seats, Erin and her parents at least twenty rows back. My stomach churned audibly.

Focus, Dakota. You have a job to do.

"I can't believe it's time," Timothy whispered as the school board walked onto the stage. My poor mother. She looked even more nervous than me.

"It's do or die," I said, glancing behind me. Mr. Dennis gave me a thumbs-up, and Addie Wilkins smiled at me.

"Looks like I'm here just in time," a voice to my left said. I knew that voice, and when I turned to the aisle, Jeremy was beaming at me from his wheelchair.

"You wouldn't miss this for the world," I said, grinning. "This place is your theater-loving sanctuary."

"You ready?" Jeremy asked, waving at Hannah who sat two chairs to my right.

"Ready as I'll ever be."

"Remember last year? When you brought this auditorium to its knees with your speech?" Jeremy said. "Think of that. The rest will fall into place."

"I hope you're right."

The school board had assembled at a long table, all the members facing the audience a la Da Vinci's *The Last Supper*. My mother was second from my left. All the members had little microphones clipped to their clothing, while Superintendent Carlson wrestled with a mini-mic stand in from of him. The feedback was mating-cat horrendous, but it served to snap the murmuring crowd into silence.

"If we could have everyone's attention, we would like to begin the school board meeting," Superintendent Carlson said through a screech of feedback.

And begin they did. The school board, like any other public and/or professional organization, went through the goofy opening-the-meeting-junk. The formality of it all was almost humorous, the attention to detail precise and painstakingly thorough. They knew they couldn't mess anything up, not with the whole town watching, and especially not before they were about to get lambasted by the coalition, Addie Wilkins and whatever surprise Mr. Wayne Dennis had cooked up.

Relax. It'll all be over soon...

***

The school board steered itself into shark-infested waters when it proposed the absolute and immediate cutting of the tennis and gymnastics teams. The people of Infinity, used to sitting at sporting events and voicing their displeasure at terrible calls by the officials, went into an uproar. The board president actually banged a gavel to get the crowd to settle down. The board voted three to two to cut the programs, my mother and Mr. Thompson the only nay votes. The crowd went ballistic, and more gavel-banging ensued.

The district treasurer, Sally Gonterman, reported that the cafeteria had lost over fifteen thousand dollars in the last month due to "lack of student lunch purchases." The coalition members grinned from ear-to-ear as she read the report, and Timothy slapped me on the back. The boycott had been an overwhelming success, a success that couldn't have come at a better time for the reeling student body.

The school board decided to go into executive session to discuss personnel contracts. They left the stage for over thirty minutes, and I could only imagine who they were deciding to cut back in the wings.

"They're stalling the process on purpose," Hannah said, as we all stood up to stretch our legs. "They want the crowd to get bored and leave."

Craig Henderson slapped me on the back. "Don't worry, I'll take care of keeping their butts in their seats." With that, he jogged to the front of the auditorium, jumped onto the stage and walked to Superintendent Carlson's mini-mic stand, his boots clopping against the wood stage the whole way. He pulled the microphone up, and a nasty peal of feedback quieted the crowd.

"Ya'll stay in your seats. The good stuff's coming. It'll be a hoot and a holler." He jumped off the stage and I shook my head.

"Did he really just say hoot and a holler?"

"I believe he was using a jargon relatively unknown to the general population but certainly embraced by the agriculturally-minded," Bertrand said, squinting from behind his glasses. The poor kid's black suit was too small, and his unfortunately-chosen white tube socks peeked out from beneath the cuffs of his suit pants.

"What Bertrand said," Timothy said.

I barely heard him. I was looking at Erin.

★★★

The school board's attempt at boring the crowd to death didn't work. They walked back onto the stage to a full house. My mother looked more confident than she had when she had left. I wondered what had gone down behind the scenes that had given my mother some much-needed swagger.

"Ready?" Timothy leaned over and whispered.

"As I'll ever be," I responded, fingering the notecards in my suit coat pocket.

My mother had given me a heads up about the school board's agenda. After going into executive session, they would view our presentation. I had gone through all the proper channels to ensure we would have the opportunity to speak. After a back-and-forth meeting with Principal Stemwalter and Superintendent Carlson, I had finally procured the okay to speak in front of the school board.

"We will now we treated to a special presentation from sophomore Dakota Lester and his constituents," I heard Superintendent Carlson say into the microphone. My palms immediately clammed with sweat.

It's okay—you're going to be okay!

I felt myself stand, my feet begin to move to the front of the auditorium. I was conscious of every step, my brain on hyper-sensitive alert. I walked up the stairs to the stage as two custodians carried a large podium out from the wings. They set it to the side of the school board's long table and angled in such a way that I could address both the board and the audience at the same time. Taking my note cards out of my pocket, I placed them atop the podium and grabbed the skinny microphone that sprouted from its front. When I heard the grating of the microphone when it bent, I realized this was the same podium I had stood behind to deliver my now famous speech to the student body.

Home field advantage…

I looked to the school board and licked my lips. Three of the five stared back at me with smug grins on their overly-tanned faces. Mr. Thompson's smile was genuine, and my mother winked at me. I looked out at the crowd, saw Bertrand with his pad open, pen poised to dictate my every word. I also saw Barry Yuckerman, editor of Infinity's hard-news (sarcastic) paper. I had called Barry and made sure he'd be here when I gave my speech. I wanted to the town to see this in print, wanted them to see the coalition in action.

My eyes swept over the crowd and stopped on Erin. She looked up at me with her new blank stare. She was hollow, not even a shell of her former self. I had a flash-memory of her smiling at Pop's Diner on the fateful night of the accident. She'd been so alive, so vibrant, so full of hope despite the fact the school board I was about to address had all but ripped her dreams from her fingers. I tried to shove any thought of her out of my mind. I had a job to do, and it required absolute concentration. I took a deep breath.

"Friends, family, members of the school board, administration and faculty, I am thankful for the opportunity I've been afforded to be here this evening. While it is an honor to stand before the distinguished school board and the citizens of this great town, it is with a deeply troubled spirit I am about to say

Dakota Defined

my next few words.

"In recent months, the Infinity School District's school board has voted to drastically decrease spending to certain academic departments and athletic teams. In some cases, these departments and athletic programs have been altogether cut. Even tonight, the boys' and girls' tennis programs and gymnastics teams were exterminated, thus leaving over twenty-five capable athletes without a means by which to display their skills." I swept my eyes over the auditorium. I held a captive audience.

So far, so good...

"The Infinity High School student body's morale is diminished, to say the least. We walk the hallways every day wondering if our favorite program will be cut. We are virtual zombies in a school we once had pride in, but find no reason anymore to pledge allegiance to. We have been uprooted from our dreams, forced to abandon our goals and scared every time we walk through the front door the axe will fall. I ask you, citizens of Infinity: is it worth spoiling the hopes, dreams and bright futures of your youth to save a few bucks?" I let the question hang in the air for a moment. No one coughed, no one murmured. The auditorium was as silent as death.

"Not only have we lost our dreams, but also we've lost some of our dream-weavers. The Infinity school board has seen fit to let go—let's call it what it is—*fire* five teachers thus far in the name of economic frugality. Three of the five teachers the school board has fired have moved on to other districts, taking their talents to rival school systems who are gloating at our loss and their gain. One fired teacher is here tonight." I pointed at Mr. Dennis. Every head in the auditorium turned to see him.

"Mr. Wayne Dennis was fired, not because he was a poor teacher, but because he chose to speak out against the beasts of the board. He was effectively silenced for doing his job: showing teenagers how to stand up to injustice and how to be better

Josh Clark

citizens of this great community." I looked at the school board. Three of the five faces were fixed with death glares.

"Elected officials of the Infinity school board: you should be ashamed of yourselves. Your sins are far-reaching, and they reach farther by the day. Mr. Wayne Dennis is the best teacher—the best *man*—this high school has ever seen, and you saw fit to can him because he told you your hands were dirty. Well, you can't fire me when I tell you that your hands are filthy."

The audience burst into applause. Scattered whistles and accentuated 'that's right' and so-forth worked through the auditorium for a full thirty seconds. I chanced another look at the school board members, and their looks attempted to kill me where I stood. I raised my hands to quiet the boisterous crowd. I addressed the board again.

"As you all know, a coalition has sprung up to thwart your penny-pinching ways. But wait a minute—did I say penny-pinching? Are you the same school board who cut athletic programs, art and music departments, et cetera, and then voted to give your administrators a *three percent raise*?"

The audience went ballistic. I raised my hands to quiet them again. I looked directly at Superintendent Carlson.

"So, what are you up to now, Mr. Carlson? Oh, wait, I have the figures right here." I theatrically reached into my suit coat pocket and took out a folded piece of paper. I flipped it open like a showman. Jeremy had to be proud of me.

"If my calculations are correct, and they are, you are slotted to make one hundred eight *thousand*, two hundred twenty-nine dollars and sixty-four cents next school year." The crowd went nuts. I raised my hands again.

"I wonder how many art supplies, musical instruments and football helmets one hundred eight thousand dollars can buy? I guess we'll never know."

More buzz from the crowd.

"Principal Stemwalter, I won't bother to read your salary. We should just know that three percent tacked onto a seventy-eight thousand dollar salary isn't chump change." Superintendent Carlson's face was beet red, the zigg-zaggy vein in his forehead bulging something fierce. Stemwalter wasn't on the stage, but I knew he was somewhere in the crowd with a face to match Carlson's.

"As I was saying, a student coalition has sprung up to thwart your *perceived*-penny-pinching ways. The coalition, made up of student representatives from every cut department and athletic team, is behind the cafeteria boycott and the athletic walk-outs. We have no plans to end the boycott and walkouts until we are given back our hopes and dreams in the form of our cut extra-curriculars. But, if that doesn't faze you, maybe this will."

Here it was, the climax of my speech, the moment that would bring the school board to its knees. As one body, all the coalition members reached into their suit coats and/or purses and each produced a piece of paper that might just win the day. I took the skinny microphone from its holder and walked in front of the podium. I raised the yellow paper in my hand over my head. The coalition members in the first three rows did the same thing with their multi-colored papers.

"Members of the school board, in my hand I hold an open enrollment form to Clearton High School. It is filled out and ready to be filed. Since the great state of Ohio allows open enrollment, I'm leaving Infinity High School for the greener pastures of Clearton High School where corruption and tyranny does not rule the day. As you will see, I am not the only one planning to leave. Our thirty coalition members are holding forms from fourteen different school districts. Not only will our leaving have a devastating effect on the school's population, it will also make local, state, and, perhaps, national news. I have press release drafted and ready to submit to every county newspaper in the state as well as to the major newspapers across the country. This way, the nation will know the truth behind the mass exodus from the Infinity school district."

The crowd buzzed, shock sweeping through the citizens of Infinity like a live current. I held up my hands, ready to deliver the final knock-out blow.

"Think this sounds bad, school board? How does this sound: to date, the coalition has gathered sixty-eight percent of the student body's support for this cause. That means that sixty-eight percent of the student population will be walking out of the Infinity High School doors never to return again. And if you think we're bluffing, every single student of the sixty-eight percent of the students who have filled out open enrollment paperwork have parental or guardian signatures attached to their respective forms. It's a done deal if we don't get every department and athletic team that we've lost back, effective immediately. We are also demanding new contracts for Mr. Wayne Dennis and Ms. Emily Tannerly. They are to be reinstated tomorrow. Those are our demands. They must be met, or sixty-eight percent of your high school population is walking." I paused for effect. "The ball's in your court."

The crowd went nuts. They were on their feet cheering and whistling themselves into a frenzy. And since it felt like the right thing to say, and since I had ended my student body speech with it last year, I raised my arms into the famous Nixon pose and delivered my final words:

"And God bless America."

I walked off the stage knowing the coalition had successfully wrestled the axe out of the hands of the school board and we were now wielding it ourselves.

***

Addie Wilkins took to the stage and sashayed in front of the school board and the citizens of Infinity like only Addie could. She was wearing a form-fitting blue dress, her long legs supported by sizable heels that gave her even more height than she already had. As Mr. Dennis and I had thought she would, Addie nailed her presentation. She looked at the school board's budget-slashing through the lens of an alumnus and was "appalled and disturbed" at how the board had decided to get rid of teachers like Mr. Dennis. She ended by endorsing the coalition's movement to support open enrolling at different school districts—she coined the term Operation Mass Exodus-- if measures were not taken to give students and fired teachers back what they deserved.

Bottom line: Addie followed my presentation with a more than solid one of her own. Now all we had to do was sit back and wait for Mr. Dennis's surprise.

But it never came. And if it was supposed to come, it didn't have time to. All hell broke loose when standing microphones were placed in all four aisles of the auditorium and the public was allowed to weigh in on the budget-cutting issue.

The school board got skewered. If I didn't know better, I would have actually felt bad for them. There were a few members of the voting public who knew where my mother and Mr. Thompson stood on the issue, but mostly the school board was slammed for its "totalitarian rule" and its "stupid approach to running an educational institution." I sat back and took it all in, occasionally exchanging grins with Jeremy and Timothy. If we didn't win this thing, I'd be absolutely shocked.

At one point I chanced a glance at Erin. To my surprise, the seat between her parents was empty. I couldn't help but wonder how she'd feel about the whole presentation. Was she proud of me? Would she say so? Would she allow me to talk to her after?

I felt my phone vibrate in my pocket. Taking it out and seeing whom the text was from made my heart swell. My heart plummeted to the floor when I realized what it said:

You were great. I'm sorry I couldn't tell you in person. It has to be this way. Please don't cry for me. I've finally found peace. Remember me.—Erin

My fingertips tingled and dark spots floated across my vision.
Please, God—no!

sac·ri·fice   \ˈsa-krə-ˌfīs, *also*
-fəs *or* -ˌfīz\

VERB: To offer yourself so that another might live

chap·ter 49
noun

WHEN LOVE RUNS

I had to get out the auditorium, had to get to Erin. Time was of the essence; the more precious seconds that ticked by were seconds Erin could be using to...

Focus! Stayed focused! Just get out of the auditorium!

I stole a glance at Erin's parents, saw them snug in their seats in the middle of the auditorium amongst a sea of Infinity's faithful, and knew there was no time for me to climb over fifteen people to alert them to the situation. I had to do this alone and I had to act now.

Please, God...please, God...

I stood from my seat and eased past Jeremy in the aisle as a man across the auditorium was asking the school board a question from one of the standing microphones.

"Gotta pee?" Jeremy whispered. I didn't answer him. Instead, I hurried up the aisle and out the auditorium doors.

She probably told her parents she was going to the bathroom...but she went home. I know she went home. Please, God—don't let me be too late!

I took off in a dead sprint for the glass front doors, ripping the knot of my tie down my solar plexus and shrugging out of my suit coat. I threw the coat next to the big, fake potted plant by the front door and shoved into the chilly April evening air

She planned this—her parents told her she would be going to the in-house rehab facility and she used tonight as the perfect set-up for—

I couldn't think about the rest, couldn't allow my mind to wander into the abyss. I willed all my focus, all my energy into forcing my feet to beat against the pavement. I had to get to her, had to stop her, had to make her *live.*

The Taylors' house was a good seven blocks from Infinity High School, and as I sprinted down Charles Street my lungs burned and my air came in short, hyperventilating breaths. I knew I had to suck down the panic, knew I couldn't allow hyperventilation to take over my body. If I had to stop to regain my composure, I knew I'd be too late. And I couldn't be too late.

I should've used the gun...

Erin's words from the hospital flickered through my head like a shorted wire. It didn't take a genius to know Erin wouldn't be popping pills this time, nor would she be applying a razorblade to her wrists. No, she would be cutting the lock from the old school locker in the garage and using her father's gun to—

Please, God! Please let me get to her in time!

I turned onto Winston Avenue and my stomach lurched. What was I about to see? What scene was about to unfold? If I was too late, could I live with the images for the rest of my life? Could I live with myself if I showed up too late? And even if I was early enough to intervene, would I be successful? How could I possibly be capable of talking her out of it?

Because you love her, Dakota. You love her more than you even realize...

I jumped the curb at the end of Winston Avenue and took to the grass. Cutting through side lots and jumping more than one hedge I raced through backyards and front yards alike. In one back yard, my foot caught the side of a child's sandbox and I went sprawling atop the closed box, my face slamming into the wood, the palms of my hands becoming a pincushion for splinters. Staggering to my feet, I put my hand to my forehead and felt the wet of blood as it seeped from a nasty gash. But there was no time to focus on my pain. Erin's was more important. I was into a sprint again in a matter of moments, running faster than I ever had before through backyards and front yards, over sidewalks and streets. I would have run ten thousand miles if it was what it took to save Erin's life. I was desperate to get to Erin, desperate to save her from herself. I ran until my lungs nearly burst, until my heart threatened to beat out of my chest.

Because sometimes love runs.

chapter 50
noun

DAKOTA DEFINED

I ran up the Taylors' driveway and leapt over the three porch steps. Turning the doorknob and putting all the weight of my body into the heavy door, I stumbled into the Taylors' dark living room. The air was heavy, the smell of fear palpable in the small living area.

Dear God, am I too late?

I froze for a moment in the middle of the living room, the silence of the house squeezing against both sides of my skull. Blood from the gash on my forehead trickled down my cheek and onto the Taylors' carpet, my heartbeat slamming like a sledgehammer against my sternum. It was quiet. Too quiet.

Oh...oh...

My brain was in shut-down mode, logical thought processes unable to bridge the synapses, and a sense of overwhelming fear and profound grief swept over me.

She's in her room—dead. I'm too late.

The unmistakable sound of a gun cocking shattered the silence and set my brain and feet to motion.

She's alive—in her room—there's still time!

I sprinted into the hallway, knocking over a vase of flowers in the process. It thumped onto the ground, water soaking into the heavy carpet like a macabre blood stain. Erin's door was partly closed, and when I got to it, I slowed down and slowly pushed it open. What I saw nearly killed me.

"Erin—what are you--" But I couldn't finish my sentence, the scene too horrible for words. Sitting on the edge of her bed with the barrel of her father's .40 Smith &Wesson inside her mouth, Erin slowly turned and looked at me through far-gone eyes.

Oh, God, no--please, God...

I slowly stepped into the room, afraid any sudden movement on my part would spook her finger into jerking the trigger. And her finger *was* on the trigger.

"Erin—please—put the gun down," I said softly. I took a step forward and Erin tensed and inhaled sharply. I stopped in my tracks. A thin spindle of saliva trickled down the barrel of the gun and dripped to the floor. Erin's eyes were lifeless as she studied my every move.

"Erin, you don't have to do this," I said, desperately warring with myself to keep my emotions from bubbling into panicked tears. I had to be strong, had to exude a sense of calm I wasn't close to feeling.

"I can't let you do this, Erin. I can't let you end your life when you have so much to live for, so much to give to the world."

Erin's lifeless eyes only stared at me, her finger still poised on the gun's trigger.

"You're the best artist I've ever seen. Your paintings speak to emotions I never knew I had. You're going to get into an art school in New York, paint circles around everybody else and take your gift to the world."

Erin blinked.

"You're the most thoughtful, compassionate and caring person I've ever met. Please don't let the accident define your life. It was what it was, an accident."

Erin lowered the barrel of the gun from her mouth. Her words came out monotone and void of any emotion.

"It's over, Dakota. It's all over. Please leave."

I took a step forward and Erin pulled the trigger. The blast was deafening in the small bedroom, and ceiling plaster rained down on us in a hazy white cloud. My ears rang, my head spun, I coughed into my hand as I inhaled the white powder.

"It's over, Dakota," Erin said over the ringing of my ears. "There's no going back. I can't undo what I've done."

I glanced up at the ceiling, saw the hole into the attic. I took a step forward and Erin cocked the gun and placed it into her mouth. I put my hands up and allowed my feet to take root into the carpet.

"You might not be able to change what happened that night, Erin, but you can move on from it. Jeremy's going to be working really hard—he'll walk again."

Erin took the gun out of her mouth again. "One percent chance of that. One percent is nothing."

"But it's a place to start," I said, testing the waters and inching forward. Erin pulled the trigger again, this shot obliterating the overhead lighting fixture and sending more plaster and bits of glass flying throughout the room.

"Don't come any closer," Erin said through the white haze.

My eardrums felt like they were bleeding. A sharp sting in my wrist told me I'd been hit with shrapnel. When I brought my arm closer to my face to examine it, I saw a jagged piece of glass protruding from the back of my wrist. I yanked it out and threw it to the floor as Erin raised the gun.

"I won't come any closer," I said, raising my hands. "Just—please—put the gun down. Let's talk about this--"

"There's nothing to talk about!" Erin screamed, the new burst of emotion jolting me where I stood. "It's not worth it! It's not worth living if I have to feel this pain!"

"Who says you have to live with this pain?" I countered.

"Who is making you believe you have to live with this hurt? Jeremy forgave us, and so did his parents. And I--"

"You deserve better than me!" Erin said, breaking into sobs. Her body trembled but her grip on the gun remained firm.

"What do you mean? If anything you deserve better than--"

"I can't, Dakota!" Erin screamed, tears streaming down her face. Her mascara ran in inky black rivulets down her cheeks. "I can't be with you! Can't live in this town! Everybody knows what I did—*you* know what I did—and I can't do this anymore! There's no point! There's no reason! I just want to die!"

"No!" I shouted back. "You're the best thing that's ever happened to me! Now, put the gun down and let's talk about this!"

"They want to send me away!" Erin sobbed. "They're sending me away because I'm an emo-freak who can't even live life right!"

The tension in the room was elevating, Erin's arms were trembling. The gun, angled toward the ceiling, wobbled in her hand. I was through controlling my emotions. I burst into tears, the two of us sobbing, broken people in the epicenter of her devastated bedroom.

"If you do this, I don't know how I'll go on!" I shouted, tears and snot streaming down my face.

"Go home, Dakota! Get out of here and let me die!"

"*No!* I *won't* let you do this!"

"You don't have a choice!" Erin screamed, putting the gun back into her mouth.

Greater love, Dakota—greater love lays down his life for his friend...

"Then shoot *me!*" I exploded. "Shoot *me!*"

Erin took the gun from her mouth. "Why would I do that? Why would I--"

"*BECAUSE I LOVE YOU!*" I roared, dropping to my knees

and spreading my arms. "Because I love you and I'd rather die than live without you! I'd rather die than have you feel any pain! Because I've loved you since the moment we first met! Because I want to love you now and forever! Just give me a chance to love you!"

I slumped to the ground, completely spent, my forehead seeping blood, my wrist spilling a crimson stain onto the carpet. I had just given Erin all I had, had poured myself out to her and had nothing left to give. My love was my everything. My greatest sacrifice.

I raised my head, saw the gun trembling in Erin's hand. Tears poured from her eyes as I reached to her.

"It's finished, Erin. You don't need to do this. Please—give me the gun."

Erin studied me for a moment, a violent sob rocking her body. After what seemed like a millennium, she slowly handed me the gun. The moment it touched my hands, Erin groaned a sigh that sounded like a release of her burdens, an emptying of her pain. It was the most beautiful sound I'd ever heard.

I thumbed on the gun's safety lock and threw it behind me into the hallway. With hope bubbling in my chest, I stood. A laugh escaped my lips and tears streamed down my face as I made my way to Erin. Nothing would separate me from her in this moment. She was mine and I was hers.

Thank You, God! Thank You!

I sat down beside Erin and she crumpled into my arms. And I held her until she'd spent all her tears. We didn't need words, didn't need to say anything. Everything I had to say to her I said with my embrace.

My love for her spoke for itself.

chap·ter 51
noun

FOUR MONTHS LATER

"Did you hear that Superintendent Carlson resigned?" I asked Erin as I bit into my Pop's Burger. The cheese was gooey and hot, the clear burger grease running down my fingers to my wrist. Just the way I liked it.

"I can't believe it took him this long," Erin said, dipping a curly-fry into a glob of ketchup. Since I'd started working at Pop's Diner, I tended to think of everything related to the establishment as fitting into one of two categories: grease or glob.

"Yeah, Mom says he just submitted the paperwork yesterday. Said he was going to retire to Florida, but I think it's because he couldn't stomach the thought of coming back to a school district that all but tarred and feathered him last spring."

"He's just lucky they didn't throw a vote of no confidence at him," Erin said, scrunching her nose. "Ew. I don't know why I eat these fries. They're completely saturated in grease."

"Helps 'em slide right out when you need 'em to," I said with a wicked smile. Erin only shook her head, used to my frequent toilet humor.

A lot had transpired in the last four months, so much that Infinity High School didn't look like the same place. Literally.

Dakota Defined

After the school board was all but forced by the voting populace to reinstate the athletic programs, academic departments and extracurriculars and to give Mr. Dennis and all the others their jobs back, the voters had had their cake and had eaten it too. During the May school board meeting, once again held in the IHS auditorium so the less-than-adoring public could watch the proceedings with scrutinizing eyes, a proposal was brought to the board by the art, theater and vocal and instrumental music departments for a new arts-only addition to be added to the existing high school. The board, eager to please after they had narrowly avoided Operation Mass Exodus, voted three to two in favor of the new wing. The construction started the following month, as the plans had already been in existence--and the money had been set aside, go figure-- for a potential addition. In the end, the money emergency the school board had declared really hadn't been that much of an emergency at all, just a bunch of Caribbean-tanned ego-maniacs who liked to see how much power they could wield. In the end, all of them save my mother and Frank Thompson resigned. When I had called Erin at the in-house rehabilitation facility to tell her the news, she had been more than excited.

Barry Yuckerman of the *Infinity Chronicle* had written a scathing piece on the school board and had all but elevated me to a position of sainthood, saying that I had single-handedly brought the school board to its knees. Of course that wasn't true. The coalition, Addie Wilkins and Mr. Dennis had had a whole lot to do with the student body's victory. And, come to find out, Mr. Dennis never even had a surprise planned; he had just told me he did so I wouldn't be nervous and think the weight of the entire student body was on my shoulders. God bless him.

After the episode with Erin and the gun, she had submitted to going to the in-house rehabilitation facility in southern Ohio. She has stayed for six weeks, and as each day passed

I knew she was getting the care she needed, knew she would be back to the Erin of old. And one day in the middle of June, Erin had surprised me by knocking on my front door. When I opened the door, she had been beaming.

"I missed you so much," she had said, launching herself into my arms. I had taken the moment in, savored her smell, her warmth. When she pulled away, I saw her deep chocolate eyes were filmed with tears. But these hadn't been tears of sorrow, but tears of happiness and contentment.

"And, Dakota?"

"Yeah?"

"I love you, too."

She had kissed me then, and my own tears of happiness had rolled down my cheeks. Erin was back; her eyes were alive and shining, her personality warm and compassionate. Her sorrow had lasted for a long stretch of night, but joy had burst forth with the morning.

"I'm nervous about tomorrow," Erin said as she wiped the grease off her fingers.

"Don't be. Jeremy can't wait to see us," I answered, wiping a glob (there it was again!) of mayo from my upper lip.

"Still. I haven't seen him since--since before I got better. I'm just a little jittery about the whole thing."

My mother was driving Erin and me to Columbus the next day to visit Jeremy. He had been undergoing intense physical therapy, and his mother had said it was best we wait until the beginning of August to make the trip down, as that was the end of a series of programs he was doing to regain use of his legs. I had absolutely no idea what to expect, as he had been pretty mum about his progress when I talked to him on the phone or texted back and forth. I could see how Erin would be nervous; this was the first time she would see him in her current state of mind and, even though she didn't say it, I'd bet she was worried that seeing him might trigger some of the old feelings of guilt.

"You have nothing to worry about," I said, putting my hand atop hers, "I'll be right there with you."

★★★

The Stines's Columbus-suburb apartment was quaint and homey. Mrs. Stines had spruced up the too-beige living room by adding quirky purple and teal accents and framed family pictures and such. As she escorted us into the living room, I felt the sense of home oozing from the room, and I was grateful Jeremy's recovery was taking place here where there was some semblance of cozy normalcy.

After hugs all around, Mrs. Stines led us to Jeremy's room. Erin hovered close behind me, her breath coming in short bursts. I reached behind me and took hold of her hand. She clutched it and whispered her thanks as we walked into Jeremy's small bedroom.

"Here he is," I said, walking over to him and embracing him. Jeremy hugged me back, a huge smile on his face. He was sitting up in bed, a *Call of Duty* game set to pause on a flat screen television at the foot of his bed. I pointed at the screen and slapped him on the back.

"Any time you want to be completely owned at that, let me know."

"I've gotten better," Jeremy said, laughing, "I can probably play well enough to shut up Dakota Lester, a feat akin to climbing Everest."

"Can it, theater boy," I said. All the while Erin hung behind me, obviously afraid to face Jeremy after all the time that had lapsed since her last visit.

"Aren't you gonna give me a hug?" Jeremy asked Erin. "I promise Hannah won't be jealous."

Erin timidly stepped around me and approached Jeremy's bed. Jeremy laughed.

"I promise I'm not gonna bite your face off!"

Erin smiled, the tension broken. She threw her arms around Jeremy and held him tight.

"I'm sorry it's been so long."

Jeremy stroked her back and returned the tight embrace. "I'm just glad you're better. It's good to see you again."

When Erin and Jeremy broke their embrace, Erin's cheeks were moist with tears. I smiled at her and squeezed her shoulder.

I love this girl.

"Hey, I have something to show you guys," Jeremy said, throwing off his covers. Before I knew what was happening, he had pivoted on his butt, his legs and bare feet dangling over the edge of the bed. He inched toward the edge of the mattress, using his arms to propel him forward.

"Jeremy, is this a good idea--" I started.

Erin gasped when Jeremy dropped his feet to the floor. His hand gripped his bedrail and his face showed the strain of concentration. When he straightened his back and stood tall on his own two legs, I felt a chill sweep down my spine.

"Jeremy--you're standing!" I said, astounded. "When did you--"

Jeremy looked at me, mischief in his eyes. "Would you can it, D.L. Do you think *this* is what I wanted to show you?"

I stammered, unsure what to say. Here Jeremy was *standing* on his once lifeless legs. I was witnessing a miracle in the making. Jeremy pointed at the wall behind us.

"Erin, can you unfold the walker and hand it to me?"

Erin and I turned around. A gunmetal walker leaned against the wall. I hadn't seen it when we had come into the room. When I turned back around, both Jeremy's parents were watching from the doorway. Erin unfolded the walker and walked it over to Jeremy.

No way. He's not going to--

Always the thespian, Jeremy's voice assumed a showman's tone. "And now for my next trick, I'm going to do the impossible."

And with Erin, his parents and a baffled me looking on, Jeremy put one leg in front of the other and took his first step. I felt tears well in my eyes as I watched my friend take another slow, shuffling step, and then another. He was proving that one percent was just a number before my very eyes.

I felt Erin's hand wrap around mine, and I stole a glance at her. She smiled at me through her own tears. I squeezed her hand, and together we watched Jeremy walk.

Yes, I believe in miracles.

Josh Clark

love \'ləv\

(See Never-Failing)

Author Acknowledgments

It is hard to know where to start the thank yous for a book that was never supposed to be written. I had thought Dakota Lester had experienced and said all he needed to in *Dakota Divided*. I guess I was wrong. This whole project started when my students told me I should write another Dakota book. I was reluctant at first, but when a plotline started to circulate in my mind, I knew there was no way I could deny Dakota another story. To make a long story short, I told my students that if I were going to write another Dakota book, they would have to think up another alliterative title. I made it a contest, saying that the person who came up with the best title would find him or herself as a character in the book. In the end, Hannah S. and Craig H. both came up with *Dakota Defined*. I loved it, and Hannah became a member of the Hodgepodge table and Craig became the head of Infinity High School's farmer federation. It was fun writing them into the story. I hope they are happy with the result.

I'd like to thank my students for inspiring me to be a better teacher and a better writer. Without you, I'd have no reason to write and nothing to write about. You bless me on a daily basis. Thanks.

Thanks to Hannah and Craig for the great title. It's one that makes me say "I wish I would've thought of that!"

Thanks to Skip Coryell for being a great mentor, friend and publisher. I am proud to be a part of the White Feather Press family!

Thanks to the Northwest Ohio writer's group. It is great to be around passionate, creative people who aren't afraid to tell you when your stuff stinks. You guys rock.

A huge thank you to my friend, Mary Mueller. You are more than a mentor, and you have impacted both my writing and my life in more ways than you can possibly know. Thanks for putting up with my dreaming and scheming. We truly are a dangerous team. I can't wait to co-write the next book with you!

To Landon Elijah, my joy and my heart. You have brought your daddy so much happiness. I thank God for allowing me the privilege and honor of being your father. Your laughter and wet kisses make me look forward to getting up in the morning. I love you, Doosker!

To Cindy. You allow me to write and travel and chase a dream. Never forget that *you* are my first love, my first dream. Dakota's love for Erin is born out of the love I have for you. You are my constant, my rock, my best friend. I love growing older with you. I love you!

Jesus, my Savior, my Greater Love. You sacrificed Your life so we might live. No thank you will ever be enough. Thank You for your provision and guidance. Though our sorrows may last for a night, Your joy comes in the morning!

About the Author

Josh Clark is an English teacher in Ohio. Like Dakota, Josh likes to ride around town on his trusty Schwinn. He is married and continues to write for young adult readers.

Made in the USA
Charleston, SC
31 July 2012